AMBUSH!

Ben Raines's eyes caught the glint of sunlight off metal or glass in the tall grass by the side of the overpass. Might be a sniper up there, he thought. He turned back to Big Louie.

"What about it?" Ben asked.

Louie's lips grew pouty. "Ultimatums, general? That's not a very nice way to begin a relationship."

The man standing beside Louie suddenly turned, stepping to one side, a movement that put him directly in front of Ben.

A moment later the sound of a rifle booming reached them.

The slug hit the man's battle harness, and an explosion momentarily deafened Ben just as the man in front of him seemed to disintegrate before Ben's eyes.

Then the rifle cracked again and something smacked Ben on the back of his head, dropping him into darkness . . .

BOOK ONE

BOOK ONE

1

The young man listened to his mother's screaming harangue, but paid scant attention to her shrieking. It was always the same. Everything bad that had happened was the fault of Ben Raines. Ben Raines was the Great Satan. Ben Raines this and Ben Raines that and Ben Raines must die.

The young man had known for some time that his mother was very nearly a basket case. But she was still his mother, and—What was that old saying? Blood is thicker than water, or something like that.

The young man stepped further back, in order to better inspect the crowd who listened with rapt attention to the woman's words. The expression on their faces was one of love and devotion and fanaticism.

Hell, they're just as crazy as she is! the young man thought.

Poor, misguided, foolish people.

The young man looked at the new additions to his mother's army. Those scabby, savage motorcyclists who had come roaring in from the west, after being soundly defeated by General Raines. He had listened to his mother speak to them when they first arrived.

Same old shit.

The young man backed further away from the mob

and shook his head sadly. He thought: You made a mistake, Mother, when you insisted I be educated. When you insisted I learn languages and study the writings of the ancient intellectuals. Patrick Henry said it, Mother: I have but one lamp by which my feet are guided, and that is the lamp of experience. I know no way of judging the future but by the past.

And if I stay with you, Mother, I'll soon be as crazy as you are. And you, Mother, your babblings, are not the answer. Your hate has consumed you.

He saw movement to his right and just to his rear. He cut his eyes. An old man motioned to him. He walked to the old man.

"I see your motorcycle is ready for the road," the old man said. "You've made up your mind then?"

"Yes."

"Good. It's past time for you to get away from your mother, before she poisons you, like she has done so many."

"I fear I shall never see you again, old man."

"You won't. The cancer is growing. Sometimes the pain is almost too much to bear. I think I only lived this long to see you gone and free from your mother."

"Is he really my father, old man?"

"Yes. Of that I am certain. You have his eyes, his intelligence, his bullheadedness, and his drive to organize; to pull something better for all out of the ashes of this horror we've been living in for years."

"Should I, when we meet, tell him the entire truth, old man?"

"Oh, yes. Don't try to lie to him. He'd see through that instantly."

"Is he really a god?"

The old man hesitated. "I . . . don't know. I rather doubt it; but I can't be sure." He gripped the young man's thick, strong arm. "Go now, boy. Turn away and never look back. And may the true and only God ride with you."

The old man limped painfully into the timber.

The young man walked swiftly to his motorcycle and cranked it into life. He toed it into gear and rolled out. He did not look back.

"How would you have changed history, General Raines?" a young Rebel asked Ben.

The Rebels were bivouacked by the shores of a small lake in Central Kansas. They had pulled over early in the day to make some much needed repairs to some trucks.

"That's a very interesting question, son," Ben said with a laugh. "What time frame in history are you speaking of?"

"Ten years before the Great War," another young Rebel said.

Ben started to ask, "Which Great War?" But he knew which one the Rebel meant. The world war that brought the entire world, free and otherwise, to its knees. The war from which the world had never recovered.

How would I have changed history? Ben silently mused. He hid a smile, thinking: I would have shot every goddamned liberal.

But he knew he would not have done that, for while Ben Raines sometimes leaned so far to the conservative right some wondered how he managed to walk upright, figuratively speaking, Ben shared many of the liberal views. The difference was, Ben backed up his views with gunpowder.

"What do you know about that time before the Great War?" Ben asked, looking at the young Rebel who had asked the question. The young man could not have been much more than ten years old, if that old, when the world collapsed.

Several hundred Rebels, including Ike McGowan, had gathered around. Ike had been with Ben from the outset; had been with him, working beside him, when Ben's dream, the Tri-States, had become reality. The ex-navy Seal was just about Ben's age; both men's hair peppered with gray.

Ike winked at Ben.

The young Rebel said, "I know that it was a time of great confusion. Of a lot of people being rich and a lot of people being poor, with not much in between."

Ben also knew the young man had no real knowledge of what being rich or poor meant. The dollar had not been in use for some time. And within Rebel-held territory, no one went hungry, or went in rags, or lacked proper housing or fuel to keep warm. But outside of Rebel-controlled territory in this, what was left of America, roaming gangs of thugs and punks and killers ruled. Men and women and children lived in daily fear for their lives.

Again, Ben had to hide a smile. Hell, he thought, maybe that much hasn't changed in this, the second decade after the Great War, and the government smashing of the Tri-States.

"It was a confusing time," Ben said. And the gathering of Rebels, young, middle-aged, and old, fell silent in order to better hear the words from General Raines. "It was also a time of great greed. The philosophy of many was: Give me more money for less work. I want everything my neighbor has. Many companies literally priced themselves out of existence while the quality of their merchandise went to hell in a bucket. Not all people felt that way, but enough did to tip the balance.

"It was a time when the criminal had more rights than the law-abiding citizen." Don't they ever get tired of hearing this? Ben thought. How many times over the years have I made this same speech? A hundred? More? Probably.

"The United States was surrounded by nations who called themselves our friends, but not so secretly hated us. Britian, and in some respects, Canada, stayed with us to the end. If the germ-carrying bombs had not come, we would have probably had to fight a war with Mexico. Communism had already crept up to that nation's southern borders. Our United Nations was nothing more than a cancerous wart sitting in New York City. All anyone would have had to do was count the votes against us every time a vote was taken, and they could have seen what was happening. Many of the so-called Third World nations wanted our money, our aid, and then turned around and farted in our faces every chance they got."

Ben took that time to roll one of the few cigarettes he allowed himself daily. Piss-poor cigarettes they were, too. Good tobaco, if there ever was such a thing, was no more. Like coffee, a free ride, welfare, Legal Aid, the ACLU, unions, the stock market, General Motors, apple pie, and the girl next door—all gone. When the government crumbled, it was the end.

"What would I have done?" Ben asked the question. "It was so complex, and yet so simple. I—"

"General?" an aide interrupted. "Sorry, sir. But we've got company."

Ben ground out his hand-rolled smoke and stood up. "Where and how many?"

"Comin' from the east, sir. Half a dozen cars and trucks. Scouts say four people to each car, the trucks

13

are full of people."

"How far away?"

"Couple of miles out, sir."

Ben picked up his old Thompson SMG, knowing all eyes were on him as he did so. "Let's go see what we've got, people."

"Pitiful," Ike said. "No matter how many times I see it, it's still pitiful."

The men were beaten down; the eyes of the women frightened; the kids dirty and probably hungry.

"I know," Ben said.

"We don't mean y'all no harm," a man spoke from out of the ragged group. "But we'd be much obliged if y'all had some food for the kids."

"Alabama?" Ben asked the man.

"South Carolina," the man replied. "We don't look like much now, sir, but we was doin' all right until Khamsin and his people blowed in. We had us a co-op farm, nice gardens, ever'thing. We'd fought outlaws, motorsickel gangs, white trash, and black trash and you name it, and we'd pulled through all right. But Lord have mercy! That Khamsin and his bunch of heathens was just too much."

All the Rebels gathered around had noticed the black family among the whites. One good thing had come out of the horror of germ and nuclear war: Blind prejudice, among most, was a forgotten thing.

From the intelligence Ben had received about Khamsin and his troops, the residents of South Carolina were indeed having a bad time of it. Ike had just returned from Khamsin's HQ, where the ex-Seal had led a small team in to rescue his ladylove, Nina. During the raid, the so-called invincible Khamsin, The Hot Wind, had been wounded in his Libyan ass.

14

Ben said, "You people get something to eat. We'll talk later." He motioned Col. Dan Gray to one side. "Find out as much as you can from these people, Dan. They seem like fairly decent folks to me."

"My first impression agrees with that, general," the Englishman said. "This would be a fine place to start another outpost, right, sir?"

"You're reading my mind again, Dan," Ben replied with a grin.

Gen. Ben Raines's latest dream was to build a series of outposts across the land, stretching from east to west, and eventually, from north to south, each outpost about a hundred miles apart. The outposts would be staffed by civilians, with a small contingent of Rebels to beef them up. Maybe then, yes, *only* then, could the nation begin the slow, painful process of pulling itself out of the ashes of ruin and war and desperation.

It damn sure was worth a try. The people certainly had nothing to lose and everything to gain.

Since the Great World War, no country had been able to pull itself out of the rubble and form even a semblance of workable government.

No one except Ben Raines and his Rebels.

Tri-States had worked. It had not worked to the satisfaction of all, but it had worked to the satisfaction of all those who lived within its borders. But then the struggling government of the United States, with all the fury and intolerance of a government toward any type of change, had smashed the Rebels' dreams.

Shortly after that, Ben Raines and his Rebels had taken over the government of the United States, and Ben had been installed as president. It was to be a

15

short tenure, for after the horror of germ and nuclear warfare, there followed the plague that threatened to completely wipe out humankind worldwide.

But the human spirit is difficult, if not impossible to crush, and many more people than Ben and his Rebels first thought survived through the disease-carrying rats and fleas.

But there was not a stable government anywhere in the entire world. The world, the countries of the world, the government of those countries, large to tiny, from Russian to Monaco, were no more.

Ben had not traveled outside the boundaries of the United States since the Great War, but he had no reason to doubt the stories that had drifted to him. The stories were appalling. Many people around the world had reverted back, in such an amazingly short time, to barbarism. Even in what remained of the United States, warlords had risen out of the rubble and ruin, to claim all sorts of territory, to enslave the people, to rob and rape and loot. There were people within the borders of the United States who had reverted back to the caves, calling themselves the Underground People, rarely venturing out during the daylight hours. All sorts of cults and so-called religions had sprung out of the ashes, preaching all sorts of semi-religious bullshit. Most of it hate filled. And a lot of the hate was directed toward Ben Raines and his Rebels.

The far Northeast was out of bounds for anyone, human or otherwise—so far as Ben knew. That area of the country had taken several nuclear hits, along with a few other cities. Most had died from the germ warfare.

And there were mutants that roamed the land, products of the germ and chemical and nuclear bombs. Part human, part animal, and God alone knew what else. Great hairy beasts, the adults as large as the biggest polar bear, and twice as dangerous because the mutants had some capacity for thought and reason.

There was danger anywhere one ventured. No one dared to go unarmed. To do so, to be unprepared, to drop one's guard for even a moment, in this now savage land, was to court death—or worse.

And in South Carolina, waiting to spread like a wildfire, was the Libyan, Khamsin, The Hot Wind, and his thousands of troops. For now, Khamsin and his people were contained; Ben's Rebels and the civilian fighters along the borders of South Carolina were holding The Hot Wind, allowing it to blow within that state, but preventing it from spreading.

But while some of his people may have been kidding themselves, Ben Raines knew that Khamsin and his troops could break out wherever and whenever they chose to do so. Why they had not done so was something that still puzzled Ben.

But he knew that before he could really, effectively start his outposts across the land, Khamsin had to be dealt with. And dealt with in extreme prejudice.

In other words, kill the son of a bitch!

"Now I think I'm a good Christian man, General Raines," the spokesman with the group from South Carolina told Ben. "But I worship the God I choose. That damned bunch of heathens that's took over South Carolina is forcin' people to forsake Jesus Christ and God Almighty to worship Allah. Now, I ain't knockin' anybody's religion, but I'll worship my God, not somebody else's God. And I'll fight for that right, sir."

The man was ragged, but there was steel in his

words, and the weapons they all carried were old, but well cared for.

Ben held out his right hand and the man shook it. "You're my kind of man, sir," Ben told him. "Are there any more following behind you?"

"Not many more, General Raines." The man had gotten over his shock upon learning that he was in the company of the legendary and famed Gen. Ben Raines.

Ben looked at his map. The column was just north of Great Bend, Kansas, a small city that had, before the Great War, a population of about sixteen thousand. Ben had briefed the newcomers of his plans of forming outposts across the country. The people from South Carolina were all immediately interested and eager to be a part of it.

"It won't be easy," Ben told them all. "And it will be lonely and dangerous."

"You lead, sir," the spokesman said. "And we'll follow."

Ben smiled. "Let's go!"

2

Nothing.

A strange, almost eerie silence greeted the column as they rolled up to and stopped at the outskirts of Great Bend, Kansas.

Ben got out of his truck and stood alone in the center of Highway 56. He listened intently, but could hear only the lonely sighing of the hot, late summer wind as it whispered dark and bloody secrets from times past.

Ike joined Ben, and Ben was glad that the man had flown back from Base Camp One after Nina's rescue to rejoin him.

"Eerie," Ike said.

"More and more we're seeing this," Ben said, his voice soft in the heat that reflected up off the roadway. "People forsaking the towns to head for the deep country. Splintering off into groups of two and three families. But they don't realize, even now, they're committing suicide by doing that. Seems like

19

they'd know by now that the only strength is in loyal numbers."

"They'll probably realize it," Ike said sourly. "Right before they die."

"Hell of a way to find out," Ben said. "Sergeant!" he called. "Get a flag from the truck. Dan! Send your teams in to recon the town."

"Right away, sir!"

The long column waited under the sun. A hour passed before the recon team leader radioed back. "Nothing and nobody, sir. The town, as far as we're able to determine, is deserted."

"Cordon it off," Dan," Ben ordered. "Then begin a house-to-house, building-to-building search. Let's be sure of what we've got." He motioned for an aide to come over. "At Dan's orders, start the other teams in to label and store anything that's useful. Go."

"Yes, sir."

Ben turned to the man from South Carolina. "Are you in contact with any of the people coming up behind you?"

"No, sir. But they know the route. That was pre-planned."

"Any malcontents among them? Bigots, laggards, anyone like that?"

"No, sir. We copied our form of existence from you, general. From the old Tri-States philosophy. Everybody works. If they don't work, they don't stay. We take care of the old and sick. But able-bodied people work."

"We'll stay here with you for a couple of days," Ben told him. "If you've survived this long, you know something about defense. We'll upgrade your weapons, leave you plenty of ammo and the wherewithal to produce more. Then we'll push on. For this first winter, food might present a problem for you. You might be eating a lot of game, but I suspect you're used to that."

The man grinned. "Growed up on it, general. We'll start farmin' and putting in gardens come spring."

Ben sighed. "Well, it's a start. We might be able to pull it off. God knows, we've got to try."

"It's never gonna be the way it was, is it, general?"

"Not in our lifetime," Ben said, thinking, probably never again.

Ben was awakened by the guard commander just after midnight. "We got company, general."

Ben pulled on his boots and slipped into his ammo harness. He picked up his Thompson and said, "Who are they and how many of them?"

"Identity unknown, sir. At least a couple of hundred of them out there."

"Have they made their intentions known?"

"They're either awfully arrogant or extremely stupid, Ben." Ike's voice came through the darkness. "They think they're slipping up on us. Our forward posts reported them moving into our area about forty-five minutes ago. I decided to let you sleep until we were sure what they were up to."

Ike had moved closer, and Ben could see the smile on the man's lips. "And exactly what are they up to?"

"We captured one of them. Dude looks like something out of one of those old punk-rock movies. Of all the things I have to remember from back in the '80s, it would have to be that shit."

"They are rather unforgettable," Ben said drily. "Warlords type?"

"Right. Are you ready for this, Ben?"

21

"Give it to me."

"They follow some guy calls himself Zorro."

"Does he wear a mask and a cape?" Ben asked with a smile.

The young guard did not have the foggiest idea what General Raines and General McGown were talking about. Zorro was a new one on him.

Ike laughed. "Let's hope not. I'd be laughing too hard to shoot him."

"You're in our territory," the young man told Ben. "And for that, you all will die."

Ben sat and stared at the odd-looking young man. His head was shaved, all except for a strip of hair down the center of his head. And that was colored orange and green. He wore high-topped boots, leather britches, and a sleeveless T-shirt.

"You're the goddamnedest thing I've ever seen since the days of Alice Cooper, boy," Ben told him. "Do you know who we are?"

"I am not a female!"

"Neither was he. Answer my question."

"You are invaders in our territory. You will all die."

The young man's body odor was getting a bit much. Ben wondered if the young man had ever been introduced to soap and water. "My name is Ben Raines."

"You lie!" the young man shouted. "Ben Raines does not exist. He is a myth. No man can do what he is said to have done. You're an imposter!"

"Sorry to disappoint you, boy," Ike said. "But you're lookin' at the real article."

Obviously, the stories about Ben being a god either

22

had not reached Zorro and his group, or else they simply chose not to believe them.

The young man spat in Ben's face.

Ben backhanded the strange-looking young man clear out of his chair.

With the young man staring up at him, blood leaking from a cut lip, Ben said, "You've been treated pretty good in this camp, boy. If you'd been wounded, we'd have patched you up; if you're hungry, we'll feed you. But if you ever spit in my face again, I'll kill you!"

The sounds of gunfire split the still night air. The yammering of M-60s and .50 caliber machine guns hammered and chugged.

The young man had jerked on the floor as the guns erupted. Ben had neither blinked nor moved, but just continued staring at him.

"Cease fire." Dan's voice roared over the noise. "Cease fire. Someone's out there with a white flag."

Ben turned to the young Rebel who had captured the—whatever the hell he was, and Ben wasn't all sure. "If he moves, shoot him, son."

"Yes, sir!"

Ben stepped out of the building with Ike just as a runner came panting up. "One of those funny-lookin' people has come up with a white flag, general. Says he wants to talk with our leader."

"Well . . ." Ben had to fight back a chuckle. "Take me to him."

"Ben," Ike said. "This is getting ridiculous! What's with these people? Have they been freaking out on old movies?"

"I don't know, Ike. But their guns are sure real."

"For a fact."

Both men came to a sudden halt at the sighting of

the truce-flag bearer. Ike had to choke back a laugh. But his stifled humor was infectious: Ben had to cover his mouth with a hand to keep from laughing.

Old Doc Chase appeared in the night and stood with his hands on his hips, glaring at Ben and Ike. "It's not funny! It's tragic. And you both ought to be ashamed of yourselves!"

The young man with the white flag was dressed almost identical to the young man guarded by the Rebel. With a couple of exceptions:

He wore a black mask over his eyes and had on a long black cape.

Perhaps it was because of the long and brutal fight that Ben and his Rebels had just endured, defeating the Russian, Striganov, and Ben finally killing his old adversary, Sam Hartline. Pent-up emotions and wire-tight nerves, perhaps. Whatever the reasons, Ben and Ike sat down on the curb by the littered street and laughed until tears were rolling down their cheeks. The two men were so weak from laughing at the sight they had to lean on each other for strength as their laughter wound down.

Other Rebels had gathered around, most of them young, too young to know anything about Zorro. They thought the flag-bearing person was dressed a bit oddly; but from the way General Ike and General Ben were laughing, you'd have thought they'd just heard the funniest joke in the world.

"You're laughing at me!" the orange-haired, caped young man screamed.

Ben waved at him. "No, son. Not you. I would explain, but I think it would take too long." Chuckling, Ben got to his feet, helping Ike up. "Anybody hurt in all that gunfire?" he called.

"None of our lads and lassies!" Dan Gray called.

"But we dropped a dozen or so of . . . whatever in the world these misbegotten folks might be."

"Zorroettes!" Ike burst out, and both he and Ben started laughing again.

Now Dan started chuckling. Soon his chuckling had grown into full-throated laughter.

The younger Rebels stood smiling at the antics of their senior officers, but they didn't really know what was going on.

CSM James Riverson walked onto the scene and stood for a moment, smiling and shaking his head. He looked at the caped young man, anger on his unshaven face. "You foolish young man," James told him. "Do you know who your people attacked this night?"

"No. And I don't give a shit, neither."

"Gen. Ben Raines and the Rebels."

That shook the young man down to his high-topped boots. His face paled in the dim moonlight. "General Raines does not exist," he said, his voice very shaky.

James pointed toward Ben. "General Raines, meet . . . Zorro." Then James started laughing.

"Stop laughing at me!" the young man screamed. "I command you to stop it!"

Ben walked to the young man, stopping a few feet from him. "What is it you want . . . Zorro?" He managed to keep a straight face.

"I want my brother's body. You have it."

"No, I don't have your brother's body. But I do have your brother. He's very much alive. But what do we get out of this exchange?"

"I'll . . . allow you to live."

"That's big of you, son. Now I'll tell you something. You can have your brother, and welcome to him. I hope to God you both go somewhere and take a bath. Preferably with soap. A group of Rebels will be resettling this town, this area. And I am giving the orders that if they see anyone with hostile intentions, they are to shoot them on the spot. Do you understand that?"

"You have no right to come in here giving orders to me!"

"Now you listen to me, you . . . Hollywood reject." Ben felt certain the young man had absolutely no idea what Hollywood meant. He pointed a finger at the caped and masked young man. "Do you have farms, gardens, windmills to pull water up?"

Zorro shook his head.

"Do you have schools, hospitals, newspapers, libraries?"

He shook his head again.

"I figure you for about twenty/twenty-two years old. That means you had time for some schooling before the bombs came. And you had ten years after that for education. Right?"

Zorro glared at him.

"Can you read, you bastard!" Ben lost his temper, as he so often did with people who seemed hell-bent on wasting their lives, and more importantly, the lives of others; who seemed content to just exist. In Ben's mind, and in the minds of all who followed him, in this age of no-free-ride, no one had the right to just exist. If there ever was to be another America, everyone had to work toward that goal.

"I can read," the young man replied sullenly.

"How many of your followers can read?"

"Some."

"Are you making any effort to teach them?"

The silence answered Ben's question.

"You stupid young fool!" Ben's voice lashed out at him. "Even the Underground People are teaching their young to read and write and figure. Without education, you're doomed. And you're damning those who follow you."

"We get by."

It's worse than trying to teach social codes and manners to a redneck, Ben thought. "Bring Zorro's brother out here," Ben said.

The young man was led out.

"What's his name?" Ben asked Zorro.

"Lash."

Ike started laughing. Ben struggled to keep a straight face. "I don't *even* want to know how he got his name. Now listen to me. If you and your followers want to live in peace with us, that's fine. If you want war, that's fine. But if it is the latter, I'll wipe you and all that follow you from the face of the earth, then I will stack your stinking, ignorant bodies out in the prairie for the buzzards to eat. Is that understood?"

"Understood, Ben Raines."

"Get out!"

When the two young men were gone, escorted by Rebels, Dr. Chase walked to Ben's side. "You're getting harder, Ben."

"Yes, I am, Lamar. And I'll tell you why. If we—you, me, Ike, Cecil, all the Rebels—we don't get a grip on the handle of this thing and start twisting it around, we will have nothing to leave our children. Nothing except savagery, barbarism, and years of ignorance. Education is the *only* way we're going to pull out of this mess. And don't you think for an instant that Zorro what's-his-name doesn't know that. He knows it. But he's smart enough to know

27

that with education, his followers would leave him.

"Lamar, I have hated ignorance all my life. In every one of the books I wrote, under whatever name, somewhere in those books, I made my comment about education being important. Now, more than ever, we've got to stress education."

Chase waved him silent. "Don't lecture me, Raines. Hell, I agree with you. But what leadership have people like this . . . Zorro had to follow? None! And *you* know *that*."

"That's their problem, Lamar. All that shows me is that they're ignorant to the core, and worse, proud of it."

The doctor, another Rebel who had been with Ben from the outset, having met him outside the ruins of Denver a few months after the Great War, stared and glared at Ben in the dim natural light of night. "What would you do with people like that, Ben?" he asked softly.

Ben returned the stare, letting his eyes speak silent, cold words.

"I see," Chase said.

"I'm glad you do," Ben replied. He turned around and walked up the silent, littered street, to his billet for the night.

Dan Gray stepped out of the night to stand by Dr. Chase. "If Ben's dream could come true, Lamar, we could all lay down our guns and live in peace."

"Laying them down on the ground that covers the bodies of those who chose not to read Themistocles, Aeschylus, and Pindar, Dan?"

"You've read them, yet you're here," the Englishman said softly.

"Yes," the doctor said quietly. "I suppose you're right. But I am so weary of war."

"And you think Ben Raines is not?"

"Dan, I'm sure he is. But I'm wondering if he knows that on this night, he made a mortal enemy of that Zorro-type?"

"He knows."

"I have this uneasy feeling that he did so with careful deliberation."

"Your feeling would be correct, I should imagine."

"For God's sake, Dan!"

"It isn't so awful, Lamar. So one or ten or twenty dies in order to salvage two or three hundred. You've seen Ben do it before. Why should his actions on this night offend you so?"

"In other words, Dan—you can't make an omelet without breaking some eggs?"

"Something like that, doctor."

"Perhaps it's time for me to stay behind, Dan. To run my hospital and care for the sick at Base Camp One." The words were not phrased in question form.

"That is a question only you can answer, doctor."

"You think it's going to get worse before it gets better, don't you, Dan?"

"Most assuredly, doctor."

"Well, to hell with it!" Lamar Chase said. "Someone has to tag along to look after that damned long lean drink of water. Might as well be me."

"I thought that would be your answer."

"You're all going to die!" The angry words sprang out of the night. "If you stay here, you're all going to die. Die! Die! I am Zorro, supreme leader of this area."

"Hold your fire!" Dan called. "Pass the word," he ordered. "Let the fool sign his own death warrant."

"What price peace, Dan?" Lamar asked.

"One look at the graveyards of the world should

answer that, Lamar."

The doctor and the warrior parted. The night once more grew silent.

Not quite as silent as a graveyard—but close.

3

The outline of Great Bend gradually faded in the rearview mirror of the last vehicle in the long column. Everyone in the Rebel column felt a small sense of loss; they had all left friends behind in the prairie outpost, and all wondered if they would ever seen them again.

The Scouts were ranging miles in front of the column, and as was his custom, Ben drove at the head of the column, in his pickup truck, alone.

"We have company, general," a Scout radioed back. "On both sides of the column. Motorcycles and dune buggies. I think it's the caped-terror and his bunch." Ben pulled over, halting the column.

Ben's smile contained no humor as he looked at the battered, rusted, and bent road sign: Chase 6 miles. He lifted his mike to his lips. "Is there anything in Chase?"

"Nothing, sir. It's a ghost town. That's where we've pulled over."

"How many people you need to pull this off?"

"One platoon, sir."

"You listening to this transmission, Ike?"

31

"Ten-four, Ben. I've got a platoon leader moving out now."

"Keep me informed."

"Ten-four, Ben."

Ben sat in his pickup, listening to the silence build around him. Most of the vehicles in the long column had shut down their engines. Ben was not particularly proud of what he was doing. But he'd done it too many times in the past to expect to lose much sleep over it.

To kill the snake, one had to cut off the head.

In his side mirror, Ben could see Ike walking slowly up to him. Ben got out of his truck and waited on the cracked highway for his friend.

"You and Dr. Chase have a few words last night, Ben?"

"Nothing serious. Chase has always been a good balance point for me, Ike. I really expect this run to be his last. I'd like to see him slow down. Maybe stay back at Base Camp One and run his hospital. As a matter of fact, I think I'll suggest it — in a very tactful way. He'd be much more valuable to us as a teacher."

Nodding his head, Ike said, "Oughta pop anytime now."

"Yeah. Chase thinks I enjoy this, Ike."

"No, he doesn't, Ben. He's just tired of this endless war. I think he'd like to try another way of settling things — like with this bunch of kids — but he knows, down deep, that what you're — *we're* — doing, is the only way."

"I wish somebody would show me another way, Ike. If it had just a chance of succeeding, I'd damn sure try it."

Two quick rifle shots split the late summer air. They came from the rear of the convoy. Ike lifted his walkie-talkie to his lips. "Ike. What's that shooting about?"

While Ike was listening, Ben's ears could just pick up the very faint sounds of heavy gunfire; his eyes seeing black plumes of smoke rising from out on the seemingly endless prairie.

Ike lowered the walkie-talkie and looked at Ben. "Zorro and his brother, Ben. Rear guard caught them trying to plant charges under one of the fuel trucks. They're both hard hit."

"Come on."

Ike got in the passenger side, and Ben pulled off the road and onto the once wheat and corn-filled land, now long grown over with weeds and wild runners. As they drove, Ben's radio crackled. Ben lifted the mike to his lips and said, "Go."

"We broke the back of Zorro's boys and girls," one of Dan Gray's Scouts reported. "We followed your orders and took a lot of prisoners, general."

Ben had broken one of his rules this day and allowed the taking of prisoners. Solely for the sake of Dr. Chase. Ben wanted to prove a point, but he hoped to hell his point was never made. He also feared it would be made—the hard way—in this deadly crap shoot.

"Hold them there," Ben radioed.

The two young men lay in the center of the old highway, Dr. Chase and his medics working on them. Chase looked up as Ben walked over to the blood-splattered spot on the highway.

"Both these boys are gut-shot," Chase said. It was not spoken reproachfully; just stating a fact.

The Rebel cradling the 7mm Magnum looked at Ben.

"Nice shooting," Ben told him.

The sniper smiled.

Chase muttered something under his breath.

"Are they going to live?" Ben asked.

"You know better," Chase replied without looking up. "One has a shattered spinal cord and the other's guts are torn apart. There is nothing I can do for them except try to ease the pain."

"Put them in the back of my truck and we'll take them up to the next town. By the way, doctor—the name of the town is Chase. Do you suppose that's prophetic?"

"Why take them there?" Chase asked, ignoring Ben's question.

"I want the prisoners to see that the caped-avenger and his sidekick are mortals."

"*You* ordered prisoners taken?" Chase asked. "Getting soft, Raines?"

"No, Lamar. You seem to think there is hope for people such as these." Ben pointed to the dying young men. "You can have your chance."

"You mean that, Ben?"

"I said it, didn't I?"

Chase looked long at him. Finally, the doctor sighed. "Put them in the truck," he ordered.

The Rebels had killed or wounded about a third of the attackers. They had the others sitting in a vacant lot of the tiny deserted town, their hands behind their heads, fingers laced.

"See to the wounded," Chase ordered his medics.

"Personally," Ben said, "I'd drag Zorro and Lash out of the truck and dump their bodies in the street, doctor. But this is your show; you handle it the way you like."

34

"Thank you so much, Ben." The sarcasm was rather thick in his voice. "But how do you know the boys are dead?"

"I just looked."

A medic confirmed it.

"Put them on the sidewalk," Chase ordered.

"Charlie Company," Ben ordered. "First and second platoons. Stack arms here." He pointed to the sidewalk.

Chase paid no attention to the orders. Ben looked at Ike.

"Everything set, Ike?" he whispered.

"Right. And I hope to hell this doesn't backfire, Ben."

"You and me. Since we're going to be right in the middle of it."

"You people!" Lamar shouted at the prisoners, young men and young women. "Look at your leaders and tell me what they died for?"

The eyes of the prisoners looked at the bloody pair on the sidewalk. "They died fighting for our right to claim territory," a young woman said.

"I'll give you that much," Chase conceded. "But what have you been *doing* with this claimed territory?"

"We don't have to do anything with it," a young man said. "It's just ours."

"I've seen no signs of farms or gardens or anything like that," the doctor said. "Where do you get your food?"

"People pay us tribute to live here."

Ben smiled, and his smile annoyed Chase.

Doing his best to ignore Ben's smile, Chase asked, "Suppose you were given the chance to better yourselves, would any of you take it?"

Ben and Ike picked up very quietly on the furtive glances that passed between the prisoners.

"How do you mean, 'better ourselves'?" a young man asked.

"Have an education. Live in . . . relative peace. Work and build and plan for the future. That's what I mean."

Several of the prisoners exchanged soft whispers. One of them who squatted near a stack of weapons cut his eyes to the weapons, very quickly, and then looked back at Chase. "Can I stand up?" he asked. "I hurt my leg and it's crampin'."

"Of course," Chase told him.

Ike very quickly clicked his CAR-15 off safety. James Riverson shifted positions, a seemingly harmless movement. But the muzzle of his M-16 was now pointed toward the large group of prisoners.

Dan Gray and Ben very briefly locked eyes as the Englishman turned. Now the muzzle of his automatic weapon was pointed directly at the front row of prisoners.

The young man stood up, rubbed his leg, and took a step toward a stack of weapons. Just one step, but it put him very close.

"Work?" the young man said. "What kind of work you talkin' about?"

"You have to work to live," Chase said patiently. "It's wrong to force people to give you tribute if they don't want to give it."

"Who says it's wrong?" a young woman asked, rising to her feet.

She scratched her head, and Ben could practically see the fleas hopping about on her head.

The smell of unwashed bodies was rank in the still, breezeless summer morning.

"God says it's wrong," Chase told her.

"Not our god," the young woman said.

"What God do you worship?"

"That one," she said, pointing to the bloody body of Zorro.

"But he's dead!" Chase said. "That should tell you something about your choice of whom to worship. Doesn't it?"

"Naw." She shook her head. "We'll just find another one."

"Is it that easy?" Chase asked.

"Sure. We have a dance-thing. The one who dances the longest is the chosen one."

"A . . . dance-thing?" Chase said slowly. "Can you read?" he asked her.

"What for?"

"So you can teach your children!" Chase's voice held a definite note of annoyance.

"Why do that? Readin' don't put food in our bellies. It don't protect us from the rain and the cold. It don't do nothin'."

Many of the prisoners were now standing, and several had moved much closer to the stacks of weapons.

The Rebels did not order them to get back on the ground. Many of the Rebels had turned their backs to the prisoners, seemingly uninterested in the proceedings.

"Suppose we turned you all loose?" Chase asked. "What would you do?"

"What do you want us to do?" a young man asked.

"If I didn't know better," Ike muttered, "I'd swear he had some experience talking with a social worker."

"I want you to make something of yourselves," Chase told him. "To help us in rebuilding the United

37

States."

"You mean, laws and rules and all that shit?" the young woman asked.

Chase looked at Ben, a helpless and annoyed look in his eyes. Ben shrugged.

"To have any kind of workable, productive society," Chase said, "one must have rules and laws. Without them, you have anarchy."

Ben had clicked his Thompson off safety.

Ike and Dan had seen the movements of the prisoners toward their high-topped boots and suspected they had knives tucked in there.

"Have what?" the young woman asked, taking yet another step toward the stacks of weapons. She was within reaching distance now.

Ben cut his eyes upward. Several Rebels were on top of a nearby building with M-60 machine guns. Ben carefully eased his finger onto the trigger.

"Anarchy," Chase persisted. "Lawlessness."

"Oh, yeah," the young woman said. "We sure don't want none of that. That'd be terrible."

Chase looked at the young woman. "Everything I've said. It's just a big joke to you, isn't it?"

She shrugged. She would have been a pretty woman had she cleaned up and got the fleas off of her.

But now she wasn't going to have time to do anything. Except die.

"You got your way of life, we got ours," she said. "You're not going to change, and we're not going to change."

"That's a pity," Chase said. "But I had to try."

"Big Louie is waitin' for you folks 'bout a hundred miles further," she said. "Some of you might make it to his turf. I hope so. He likes to burn people alive."

"Sounds like a perfectly delightful fellow," Chase said. "But why would you think that just some of us would make it?"

Screaming, the young woman leaped toward the stack of weapons. The slugs from Dan's M-16 stopped her in mid-air, flinging her backward, dead before she hit the concrete.

The prisoners charged Dr. Chase and Ben and Ike and Dan, knives in their hands.

It was carnage. And it was over in less than a minute.

Twenty-odd of the prisoners had not moved from their spots on the vacant lot. When the gunfire started, they simply hit the ground and stayed there.

When the gunfire had echoed away and the gunsmoke had cleared, Ben looked at those who had elected not to fight, and thus stay alive.

"If I decide to turn you loose, what are you going to do?" Ben asked.

"Git away from this spot just as fast as I can," a young man said. "I might join up with another gang. I might not. I ain't sure. But one thing I am sure of. I ain't gonna fuck around with you people no more."

"Clear out," Ben said. "And I don't ever want to see you again."

The last glimpse any one had of the young man, he was loping across the plains. He did not look back.

"How about the rest of you?" Ben asked the group of young men and women.

"Just let us get away from here and you," a young woman said. "I know me a fellow down in New Mexico wants me to come live with him and raise sheep. I figure now is a damn good time to do just that."

"Your religion must not be too strong." Chase

couldn't resist one more shot at it.

She looked at him. "What religion, you old fart? Stealin's just easier than workin', that's all."

Chase shook his head and walked back to his vehicle.

"Aren't you going to patch up the wounded, Lemar?" Ben called after him.

"Fuck 'em!" Chase said.

4

The column pulled over early that day and made camp, while recon patrols were sent out to check on Big Louie's whereabouts.

"He's pretty close," Ike said. "What's left of Kansas City is gonna be hot for another three/four thousand years."

It was late afternoon, and Dr. Chase, Ben, Ike, Dan, and a few other Rebels were sitting in the shade of a tree, drinking a concoction called Rebel Rouser—homemade whiskey, actually.

And Lamar Chase was hitting the sauce harder than anyone else.

"What a blind, stupid, idealistic old fool I've become," he said.

"That's bullshit, Lamar," Ben told him. "You just got tired of it all. All the killing . . . the whole nine yards. We all do at one time or the other."

"Yeah," Ike said. "You got the 'that's it, I quit, I'm movin' on' syndrome."

"Sam Cooke," the doctor said, refilling his cup with booze.

"What?" Ike said.

41

"Who?" Dan asked.

"Goddamn, Lamar!" Ben said. "You are gettin' old. Or drunk. Or both. *I* don't even remember that one."

"Sam Cooke recorded that," Lamar said. He hummed a few bars.

Dan grimaced. "I hope it sounded better than that."

Lamar, quite uncharacteristically, gave the Englishman the finger.

After the laughter died down, Ike said, "I wonder what this Big Louie is going to turn out to be?"

"Oh, another loser, I should imagine. Don't you agree, general?"

"Sure. Just like Zorro and Lash and all the others we've encountered over the long and bloody years we've been together. It really wouldn't have made any difference. War or peace; prosperity or depression; full working government or anarchy—they'd have been losers of one type or another, no matter what."

"Raines, do you really believe that?" Chase challenged.

"Certainly. How many people did you know back when the world was whole, more or less, who fucked up everything they tried to do? When they lost a job, it wasn't their fault; it was somebody else's fault. If they lost at cards, somebody cheated. If they got a ticket, the cops were picking on them. When they got caught cheating on their income tax, they'd lie to the examiner; and they could lie so well, they actually believed it themselves. If they made a hundred thousand dollars a year, they'd live on a hundred and ten thousand. And when they went bankrupt, it was never their fault. Losers. This situation we're all in now is just perfect for them. It was made to order. They were losers in a land of plenty, and they'll be losers until the day they finally do the world a favor and die."

"You really are a jaundiced bastard, Raines!" Lamar said. "What a perfectly horrible opinion of humankind you have." He tossed back another belt of Rebel Rouser.

"You're a minority of one, Lamar," Ben told him.

"Oh, of course I am!" the doctor cheerfully admitted. "I just like to hear you rant and rave, that's all. I'm sure as hell not going to tell you that you're right. You're such an insufferable martyr as it is."

Ben laughed. This small group he had around him now—the only one person missing being Cecil Jefferys—could always be counted on to tell him the way it was. Without pulling any punches.

"I didn't ask for this job," Ben said with great indignation.

"Oh, God!" Lamar said. "Here he goes again."

Dan excused himself, leaving to go check on the guards and to see if any intel had been received on Big Louie.

The column had left Highway 56 just east of Marion, Kansas, angling south on Highway 77 for a few miles, then once more heading east on Highway 50, picking that up at Florence. They were camped along the banks of the Cottonwood River. Chase's medical people had tested the waters of the little river and found no contamination from radiation. Kansas City was hot, but like so many of the cities around the world, the bombs were of the "clean" variety: killing the people, but leaving the buildings standing.

The convoy was going east on their present route only as far as the junction with Highway 75, about fifteen miles past Emporia. If they didn't encounter Big Louie by then, to hell with it. They would cut south down to Highway 54 and continue on east, avoiding Kansas City.

Dr. Chase poured another cup of Rebel Rouser and said, "What about the next outpost, Ben?"

"Iola, I'm hoping. Scouts report about two hundred and fifty or so people in and around that area. They seem to have some organization. But they've been having some trouble with roving gangs. Probably this Big Louie character. We'll meet with the people in Iola and see if we can't punch Big Louie's ticket. See about setting up an outpost there."

A Rebel said, "Seems like whenever we put one gang out of business, three more pop up."

"It's going to be that way for a long time to come, I'm thinking," Ike said, eyeballing Lamar as he knocked back the booze. "And with the exception of Zorro and his bunch of nitwits, the gangs seem to be getting smarter. You agree, Ben?"

"Many of them, yes. The really smart warlords know we're after them; and they're doing their best to avoid us. We can't let up, either. We're going to have to keep the pressure on."

Lamar looked at his cup. "It's never going to end, is it, Ben?"

"No, Lamar. It isn't. I thought for awhile it would. I thought for awhile it would take us two, maybe three years to clean up the country. Then we could all settle down and live out our lives in relative peace. I was wrong."

"You're not the only one who was wrong, Ben," Ike said.

Ben looked at his friend.

Ike poured a short two-fingers into his cup. His smile was both knowing and sarcastic. "You remember all the talk shows and books and magazines back in the late '70s and '80s—all that crap about how the military sucked and how peace advocates were always

44

blabbering about *they* would be the ones who would build a better society if any major tragedy ever occurred. And *their* way was the only way. Just a more articulate extension of the peace and love bull-shit of the '60s." He knocked back a belt of booze.

"Well, guess what, folks? Where are they now? Guess who is out here trying to put this nation back together again? Old soldiers. Surprise, surprise! And where are the peace and love and lay down your weapons advocates? In the grave, I guess. I sure haven't seen any lately. But more than likely, any who survived are high up in the mountains or in the deep woods, in little-bitty communes, keeping a very low profile. And not doing one goddamn thing toward rebuilding this country. But what galls my balls is this, and you all know I'm speaking the truth: When we get this outpost system complete, coast to coast, and some semblance of law and order, you just wait and see—here they'll come, whole bunches of the little mouthy bastards and bitches, all of them say-ing, 'Oh, we're so happy to see you big, brave people. Is it safe now? Can we come out and join you folks?' You wait and see if it doesn't happen that way."

"Wait a minute, Chase," Ike said. "I'm not done yet. And if we let those assholes in, they won't be in fifteen minutes before they'll start sneaking around behind our backs, making all sorts of snide little comments. Like, 'Well, we have law and order, now, so why don't we put some controls on those terrible guns? And isn't the death penalty terribly harsh? Why don't we do away with it?' And that sort of bullshit. Fuck 'em. Fuck 'em all!"

Chase looked at Ike. "Jesus Christ, McGowan! Who pulled your string? What brought on all this crap?"

" 'Cause I can see the light at the end of the

tunnel, Lamar. That's why. And I want to make my views known, up front, and right now. The light's still a long way off. We've got a lot of bloody years ahead of us; but we're gonna make it. We'll stretch this outpost system from coast to coast, and then we'll start workin' it north to south. *Us!* Not those other assholes — *us!* We're the ones going to make it work, with our blood, and our sweat, and our pain. We got graveyards stretchin' from Georgia to California, Michigan to Texas. And those Rebels didn't die so a bunch of goody-two-shoes types can come in and spew their verbal poison.

"That's it, I'm done. Me and Dan talked this over the other afternoon. That's why Dan left a while ago; so I could say it. And . . . I ain't throwin' stones at anyone here. Don't think that at all. I just wanted to clear the air."

Ike rose and left.

Ben carefully rolled a cigarette and lit it. He took a slow drag and exhaled, his eyes on Dr. Chase. "First time Ike's made a speech that long in years."

"But he's right, you know."

"I know."

"And some of those people he described will certainly surface."

"I hope they don't get near Ike. He'd probably shoot them."

"And you, Ben? What about you?"

"I'd probably help him do it. Or at least want to help."

Chase shook his head. "Going to become very interesting around here very soon." He poured another cup of Rebel Rouser and downed it.

"Lamar, are you going to sit here and get drunk?"

"That is my intention."

"You're going to have a hell of a headache in the

morning, old friend."

"Nonsense! I never have hangovers."

"How long has it been since you were last drunk?"

"Oh . . . twenty years or so."

Ben smiled. "Good luck."

"What's the matter with Lamar this morning?" Dan asked Ben.

"He isn't feeling well," Ben said.

Lamar was sitting in front of his tent, a cup of coffee on a small camp table in front of him. Using both hands, he managed to get the cup to his mouth and take a sip without spilling too much of it.

"Worse crap I ever tried to drink," Lamar bitched. "Almost pure chicory."

"Would you like to have a bit of the hair of the dog that bit you?" Dan called cheerfully.

Lamar glared balefully at him. "How would you like to be circumcised without benefit of anesthesia?" the doctor growled.

Laughing, the two men walked toward the communications truck.

"Anything on Big Louie yet?" Ben asked the young woman Rebel manning the truck jammed full of electronic gear.

"I've been putting together bits and pieces as they come in, general. I got the last transmission about twenty minutes ago. Want me to read what I've got so far?"

"Please." Ben accepted a cup of tea from Dan's batman, Carl, and sat down. Some of the Rebels liked the strong chicory-thick crap that now passed for coffee. Ben did not. Oh, he'd drink it if there was nothing else, but he preferred tea. And the Rebels had warehouses full of tea. It seems that in their haste to loot coffee, thousands and thousands of tins of tea were passed over, as well as warehouses full of it.

"Big Louie," the woman Rebel read. "Age forty-eight, approximately. Real name unknown. Until recently controlled territory from Nebraska line to Topeka, south. West to Manhattan. Now has included everything east of the old Kansas Turnpike to the Missouri line . . ."

"Very enterprising chap," Dan said, nibbling on a cracker.

"Yes," Ben agreed. He looked up as Ike entered the truck.

"What's wrong with Lamar this morning? I said hello and he told me to go screw myself."

"He has a slight hangover," Dan said.

"Shall I continue, general?" the woman asked.

"Please. Sorry for the interruption."

She gave Ike a dirty look. He grinned at her.

She brought Ike up to date and said, "Big Louie had approximately three thousand men and women under his command."

"Three *thousand!*" Ben blurted.

"My word!" Dan said.

"Where in the hell did he come up with three thousand people and where in the hell has he been hiding them so we didn't pick it up?" Ike asked.

"Here we go again," James Riverson spoke from the open door.

"I'm afraid so, James," Ben said. "Go on, young lady," he told the radio operator.

"The Scouts have picked up information that indicates Big Louie is a college graduate with a degree in economics from the University of Kansas. Knows this area as well as, or better, than anyone. Served in the Marine Corps. Officer. Captain. Runs his organization with military precision. His people are extremely well armed. Has enslaved the Potawatomi, Kickapoo, Sac, and Fox Indians. Uses them as forced labor on his farms. Extremely successful with farming and ranching. Has reopened schools and many area hospitals. Restored electricity and many social services." She looked at Ben. "The last part says that his idol is Gen. Ben Raines."

5

"He's a warlord! Has enslaved entire tribes of Indians and uses them for forced labor. And *I* am his *idol?*" Ben kicked a camp chair over. "Where does this son of a bitch think he's coming from?"

The entire Rebel contingent had made themselves busy in other parts of the camp when Ben started yelling. All except Ike, Dan, Lamar, and James. They sat and watched and waited while Ben vented his spleen.

Lamar grimaced as Ben yelled. He took two more aspirin.

"Where is this bastard's HQ?" Ben yelled.

"Topeka," Ike told him.

"Well, the guy must be crazy! What was it that girl with the orange and green hair told us? That he liked to burn people alive!" He pointed a finger at Dan. "I want as much intel as your Scouts can get me. Troop placement, location of farms and ranches, condition of the people inside his territorial claims, the whole ball of wax."

"Right away, sir."

"I'm glad the kids aren't here," Ben said, calming down a bit. "They'd want to go in there as my eyes and ears."

He thought of Lora and wondered how she was getting along. He had grown very fond of the little girl.

"Ike? Tell the people to eat and sleep and check and clean their weapons carefully. I want a full report on our ammo situation. Anything that we might need flown in from Base Camp One, order it done so, immediately."

Ike nodded his head. "Damn sure can't have a two-hundred-mile gap in our outpost system, can we, Ben? Especially one running right smack through a warlord's territory."

"We sure can't, Ike."

Ike walked off, shouting for his aides.

"Kick-ass time again, huh, Ben?" James asked.

"Looks that way, James. How's morale?"

"High. Of course, they thought they were going home. But they'll follow you anywhere you lead, Ben."

"Explain the situation to them, James."

The command sergeant major nodded and walked off, a huge man, so big his M-16 looked like a toy in his hands.

"Want a drink, Lamar?" Ben said, his good humor returning — slowly.

"Hell with you, Raines! You gonna start barking orders at me, too?"

"If I have to tell you what to do, you old goat, I'm in real trouble."

"I'm too short of everything for a full scale battle, Ben. I'll get on the horn to Base Camp One and tell

Cecil to start shipping me supplies. Where's the LZ going to be?"

"I don't know, yet." He looked at a map of Kansas. "We're sitting right on the edge of Big Louie's territory. I don't want to go as far south as El Dorado; that'd put us too far off center. Well, shit on it! We'll knock down the telephone poles and land them in the road. On Fifty-six, somewhere between Herington and Council Grove. Tell Cec I'll call in the LZ in the morning; soon as I have Scouts check it out."

"And away we go," Lamar said, rising from his chair and groaning from his hangover.

"Jackie Gleason," Ben said with a grin.

After Lamar had gone, alternately bitching and moaning, a young Rebel touched Ben on the arm.

"Sir?"

"Yes, son?"

"Who's Jackie Gleason?"

The young man had crossed into Indiana, met up with a group of pretty nice people and stayed with them for a day, listening to them talk.

Gen. Ben Raines, they had heard, was returning East, victorious after his defeat of the Russian and the mercenary, Sam Hartline. They were on their way to Ben Raines Base Camp, in North Georgia. Would the young man like to come along?

No. He thought he'd head west. Any idea where Ben Raines might be about now?

Colorado. Maybe as far as Central Kansas.

The young man pulled out before dawn. Heading west. He carried a .45 autoloader on each hip. A knife on his side and another one in a sheath on his right boot.

He was square jawed and tanned, very heavily muscled. His hair was dark and curly. His eyes could be warm or friendly, or deadly cold. Usually they were expressionless. The young man was quite handsome; but not in the pretty-boy manner. His was a rugged handsomeness.

He wore no riding helmet; only a red bandana tied around his head. A bandoleer of clips for his weapons was slung over one shoulder. Clips for the weapon he carried in a leather boot on the motorcycle.

The weapon was an old Thompson submachine gun.

Khamsin sat in his headquarters in South Carolina and listened to his field commanders as they reported. The Libyan terrorist-turned-general sat on a pillow. The wound in his ass, compliments of Ike McGowan, still bothered the man.

"We could break out at any time we wish," a man said. "The Rebels' positions along our borders are thinly manned."

"So they would have you believe," Khamsin said. "But behind them they have heavy artillery, missiles, and rockets. Oh, they'd let us break through. Then as soon as we were inside their territory, they'd put us in a box and destroy us. You all are far too confident. The black person commanding these troops while Ben Raines is out West is Cecil Jefferys. And Raines did not put him in charge thanks to some renewed program of racial equality. General Jefferys is in command because he is an excellent soldier. No,

53

brothers, no. The Rebels are accustomed to facing and fighting and winning against superior numbers." He looked at an open folder on his desk. "Each Rebel is trained and mentally conditioned to neutralize five of the enemy. Kindly bear in mind that the people who initially set up the Rebels' training program were Special Forces, Rangers, Marine Force Recon, Seals, SAS, and French Foreign Legion personnel. And kindly bear in mind that six, *six* Rebels wreaked havoc upon this very HQ, killed several hundred of our best troops, and stole a prisoner from under our noses. Six!"

And wounded me in the ass! Khamsin thought bitterly.

How humiliating!

"General Khamsin," a commander said. "Allah has blessed The Hot Wind."

Allah is not down here getting His butt kicked, Khamsin thought. Then he silently said a short prayer, asking for forgiveness for his thoughts.

"It is useless to send coded messages to our scouts in the field," another commander said. "The Rebels break the codes routinely."

"Do we have any intel on who is in charge of that section?" Khamsin asked.

"A person by the name of Lansky," he was informed.

"Naturally," Khamsin said. "Will we forever be cursed with those wretched people?"

No one offered a reply to that. Another six thousand years certainly seemed feasible.

Sister Voleta sat alone in her house. She had

gradually gotten over the shock of her only son's leaving. Now, looking back, she realized that she should have seen the signs.

He was just too much like his father: too opinionated, bullheaded. He never wanted the power she could have given him; too concerned about the needs of others—and he had consistently rejected her teachings. This was not the first time he'd left her.

Even when the world was whole the boy had been too curious about what lay beyond the next hill. He possessed a brilliant mind, but she could never channel it exactly to her liking. Stubborn little bastard! she thought.

But in her own crazied sort of way, she did love him.

But she didn't wish him well at all.

For she had a pretty good idea where he might be heading. And if the two of them ever got together—she didn't like to think about that at all. The possibilities were just too staggering in scope.

She answered the knock on her door.

"The old man is ready," she was informed.

"Gather everybody," she ordered. "I want them all to see what happens to traitors."

"The old man is singing some Christian song. He has no fear."

"He'll have plenty of fear when the flames sear his flesh, and his singing will take on a different note. I assure you of that."

"We had best curtail any further burning," Big Louie said. "We have been discovered by Ben Raines and his Rebels. I suspect them to come charging in

55

here at any time. Pity. I do so like to hear the screaming."

"Yes, sir, Your Majesty," the aide said, bowing. He left backing up.

Most of the intel received on Big Louie was correct—as far as it went.

Big Louie did earn a degree in economics. However, he never received it. When he learned that he had failed to maintain a four-point grade average, he tried to burn down the administration building.

He was not convicted of that. The only witness to the crime died in a dorm fire.

Big Louie was in the Marine Corps. But he was not an officer. He was a buck-assed private. He was dishonorably discharged after he burned down a barracks. He did some stockade time for that, too.

He changed his name and went to work on Wall Street for a brokerage firm. He was charged with insider trading and almost came to trial. But all the evidence against him was destroyed by fire. Including the man who caught him.

Then the Great War erupted worldwide.

Big Louie soon learned that a great gift of gab was not enough to keep him alive. One had to be tough and hard as nails. For the very first time he was grateful for his Marine Corps training. His only regret was that he hadn't paid more attention.

And he soon learned that many people were willing to do anything, *anything,* to stay alive.

And if you threatened to set them on fire, *everybody* was willing to do anything to stay alive.

When the Tri-States had finally opened their borders to the outside, Big Louie was among the first to go in and look around—being very careful to stay out of trouble while inside those borders. Ben Raines and his Rebels weren't like the law outside of Tri-States. Fuck up inside Tri-States and the law there would either shoot you right off the bat—or wait and hang you later.

And they didn't have any crime within those borders, and that fascinated the crazy mind of Big Louie. The whole world was staggering around trying to create some semblance of order out of the ashes, and Ben Raines and his people were just as content and orderly and happy as that bug in the rug.

It was, to Big Louie's mind, and to the minds of most everybody else, flat, flippin' impossible to do what Raines and his people had done.

But by God! They had done it.

Big Louie soon began to recognize and appreciate what Ben Raines had done. And he began to realize that if one didn't go quite as far as Raines had gone, and sort of reversed some of it, that would work, too.

If one took a certain type of person—not the type that Ben Raines had selected to live in Tri-States, but the less desirable types—and promised them free medical care, schools for the kids, enough to eat, and other social amenities, why the silly shits would do almost anything for you in return. Including turning their heads to certain, shall we say, extremes or excesses on the part of those in command.

After the second and seemingly final collapse of the government of the United States, Big Louie put his plan in operation. And it just tickled him to no end to discover that it really would work.

And what was so simple and amusing was that anyone who didn't like what Big Louie did—why, just

57

set them on fire and listen to them holler.

And Big Louie had one very large and very dark ace in the hole that only he and a very few others close to him knew about. And if Ben Raines fucked around with him too much, why he'd just push the button and let them birds fly!

Big Louie sat on his throne and laughed and laughed at that.

Yep, ol' Ben Raines was the bull of the woods, all right—and he could go on being bull of the woods; as long as the woods he was bull of wasn't anywhere near Big Louie's territory.

"What we've got, general," Dan Gray said, "is a collection of some of the most despicable people in the world gathered around this Big Louie character."

It was not yet dawn, yet Ben and his commanders had been up for several hours, going over gathered material on Big Louie.

And no one had found a thing to like about the man or many of the people who resided within his territory.

"Let's give them the benefit of the doubt," Ben said, adding, "for the moment, that is. This Big Louie character has, or so it seems, set up a workable form of government, complete with shops, stores, trading areas, farms and ranches, and his own currency backed by a gold reserve. Fashioned, in a way, after our Tri-States. Okay, we all see that on the surface. Let's dig for some dirt."

"The first spadeful contains the fact that he has enslaved four different Indian tribes," Dan said.

"Playing devil's advocate," Ben said, "I see the next

shovel containing the fact that he has set up schools and hospitals and some sort of a food-for-all program."

"He kidnaps women to keep his army happy," Chase said.

Ben couldn't think of anything else good to say about the man, so he kept his mouth shut.

"He burns folks alive for amusement," Ike said. He looked up as the sounds of rain hitting the canvas overhead intensified. "Shit! Cec said his weather people say this storm is gonna last two or three days. And the pilots ain't real thrilled about flyin' some of our old birds in bad weather; gonna be a lot of lightning with this storm."

"Let's get back to Big Louie," Ben suggested. "Anybody got anything else good to say about the man?"

No one did.

"Dan," Ben said. "We're not going to be able to do much until this storm blows out of here and we get resupplied. So tell your people to get me some prisoners. See if they can't penetrate just inside the borders and jerk some fat cats out of the nicer homes. Caution them not to kill anybody — unless they absolutely have to. We still don't have any really solid evidence to go on about this Big Louie character. And I'm not going to commit our people on hearsay."

"Right now, general," Dan said, and left the tent.

A runner entered the big tent just as Dan was leaving. "General, a message just came over the horn from Base Camp One."

"Give me the high points, son."

"One of General Jefferys's roaming patrols met up

with some folks from Indiana. They said there has been a major shake-up at this Sister Voleta's camp. A defector. Really shook the woman up bad. The defector is supposedly heading west, to find you."

"Is that it?" Ben asked.

The runner hesitated. "No, sir."

"Well, who is this person?"

"Your son, sir."

6

The heavy storms and rains were still south of the young man's position as he barreled on westward. He crossed the top of Missouri and made it into Kansas before the rains hit him, forcing him to seek shelter. He pulled under a carport, dried off, then checked his motorcycle. He carefully inspected the interior of the house and found it littered with rat shit.

He closed the door behind him and set about making his camp on the carport. After carefully inspecting the skies, the man decided that this storm would not blow away in a few hours; it had settled over the area. He made up his mind he would stick around until the storm had blown past.

Ben Raines Blackman built a small fire and cooked a rabbit he had shot while looking for a place to hole up from the weather. He carefully buried his trash, unrolled his sleeping bag, and spread it out on the floor of the carport. He then field-stripped, cleaned and oiled his weapons. Taking a bar of soap from his kit, the young man stripped and stepped out into the warm rain and bathed. He dressed in clean clothing and lay down on his sleeping bag.

He was close to Ben Raines now. He could sense it. And he could sense something else, too: Trouble. There was something in the air besides wind and rain. Buddy, as his mother had nicknamed him when a baby, was by no means clairvoyant; just a very intelligent and observant young man. His mother and her friends were, he knew, a bit around the bend, mentally speaking, but they had schooled Buddy well in the art of survival. He had been schooled in all forms of martial arts; he was an expert with nearly any weapon he could get his hands on; he knew what plants to eat in the woods and which to leave alone; he could build a shelter from practically nothing.

He was very nearly self-sufficient.

Listening and watching the rains fall, Buddy let his thoughts drift back to his mother and her whacked-out beliefs. He should have pulled out a long time back; he knew that. Much of what his mother did was totally repulsive to him.

However, she had never involved him in anything he felt was wrong. She had shielded him from her baser actions.

Of course, he knew what she was doing, and just the knowledge of it made him an accessory—but perhaps he would be forgiven for that.

On sudden impulse, Buddy rose from the sleeping bag and rolled his motorcycle into the utility room at the back of the carport, hiding it from—from whom? He wasn't sure. It just seemed like a good move to make at the time.

He rearranged his sleeping bag, placing it behind some piled-up old boxes on the carport. He decided against making some tea and put out his small fire.

There was just something about this area that was making Buddy very wary.

The storm blew in that afternoon, raging in full force, pushing every living thing into shelter. There could be no flights from Base Camp One until the storm blew itself out.

But the storm was a wet blessing to Dan Gray's Scouts, who had slipped into the territory claimed by Big Louie. The storm hid any slight noise the skilled guerrilla fighters might make.

One Scout team, led by Ben's daughter, Tina, came upon a fine, well-kept home just outside of Manhattan, Kansas. Tina peeked through a window and smiled at the sight. A fat man, his equally fat wife, and two fat teenagers were watching a movie from a VCR.

"Those at the slickest-lookin' folks I've seen in a long time," a Rebel whispered to Tina.

"Well fed for a fact," Tina whispered back. "I don't think they're going to like being marched through this weather." She smiled.

"You're breaking my heart, Tina."

"Yeah, poor babies," another Rebel said.

The Rebels stood in the pouring rain and driving winds and watched as a young woman walked into the den. The woman was carrying a tray of snacks and drinks.

"Get over here, you bitch!" the fat teenager shouted at her. The woman cringed at his voice. "Hurry up. I'm hungry."

The young woman obviously did not move fast enough to suit the fat boy. When she had placed the tray on a table, the fat boy rose from his chair with a grunt and slapped her.

"Nice kid," Tina muttered.

"That woman is wearing some sort of a dog

63

collar," said one of the Rebels.

"I think they used to call them choke chains," another Rebel said. "But that one appears to be welded together."

The extremely fat girl waddled to her feet and kicked the young woman in the butt. The mother and father thought it all very amusing.

"I want her now!" Fat boy said.

"I wanna watch!" Fat girl said.

The father waved his hand and the boy hooked a leash onto the choke chain, forcing the woman to crawl along on her hands and knees. She was silently weeping. Fat girl followed Fat boy out of the room.

"What a delightful family," a Rebel said, disgust in his voice.

"You ready to bust up their party?" Tina asked the group.

"Yeah. Let's do it before I puke!"

Tina assigned members of her squad to their places. Somewhere in the house, they could hear the sounds of screaming.

"Now!" Tina spoke into a handy-talkie. A Rebel kicked in the back door at the same instant Rebels were pouring in through the front door.

Tina placed the muzzle of her M-16 against the neck of the man. "You wiggle and I'll blow your head off."

"How dare you burst into my house!" the man blustered. "I'll see you burned alive for this!"

Fat boy and Fat girl were herded out into the den, a Rebel poking the boy on his bare ass with the muzzle. Fat girl was bawling. The young woman wearing the choke chain was struggling into her clothing.

"How do you get that chain off of her?" Tina asked the man.

"You don't. They're welded on at the prison. Who are you crazy people?"

"Get up," Tina told him.

"I must certainly will not!"

Tina popped him on the mouth with the butt of her rifle. Blood flew and teeth popped under the impact. "Get up, goddamn you!"

Moaning and holding his busted and bleeding mouth, the man got to his feet, swaying slightly.

"Get Fat boy some clothes," Tina said. "She looked at the man's wife. "Get up!"

The older woman jumped to her feet. "They're Ben Raines's Rebels," she told her husband.

"Right," Tina told her. "Now shut up." She looked at the young woman. "Are you a slave in this house?"

"Yes, ma'am. I'm a half-breed Indian. My mother was white, my father was Fox."

"Pack a few clothes," Tina told her. "We're getting you out of this place. We'll cut that chain off back at camp."

"You can't do this to us!" Fat boy wailed. "His Majesty said we was all safe here."

"His Majesty?" a Rebel blurted.

"King Big Louie," Fat girl said, still blubbering. She wiped her snotty nose with the back of her hand.

"Well, guess what?" Tina said. "His Majesty lied!"

"Incredible," Ben muttered. "He's been getting away with it for more than three years, and we didn't even know about it."

"Forcing minority women into prostitution," Dan said. "Or for that matter, *any* woman who tries to resist Big Louie's orders."

"My God, Ben," Lamar said, looking at the captured man and his wife and fat kids. "This Louie has

65

gathered the scum of the earth inside his borders."

"I resent that!" the man said. He was tired and haggard looking, but was recovering some of his bluster. "We only enslaved the Indians and niggers and other inferiors." The words were slightly slurred due to his swollen mouth.

"If you open your mouth again," Ben told him, "without my telling you to do so, you're going to lose some more teeth."

The man closed his mouth.

"Get them out of my sight," Ben ordered. "All except for the wife. How are they coming on the lady's chain?"

"It's off," Ike said, entering the tent. "The medics are checking her out now."

The man and his fat-assed kids were herded out of the tent. Fat girl was still blubbering. It was not a very appetizing sight.

Ben sat down, facing the woman. "You have probably guessed by now who I am, correct?"

"General Ben Raines."

"Right. Now, how much of what your husband said was truth, and how much of it was bullshit?"

"He told you the truth . . . as far as he took it."

"Well, lady, you pick it up where he left it off."

"And what do I get if I do? And he isn't my husband."

"The kids?"

"His. What do I get out of telling you what I know?"

"You can walk out of this camp alive. We'll take you down to the Oklahoma border and turn you loose."

"That isn't much, general."

Ben smiled at her. "Considering that you have taken part in enslaving people against their will;

66

taken part in burning people alive, and God only knows what else, do you want to hear the alternative?"

"I can probably guess it."

"Start talking."

"The man I was living with is not representative of most of the people living under Big Louie's rule. And neither are those lard-butted kids representative of the young people. Big Louie patterned his kingdom after your old Tri-States. Sam, that's the man I was living with, was the exception. Most others are very fit and well trained. Everyone is armed, armed well, and knows his or her assignment in case of trouble. There is about thirty-five hundred people within Louie's boundaries. And they will fight. They have a way of life that suits them, and they will defend it. And if you think I'm kidding, general, you'd damn well better think again."

"That jibes with the latest intel, Ben," Ike said. "It's not going to be a piece of cake."

"Regular army or police force?" Ben asked.

"Oh . . . probably three hundred and fifty," she said. "That's not counting the guards at the prison farm where the slaves are processed."

"How long have you been with Louie?"

"Three years. My real husband was killed fighting warlords."

"And you don't think it's wrong what you're doing?"

"No," she replied without hesitation. "It's just the way things are. The strong dominate the weak."

Ben stared at her. "You're in . . . your early forties, I'd guess."

"Pretty good guess."

"That would make you about thirty when the Great War came."

"Another good guess."

Ben had to give the woman this much: There was no fear visible in her eyes, her voice, or her mannerisms. "So I don't have to lecture you on decency or laws or moral codes."

"I hope not. You're dreaming, Ben Raines. You and your army will never bring conditions back to what they were. The whole world is a jungle, Ben Raines. Dog eat dog. For God's sake, man—if there really is a God, which I doubt—Big Louie is just one of probably two hundred or more warlords and self-styled kings. And that's just the ones that I know of. Probably twice that many scattered around the country. I work in communications, general. We know almost everything you people are planning to do. If you stamp out Big Louie, the next day you'll be fighting another warlord, and then another and another. It'll never end. Why don't you and your people just go on back to Georgia, do your little thing with Khamsin and his rag-heads, and then settle down in your own little spot? Let the world take care of itself. Who do you think you are—Don Quixote or Sancho Panza?"

"You're an educated woman."

"I have, had, a Masters, yes. And I was a very good teacher. What's that got to do with the price of eggs, now?"

"You don't teach in Big Louie's schools?"

She laughed at that. "Not hardly. I never let him know I was a teacher."

"Why?"

"Because I wasn't planning on staying around that long. Then Sam offered me security." She smiled. "You see, Ben Raines, not *that* much has changed about living."

"What's this Big Louie like?"

"Quite mad. He enjoys inflicting pain on people; likes to hear them scream. But he isn't a raving lunatic. He is usually quite lucid. And he is a genius. Hell, he built something out of nothing, didn't he?"

"By enslaving others."

"Minorities, General Raines. Indians, greasers, Jews, niggers. The strong will survive, General Raines. It's the way of the world, and it always has been. I don't have to tell you that. Or I shouldn't have to tell you. People put up with Big Louie's excesses, general. Every time he starts going off the deep end, so to speak, the doctors jack him down with Thorazine and let him float for a few days. He's a joke, general. The man who really runs things is named Ashley. I don't know whether that's his first name or his last name."

"Why do people put up with Louie?" Ben asked.

"Because they're *comfortable*, general. They live in nice homes. They have plenty to eat. They're safe. We have electricity, running water . . . all the things we had before. Currency, shops to spend it in. Just like before. And no taxes."

"And slaves."

"That's right, general. Slaves. And down near Ponca City, Oklahoma, there is another place very similar to Big Louie's. And they have slaves. And over near Fayetteville, Arkansas, there is yet warlord's headquarters . . . with slaves and whores and all the so-called abuses you've got your ass up over your back about. You're fighting a losing battle, general."

Ben turned to a Rebel sergeant. "Arrange for this . . . lady and her family to be transported down to the Oklahoma line. Turn them loose down there. No weapons."

"You don't give us weapons, general," she said.

"You're condemning us to death."

Ben's smile was not pleasant to view. "You want me to just shoot you here?"

She stood up and walked to the flap of the big tent. "I guess we'll take our chances out there. You're a hard motherfucker, Ben Raines."

"So I've been told, lady. So I've been told."

70

7

Ben interviewed the other prisoners taken by Dan Gray's Scouts. Their stories were much the same. And under prompting, the name Ashley surfaced in each interview. And not much about the man proved to be in the least admirable.

When the last prisoners had been interviewed, then transported many miles away, Dr. Chase said, "This Ashley appears to be the real power behind the throne, Ben."

"Yes. But who in the hell is he? Where does he live? No one seems to know."

"They might be lyin', Ben," Ike said.

"I don't get that impression. But I do get the feeling that everyone, including Big Louie, is very much afraid of this Ashley. But why?"

"And I get the impression that he knows you, Ben," Ike said.

"Yeah. I picked up on that, too. But I don't recall ever knowing anyone named Ashley. Wait a minute! Wait just a minute." He was thoughtful for a moment. "No. Hell, no. It couldn't be."

"Something, Ben?" Lamar asked.

"Just for an instant, that name rang a little bell in my head. But it slipped away as quickly as it came. I just don't know *anybody* named Ashley. Of course, it might not be his real name."

Outside, the rain picked up, slashing against the squad tent. "It's supposed to clear out of here in a couple of days," Ike said.

Ben nodded his head. "Was that woman right, Ike? Am I, are we, dreaming? Do we have any kind of a chance of restoring some normalcy to this nation?"

Ike, Lamar, Dan Gray, and James Riverson all stood silently for a moment. The rain and wind lashed at the tent. Ben looked at each man.

"Yes," Ike finally said. "Not like it used to be. Never that; not in our lifetime. But, yes, Ben, we can do it. But we're all going to be fighting for the rest of our lives to do it."

Ben sighed. "Sometimes I get so discouraged."

The flap of the tent was opened. A Rebel stepped in, the woman Tina and her team had rescued right behind him.

Ben stood up and smiled at the woman. "Miss. You look a lot better without that collar around your neck."

"First time it's been off in months," she told him. "Are you planning on making war against Big Louie and his people?"

"Yes."

"I wish to join your army, Ben Raines."

"All right. But I'd like to know your name."

"Denise. Denise Vista."

That brought a smile to the lips of all the Rebels.

"Something amusing about my name?" Denise asked.

"Not at all, ma'am," Ike said. "Vista was the name of the capital of the old Tri-States. Brought back a lot of memories, that's all."

"I see," the woman said softly.

Denise was perhaps five-five, very nicely proportioned, and had dark brown hair, dark eyes, and an olive complexion.

A survivor, Ben thought. She's tough. "Denise, what do you know about a man called Ashley?"

"Very little. I've seen him, two, no, three times. He's tall, perhaps forty years old. Speaks with a heavy southern accent. He's the real power behind Big Louie."

"Where does he live?" Ben asked.

"I don't know. It is whispered among the slaves that he has several homes, not all of them within the boundaries claimed by Big Louie. He is always armed, and always has many bodyguards with him."

Ben shook his head. He felt like he should know this Ashley person, but could not put a face to the name. Perhaps it would come to him in time.

He was conscious of the woman's eyes on him. Ben met her gaze. "A question, Miss Vista?"

"You don't look like a god, general."

Ben laughed. "I'm no god, Miss Vista. I'm just a very mortal man, with more than my share of the normal human weaknesses."

"Not all gods take the same form, General Raines," she said.

"I know little about gods, Miss Vista. So I almost never argue the subject."

"I see," she spoke softly, her voice just audible over the storm. "Well. Do you have any other questions for me, general?"

"Not at this time."

"Where do I sleep?"

"The corporal there will show you to quarters, miss. Someone will check you out with weapons and outfit you with uniforms tomorrow. Good night, Miss Vista."

"Good night, general." She turned, stepping out into the rainy night, and was gone.

"Very attractive woman, Ben," Dr. Chase said, a twinkle in his eyes and a slight smile on his lips. Chase knew Ben well and could see the stirring signs of interest within the man.

Ben turned, facing him. "Oh? Yes. I suppose so. I hadn't really noticed."

Ike laughed, winking at Dan. "Ben, I sure am glad you fight a whole lot better than you lie."

The sounds of a slow-moving vehicle woke Buddy from a sound sleep. He slipped from his sleeping bag, pulled on his boots and laced them, then picked up his Thompson, easing it off safety. He crouched in the darkness of the carport, waiting.

The headlights of the car appeared, dimly at first, cutting through the heavy rain. The car slowed, then pulled into the drive. Buddy waited behind the wooden boxes, silent and unseen. And deadly.

Buddy watched through a small opening between the crates as two men got out of the car, both of them armed with M-16s. They stood for a moment, outlined against the glare of headlights.

Not very professional of them, Buddy thought. How easy they would be to take.

But he waited, sensing that these men were not a part of the Rebels. From all he had heard, the Rebels were the most professional and well-trained army operating anywhere in the world.

"Long ways out," one of the men said. "You reckon some of them goddamned Indians kidnapped them folks?"

"I can't see that, Jack. We got them Injuns beat down to nothing. They so whipped out they nearabouts ask permission to shit."

"Some of them squaws got some fine pussy, though," his partner said.

"Like a nigger; that's all they good for."

Racists, Buddy thought. But who are they and what do they represent? Or who do they represent?

"You got your flashlight?"

"Yeah."

"You take the left side, I'll take the right. Be careful; can't see crap in all this rain."

Buddy laid his SMG aside and silently pulled out his long-bladed hunting knife. The knife was a full fourteen inches long; a battle knife. The blade was honed to deadly sharpness. He carefully slipped out the rear of the carport, between the house and the utility room. He waited by the corner of the house.

The man who had taken the right side of the house appeared, ghostlike in the night storm, moving carefully, his weapon at combat ready.

Buddy gripped the handle of his knife, holding the blade against his leg to prevent any glint of light off the heavy blade.

The man stepped closer. Now he was muttering to himself, his words drifting out of the stormy air. "Fuckin' Ben Raines and his Rebels. I hope they do try to pull some shit in here. I'll cut that bastard's head off and stick it up on a pole so's people can see Raines ain't so damn tough."

Buddy stepped out and swung the heavy blade. The man's head plopped wetly to the soaked ground. Blood arched from the severed neck, mingling with the torrents. The eyes were still open on the head, staring at nothing, seeing only darkness.

Buddy grabbed the body before it could hit the ground and possibly alert the other man. Quickly, Buddy laid the M-16 to one side and slipped next to the house. He raised the bloody knife, waiting.

"Jack?" The voice came just a few feet from where Buddy was pressed against the house. "Jack? Can you hear me?"

Jack could not answer, and the questioner would never utter another word.

Buddy's knife flashed in the rainy night. The blade struck the man on the back of his neck and came out just under the man's chin. The head spun in the wet night and slopped to the ground, as blood squirted.

Buddy quickly took the men's weapons and all their ammunition. He cut off the motor and headlights of the car and searched the vehicle. He found several days' rations of food and took that to add to his own supply. He stood for a moment in the rain, oblivious to it, and listened, all his senses working hard.

He could not see, hear, nor sense anything that might alarm him.

Buddy searched the yard and found two long poles, almost identical in length. He went back to the bodies and recovered the heads, sticking one on each pole, then sinking the poles deep into the wet earth, about five feet apart. The bug-eyes open, the faces grimacing in that last hot moment of pain, the heads stared sightlessly from their height.

Returning to the car, Buddy found a pad and pen and wrote: *Compliments of B.R.B. Now you have two of us to deal with. Have a nice day.*

Buddy had wrapped the weapons up in his piece of canvas and secured them to his motorcycle with rope. He rode through the night before braking at an old rusted and warped road sign. Hiawatha 9.

Using the headlamp of his motorcycle, Buddy checked his maps. He was undecided as to which direction to take. He was very wary of this country he

76

was in; something was very wrong around here. But he wasn't sure about it. Was this an area controlled by some warlord or self-styled king? Possibly, he thought. That would explain the hate he had heard in that man's voice; the hate directed toward Ben Raines. For all knew Ben Raines could not and would not tolerate warlords and their oppressive measures.

Buddy smiled as the rain slicked his handsome face. He was sure that when those heads were found, probably around daylight, someone was going to want to do some headhunting of their own.

Buddy decided that the next house he came to, one that looked occupied, he'd just find out what was going on.

It was a man and a woman, both of them about Buddy's age, he guessed. He squatted in the darkness of their bedroom and looked at the sleeping couple. He had silently, moving like a slight soundless breeze, inspected the house. It was empty except for the couple.

The man looked rough and mean, the woman looked—cheap, the word came to him. He really was not sure what that meant, but he'd read it in one of Ben Raines's books. What always bothered him about it was, what does a cheap woman do to get that way?

Baffling. Perhaps he could ask Ben Raines about that someday.

He placed the muzzle of a .45 against the man's cheek. The man opened his eyes as Buddy jacked back the hammer.

"Do you want your brains splattered all over your woman's face?" Buddy asked, his voice low.

"I don't want my brains splattered nowheres," the

77

man whispered. "How the hell did you get in here?"

"Your locks are silly. Awaken your woman and advise her if she wants to live, she will open her mouth only when I tell her to do so."

"I'm awake," the woman whispered. "My God, Gene! What's goin' on?"

"I reckon this fellow will tell us when he's a mind to."

"This part of the country," Buddy said. "Is it controlled by a warlord? And tell me the truth if you want to live."

"Big Louie runs it," Gene said, his voice soft in the darkness of the bedroom. "I don't know how in the hell you made it this far alive."

"Big Louie. Ah!" He had heard his mother speak of Big Louie. They shared a common interest: They both like to burn people alive. "My father is close by. When he hears of Big Louie, I should imagine he will take the appropriate action. It would not be wise for either of you to remain. Unless, of course, you have a death wish."

"Your father?" Gene said. "There ain't nobody strong enough to come in here and push us out, boy."

Buddy grinned. "Wanna bet?"

"Yore daddy mus' think he's a real war-hoss," the woman whispered. "Who might he be?"

"Ben Raines."

"Oh, Jesus God!" the woman gasped. "That can't be. He's 'way to hell and gone out West."

"Not anymore. He killed the mercenary, Sam Hartline, and defeated the Russian, Striganov. Do either of you know a man named Jack, who was on patrol tonight, a few miles east of here?"

"Yeah. We both know him. He lives a few miles on up this road. How do you know him?"

"I just killed him and his partner. I cut their heads

off and stuck them up on poles."

The woman started squalling, jerking around on the bed. Gene grabbed her and shook her until she shut up.

"Ben Raines is your . . . *father?*" Gene asked.

"Yes. Now, the problem facing me is this: What to do with you two?"

"Mister," Gene said. "You come into this house, movin' like a damn ghost. Afore that, you killed two of the best manhunters I ever knowed . . ."

Buddy kept his expression bland. He had seen Gene carelessly drop his right hand off the bed and onto the floor. The man must think I am a fool! Buddy thought.

". . . and stuck their heads up on poles. You just give me and baby a chance, and we'll clear this area faster than you can blink."

The muscles in Gene's right arm bunched slightly. Probably, Buddy thought, as his hand closed around the butt of a weapon. Buddy had removed the muzzle of the .45 from the man's cheek when the woman had begun hollering and jerking around. The muzzle was now only a few inches from Gene's side. Buddy waited.

"Yeah," the woman said. "We be gone faster than you can kiss a duck."

"I have absolutely no intention of ever kissing a duck," Buddy informed her.

"Well, then, partner," Gene said. "Kiss *this!*"

Before Gene could lift the pistol off the carpet, Buddy's .45 had barked three times, the booming loud in the quiet, night-filled house. The force of the heavy slugs turned the man slightly to one side, blowing a large hole in his side. Gene flopped on the bed as one bloody arm was flung across the woman's bare stomach.

With a scream of fear and rage, the woman lunged at Buddy. Buddy whapped her on the side of the head with the heavy .45. The woman dropped like a stone, not unconscious, but addled.

Moving swiftly, Buddy rolled the woman up in a blanket and tied it cocoonlike around her, using strips of torn sheet.

She was fully conscious now, looking at the young man. "Now what?" she asked.

"Be silent. I am thinking."

"This is awful uncomfortable. You tied it too tight."

"We all have our little difficulties to bear throughout life."

The woman called him a number of very uncomplimentary names.

Buddy waited until she paused for breath and said, "However, if you feel your present dilemma is too great a burden, I can fix it."

"How, you asshole!"

Buddy lifted the .45 and smiled.

She shut her mouth and silently stared at him.

"Did your man hold a position in the warlord's army?"

She nodded her head.

"What rank?"

"Company commander."

"He was close to Big Louie?"

"Nobody is close to Big Louie. Nobody exceptin' Ashley."

"Where is this Ashley person?"

"Your guess is as good as mine about that, handsome."

Buddy ignored the "handsome" bit. He knew what was on the woman's mind: Survival. He made a quick but thorough search of the house, finding detailed plans on what unit was to go where in case of attack from the outside. He discovered a map showing all heavy gun positions.

A slight noise turned him around.

The woman had struggled out of her bonds and was standing in a doorway, pointing a pistol at him.

"Ben Raines's son, huh?" she said, a smirk on her lips. "I think Big Louie will look favorably on me for this."

"Providing you can get me to him."

"Oh, I'll get you to him. Even if I have to shoot both legs out from under you."

Buddy hurled himself to one side just as the pistol in her hand started cracking.

8

Ben came awake with a start, his heart pounding, sweat bathing him. He looked around the big squad tent. It was empty.

What had awakened him?

He didn't know.

Ben lay on his camp bed, listening. He could hear nothing alien in the night. The rain had lessened somewhat. Where it had been pouring down in torrents, now it was only a quiet pattering on the canvas.

Silently, he slipped from his bed and dressed, pulling on his boots and lacing them. He picked up his Thompson and moved to the flap opening, pushing it aside and stepping out.

He stood for a moment, smelling the clean, fresh-washed earth as the light drizzle bathed his face, waking him fully.

He felt better, but that feeling of alarm was still with him.

Movement to his right turned his head. He watched as his daughter, Tina, walked toward him.

"Couldn't sleep, Dad?" she asked.

"Something woke me. Something strange. I don't know what it was, or is. You?"

"Something woke me," she admitted. "Like you, I don't know what."

"Let's walk to the communications truck," Ben suggested. He looked at his watch. Four o'clock. Time to get up anyway. A natural dawning, at least. If anything good ever came out of a worldwide disaster such as the survivors had experienced, it was the return of God's time; void of man's fiddling with it, called daylight savings.

The Rebel on duty looked up as Ben and Tina entered. "Just talked with Base Camp One, general. Storm's gone and the stars are out. The birds will be flying today. They'll bring all the equipment we asked for."

"Good! Have you found Big Louie's radio frequency yet?"

"Yes, sir. Just the usual radio chatter. Nothing much happening in there."

"Stay with it."

"Yes, sir."

Outside, Ben waited while Tina got them cups of hot tea, and then father and daughter sipped and talked in the pre-dawn darkness.

"I never placed much credence in the supernatural, Dad. If supernatural is the right choice of words. But I awakened with the oddest feeling."

"What kind of feeling, Tina?"

"Like, well, a part of me is . . . How do I say this? It was a feeling of danger, Dad. But the danger was not for me. Does that make any sense to you at all?"

"Yes. Yes, that was the sensation I experienced at waking. What do you think it means?"

"The report that your son is on his way out here,

Dad. Is he your son, Dad?"

Ben sighed. "Tina, I just don't know. It's certainly possible. I remember the woman. I remember the party and what happened afterward. It's certainly feasible that the young man is my son. We'll just have to wait and see."

She grinned up at him. "God, but I bet you were a randy bastard!"

"Watch your mouth, girl," Ben said with a smile. "You're not too big to spank."

Laughing, Tina tossed him a mock salute and walked away into the darkness.

Ben stood for a time, alone in the mist and the ink of that time just prior to the first silver fingers of dawning.

Are you my son? Ben projected his thoughts through the dark. Are you out there? And are you in trouble?

The woman screamed and pulled the trigger again. Buddy felt a lance of pain rip his leg, followed by a warm rush of blood. Buddy rolled, banged against a wall, and came up with a .45 in his hand.

The woman yelled at him and pulled the trigger. The slug struck the wall close to Buddy's head. He leveled the .45 and triggered off two quick rounds. The woman grunted and dropped her pistol. Cocked, it discharged when it hit the floor, the slug striking the woman just under the chin, traveling upward, through her head, and exiting out the top of her skull.

She fell to the floor, trembled for a few seconds, then was still.

Buddy limped to a window and looked out. The rain had stopped, only a very light mist now falling.

He waited for a full sixty count. No headlights appeared; no shouts of alarm cut the night. Turning away from the window, leaving the house dark, Buddy found the bathroom, closed the door, and switched on the lights. The explosion of light startled him. He was not accustomed to electric lights. They were so bright.

He fumbled in the medicine cabinet and found iodine and bandages. Removing his trousers, Buddy inspected the wound. Not too bad. The slug had taken a chunk of flesh from his upper thigh, then traveled on. Buddy bathed the wound in water, then gritted his strong, even teeth as he poured iodine onto the wound. He blinked his eyes a couple of times and carefully bandaged the wound. He pulled his trousers back on and took the bottle of iodine and fresh bandages. He turned off the lights in the bathroom, stood for a moment in the darkness, allowing his eyes to adjust, then stepped out into the hall.

The house reeked of blood and death.

Buddy made another search of the house, looking for anything that might shed more light on Big Louie and his forces. He could find nothing to add to what he'd already found.

He did find several hundred rounds of .45 caliber ammunition, in clear plastic bags. He took those. He had spotted a Jeep parked by the side of the house, and even though he hated to part with his motorcycle, the Jeep would afford him a bit more protection and, with its four-wheel capabilities, could take him through places where the bike might bog down.

He looked at the woman, sitting on the hall floor, her legs spread obscenely wide, her nightgown hiked up to her waist, two bullet holes in her chest. Her eyes were open, staring wide in death.

Buddy walked into the bedroom, to stand over the

blood-soaked bed. He turned away and walked out of the house to the Jeep. There, he transferred all his gear from the motorcycle and covered it with a cammo tarp he had found folded in a utility room.

The Jeep started at the first try, the engine running smoothly. The gas tank was full, and there were two five-gallon gas cans secured on the rear of the Jeep. Letting the motor warm up, Buddy checked the spare gas cans. Full. Walking back to the drivers' side, Buddy glanced into the back seat; one final check before pulling out. There was a knapsack on the floorboards. He checked it. Heavy with spare clips and ammo for an M-16 and eight or ten grenades.

"Well, now," Buddy said, smiling in the misty night. "The odds are improving in my favor."

He loaded the M-16s he'd taken from the headless men and laid them within easy reach. He backed out of the drive and looked up at the sky. It would be breaking dawn very soon. Best to hunt a hole right now.

Buddy clicked on the radio mounted under the dash of the Jeep and began searching the bands. He heard chatter that was almost military, except that they used nicknames. He knew that was not any of Raines's Rebels. He carefully searched the frequencies.

He smiled as he heard, "Recon four to Eagle base."

He knew that General Ben Raines was often referred to as the Eagle.

"Go, Recon four."

"We're between Delaven and Wilsey. Have secured a portion of Fifty-six for an LZ. Please advise the general."

"Ten-four, Recon. Will do. Eagle base clear."

Buddy checked his old and well-creased road map. He was well north and some east of that area. And from the communications just overheard, General Raines was some distance from the just secured landing zone. But where? North, south, or west of it? Not east of it, for that would put the general inside of Big Louie's claimed territory.

Buddy reached around behind him and took out two grenades from the knapsack, laying them on the seat beside him. He had made up his mind. There was a lake just west and south of his present position. He could make it before dawn. He'd go there and rest and hide; listen to the radio. When General Raines arrived at the LZ, Buddy would know.

The young man had a funny feeling in the pit of his stomach, and his mouth was dry just thinking about meeting General Raines. He would not deny the truth: He was afraid of Ben Raines. Most people he had ever talked with about Ben Raines admitted that they, too, were afraid of him.

Buddy had fought outlaws, warlords, crazed people, and mutants. He had killed many times in defense of his life. He had, of course, known fear many times.

But not this kind of fear. This kind of fear was different.

Buddy put the Jeep in gear and pulled out, glancing once more up at the sky. It looked like the dawn was going to bring a beautiful day.

The feelings that both Ben and Tina had awakened with had vanished, both of them experiencing the lifting of tensions just about dawn. Although they were not together at the time, each knew.

The old prop-job planes from Base Camp One had left at five o'clock, their time. They should be landing, barring any unforeseen difficulties, late that afternoon.

Ben gathered all his commanders in his big tent, around a table, a map of the area spread out.

"As usual," Ben said, "we're going to be spread thin. If we had more people, it would be a very simple matter to destroy this Big Louie. We'd just put him in a box and squeeze it tight. But we can't do that. But what we can do is terrorize those living in his territory; those who willingly accept and take part in the slavery and torture. And from all the intel we've received, that is just about everybody. We're going to hit and burn and run, freeing all slaves as we do so.

"This Big Louie has very thin control of the area south of Highway Fifty-four. The people we talked with say Louie's people are struggling to get a toehold in that part of the state. Dan has teams in that area now, quietly talking to the people and raising a little hell with Big Louie's people. The survivors are joining our ranks. I'm giving command of that area to Tina; she'll be leaving as soon as the planes arrive and she and her people can resupply."

Dan nodded his head in agreement. "She's earned her command, general."

The others gathered around nodded their heards in accord.

"Dan," Ben said. "You and your group will work north from Highway Fifty-four. In a curve. Run your teams from Iola east to the Missouri line, then curve your eastern groups north and work them westerly."

Dan studied his map for a moment, marking in his perimeters.

"We're going to have to cache supplies inside enemy territory. Where you put them is your business. We obviously can't carry enough on our backs for a sustained operation. Ike, as soon as you and your

88

people get resupplied, take off north, to the Nebraska line. When you get my word to jump off, strike south. *Everybody* stay well clear of Kansas City.

"I'm spreading my people along the old Kansas Turnpike and pushing eastward. We're leaving them lots of holes to escape; that's fine. I don't give a damn if they all run. Chances are they'll never regroup. But one thing for certain: We have to kill Big Louie and this Ashley person. That's it, gang. Now all we have to do is wait for the planes."

"General Khamsin. Many planes have taken off from the Rebels' Base Camp."

"Heading in which direction?"

"West, sir."

"Heavily laden?"

"They appear so, sir."

"Resupplying General Raines out West. He's found him another windmill to tilt. Did General Jefferys leave with the planes?"

"No, sir. No troops left."

"Damn!" Khamsin hit the desktop with a balled fist. He was thoughtful for a moment. Then he sighed and shook his head. He swiveled his chair and gazed out the window for a moment. Without turning around, he asked, "What is our latest estimate on the Rebels in North Georgia?"

"An estimate is all it would be, general. There are new arrivals daily. And General Jefferys keeps shifting his troops around, making it impossible for us to tally them."

"Your best estimate, then."

"Between two thousand and forty-five hundred."

"And here I sit with my divisions," Khamsin said,

a bitterness in his voice.

"The men will follow The Hot Wind, sir."

The wind blows hot from hell, too, Khamsin thought. He rose from his chair and walked to a large map. He leaned closer and peered intently at several spots along the Savannah River. "Gather your best, your *very best* assault troops. Start them infiltrating into Georgia. Very small teams, carrying as much high explosives as they can. Have them spread out, east to west, all across the top third of the state, staying south of this highway." He tapped the long line indicating Interstate 20. "Move the teams out one hour apart and start them immediately. In seventy-two hours, and if they're careful, it will take that long for the plan to be discovered by Rebel intelligence, I can have a thousand troops in Georgia. Tell them to seize transportation from civilians. Kill the civilian men, of course," he added, almost as an afterthought. "And the woman and children, too, if they present much of a problem. Every twenty hours, double the size of the teams." He began pacing the room, growing excited with his plan. "Yes. Yes. Not one thousand men in seventy-two hours, but five thousand men." He looked at his XO. An intense, fanatical light was shining in Khamsin's eyes.

The XO waited.

"Perhaps," Khamsin said, "if Allah smiles upon us, when Ben Raines returns from his adventures in the West, he will find his precious Base Camp One nothing more than smoking ruins and his so-called undefeatable army in headlong retreat, panic and fear in their eyes, and their women here!" He thumped his desk. "Toys for our loyal troops to play with at their leisure."

Khamsin rang for coffee.

The dark bitter coffee poured, Khamsin lifted his

cup. "To victory!"

The general and his XO toasted.

A bit prematurely, some might say, for they were forgetting a number of very important things.

Like about three thousand Rebel troops, under the command of one Cecil Jefferys.

9

"What's wrong?" Cecil asked the radio operator.

"Sorry to have disturbed you, sir," the Rebel communications officer said, "but I wanted you to hear this."

Cecil listened. "I don't hear a thing."

"That's right, sir. Nothing. I just scanned all the frequencies The Hot Fart uses . . ."

"I believe that's The Hot Wind, lieutenant," Cecil said with a smile.

"Yes, sir. Hot Wind, hot shit, whatever. He's still a lump of camel turd. But the silence is what bothers me, general. All of a sudden, about two hours ago, all the chatter stopped. I mean, there is *nothing* being said."

"And you've been searching the bands ever since?"

"Yes, sir. Total dead silence."

"Is the equipment working properly?"

"Yes, sir. I called the engineer in and had her check it. Then we contacted several of our long range recon patrols; one of them up in Ohio. Everything is five by five, general."

"I think The Hot Wind just blew out whatever surprise he might have had in store for us, lieutenant." He turned to a runner. "Get the XO over here, right now!"

"Yes, sir!"

"What do you think it is, sir?"

"I don't know. But whatever it is, it isn't good news for us. I'm very glad you picked up on this, lieutenant. Go to Code C and tell any patrols close to home base to get back in here, pronto."

His XO at his side, Cecil said, "Everybody up, Joe. Red alert. But keep the hustle and bustle down to a minimum and no talking about it. Mark and his brother, Alvaro?"

"They've got their people down near the Interstate, general. Just east of the Oconee National Forest."

"I don't want any unnecessary chatter on the air, Joe. Send a light plane down to their camp. Advise them that Khamsin is up to something. What, we don't know. Yet. Tell them to go to full alert. But do it quietly."

"Yes, sir."

Many of the Rebel company commanders had gathered around the two men, standing quietly, listening.

Cecil looked at them, then briefed them. "Get your people together, but do it easy. Quickly, but calmly. Full battle gear, five days' rations. Get your people ready."

The COs saluted and left.

Back in his command post, with his senior commanders around him, Cecil stood and stared at a large wall map.

"If I were the Libyan," he said, "I would hit us full force. He's got thousands of combat-ready troops; he could overwhelm us with numbers. It's amazing to me that he hasn't already done it. For some reason, he's very hesitant. But then I have to consider that Khamsin was schooled as a terrorist; Abu's student and his best. And because he is basically a terrorist, that makes him several things. A fanatic in his mind, totally ruthless, and a coward at heart. The troops he has is all he's got . . . right now. So Khamsin is not going to personally die for Allah. Not if he can help it. But he will send a couple of thousand to their deaths, in order to gain . . . what? A toehold? Yes. Certainly. But where? And using what methods?"

Cecil stepped back from the map and sat down at his desk. "A few thousand men, slipped into our area in very small teams, to be used as . . . *sappers!*"

Colonel Williams looked at Cecil. "Like 'Nam, general?"

"Yeah," Cecil said. "But more than sappers, Joe. Men schooled in the art of sabotage. There are no communications lines to cut—not anymore. So their mission would be multiple. Terror, sure. But more than that. They'd be good troops. Some of, if not, his best. If they could get inside our territory, we'd have a full-scale guerrilla war on our hands."

"And if Khamsin's troops could establish a front," Joe said, "it would be only a matter of time before his main forces would roll right over us. Like the Tri-States," he added softly. Joe had been a company commander back in those days, gradually climbing the rank ladder to become second in command of the eastern-based Rebels. Joe was a good solid soldier, one hundred percent loyal to Ben Raines, Ike McGowan, and Cecil Jefferys.

"Yeah," Cecil said. "Like the Tri-States, Joe."

The planes were, at first, only tiny dots in the blue sky. Then they took shape, did a fly-by of the LZ, and began setting down on the old highway.

Ben shook hands with the pilot of the first plane down. "How are things back at Base One?" he asked.

"Well, general, they were fine when we left. But the last communication we received was, well, odd."

"Odd, how?"

"General Jefferys came on the horn. Said a front was moving in, probably from the south. Advised us to stay out here. Said the old birds were too valuable to risk getting caught up in a hailstorm. General Raines, I checked the weather shack just before leaving. There are no systems anywhere back East. And there sure as hell isn't any *hail*."

"Khamsin is making a move, Ben," Ike said. "Cec isn't sure where or how; that's why he said 'probably from the south.' "

"And the hail is lead," Ben said. "What else did he say?" he asked the pilot.

"Well, odd again, sir. He said due to wind disturbances, communications would be difficult. Hell, sir. There was no wind when we took off. It was dead calm."

"The Hot Wind," Ben said. "Get unloaded," he told the gathering knot of pilots. "Come on, Ike."

They walked to a communications van. The engineer had just finished rigging an antenna. "Can you get through to Base Camp One?" Ben asked.

"Yes, sir. No sweat." In half a minute, he had contacted the Rebels in Georgia. "Stand by for traffic from the Eagle."

Seventy miles away, straight north, Buddy laid by his Jeep, tucked away in a clump of trees, and listened.

Ben took the mike. "This is the Eagle. Get me the Hawk."

The Hawk must be General Jeffreys, Buddy thought.

Cecil came on the horn. "Afternoon, Ben," he said cheerfully. "How's the weather out there?"

"Very nice, Cec. I hear you have a slight problem with the wind out there. That right?"

"Definitely picking up, Ben. The temperature, too."

The Hot Wind.

"Well, Cec, I guess all you can do is plug up any holes in the buildings."

"That's about it, Ben. Oh, I think we'll ride out the storm. I believe a surprise party was initially planned for me, but I got wind of it. I guess that blew the surprise."

Ben and Ike smiled. "Yeah, I hate to hear that, Cec. I forgot about your birthday."

"Yeah, me, too. Ben. But they're giving me my present anyway. Someone found an unopened carton of Camels."

Ike laughed aloud.

"They could be bad for your health, Cec."

"That's what I keep hearing. But I've got a carton of Luckies in reserve, just in case."

This time, it was Ben who laughed. "I heard that, Cec."

"What in the hell are they talking about?" Buddy said aloud.

"Don't hurt yourself blowing out all those candles, Cec," Ben said.

"I shall do my best not to, Ben."

"If you don't need the birds back, Cec, I'd like to keep them out here."

"I think that would be best, Ben. You might need them. You take care, Ben."

"Same to you, Cec."

"He doesn't sound too worried," Ike said. "Of course, I never knew him when he sounded worried about anything!"

"If he needs help, he'll holler. That's why he told the pilots to stay here. With these planes, we can jump in a battalion back home, if it comes to that." Ben was silent for a few seconds, his brow wrinkled in thought. He turned to James Riverson. "James, break out all those chutes we used back in California. Have the riggers unfold, stretch, and dry them. Then repack." He looked at Ike. "If Cec calls, Ike, you and your people will fly back and jump in. Understood?"

"Right, Ben. But that's going to leave the north wide open."

"Can't be helped. For the time being, if we can push Big Louie and his assholes north of Interstate Seventy, it'll have to do. And we may lose Base Camp One. I won't risk destroying everything we've managed to accomplish for a piece of ground. Not when the entire nation is open to us."

"I wasn't going to bring that up. I hoped you would."

"Cecil feels the same way, Ike. Besides, he has sealed orders he'll open if conditions warrant that. We'll move into Louisiana. I've had a small team in that area for over a year."

Ike grinned. "Close-mouth bastard, ain't you?"

Ben returned the smile. "Yep."

Teams from the Islamic People's Army, the IPA, were moving into Georgia, heavily laden with explosives. And General Khamsin, almost drunk with the thoughts of victory, had increased the numbers moving across the Savannah River. A small observer team of Rebels, located just south of Augusta, had been forced to retreat before being overrun. They got off one terse message to Base Camp One.

Hundreds of troops crossing river. Must pull back.

Another team of Rebels, also forced to pull back from their position further south, got off this message: *Faced with several battalions of IPA troops. Cannot contain them. Pulling back. Will link up with other recon teams and commence guerrilla warfare against enemy. Good luck.*

Cecil radioed back to all recon units pulling back from the river: *Negative on guerrilla tactics for time being. Pull into deep cover and keep your heads down. Maintain radio silence. Have plans for you people later. Good luck.*

To all roaming recon teams between Interstates 85 and 20, Cecil radioed: *Hunt a hole and stay low. Do not engage enemy unless absolutely necessary. Maintain radio silence. Good luck.*

Mark and Alvaro pulled their people back deep into the Oconee National Forest and dug in. They kept their heads down and waited for orders from General Jefferys.

"Joe," Cecil said to General Williams, "I think, like the old commercial used to read, we are in a heap of trouble."

"I think, sir, that you are right."

Cecil thought of the sealed orders Ben had given him. But he wasn't ready to open them just yet. For he had a strong suspicion what they contained. He knew there was no way he was gong to contain The Hot Wind's troops. Not outnumbered forty or fifty to one. Cecil had been playing games with Khamsin's recon people, constantly shifting troops around the area. He had less than a thousand regular Rebels at Base Camp One.

He silently counted his numbers. Mark and Alvaro had about two hundred and fifty people. Counting all recon teams, there might be an additional two hundred and fifty. Perhaps fifteen hundred men and women, and kids, among the untrained.

Cecil sighed.

Blunt old soldier that he was, Joe summed it up. "It's fucking impossible, general."

"Yes, I know, Joe. But I'm not going to roll over and run away just yet. Joe, order the untrained civilian women and all kids under the age of fourteen out of here. Send them across the line, into Alabama." He hesitated. "One platoon of Rebels with them. Clear the hospital of wounded. Send them, too. Order the motor pool to get every vehicle that will run ready to do so. That's just in case. Fully fueled. Fill tankers and get them rolling west. Start stripping this place right now; but load trucks and pull out only at night. War lights only. Let the civilian women drive the trucks."

"General?"

"Yes, Joe?"

"Let's send the old soldiers with the civilians."

Cecil smiled, remembering. He nodded his head. "Fine, Joe."

Buddy lay on his sleeping bag in the deep timber and let his thoughts drift back to his mother. As a child, when conditions were normal, she had been a good mother. Schools, nice clothes. Then after the bombs came, she had left him with the Old Man, returning only occasionally to visit him. Sometimes, Buddy had thought, she must have forgotten he was alive. The Old Man had really raised him. And then Buddy found out why she waited years to see him.

He pushed that from his mind.

But years back, when the Old Man was younger, he had taught Buddy to survive. He taught him to use a knife, a bow and arrow, to make deadly traps, taught him about all types of weapons—and mainly, Buddy had later learned, kept him away from his mother.

And it was only a year back that Buddy had learned the Old Man was really his grandfather.

Dawn.

Ben stepped out of his tent and almost collided with Denise. At first, he did not recognize the woman. She was dressed in lizard cammies and beret, her dark hair pulled back and tied. Her field pants bloused into boots. She wore a .38 belted around her trim waist. A hunting knife in a sheath on the other side.

She saluted and said, "Reporting, sir."

Ben tossed her a salute and said, "Never salute an officer in a combat zone, Denise. That's a good way to get somebody killed. Snipers."

"Oh! Sorry, sir."

"That's all right. Just don't do it again. Reporting for what, Denise?"

"As ordered, sir."

Ben blinked and scratched his head. "I didn't order you to report to me."

"No, sir. General McGowan did."

"To do what?"

"Well . . . I don't know, sir. He just said that you needed an aide and told me to report first thing. So here I am."

Looking around him, Ben saw Dr. Chase, Ike, Dan, and Tina all standing together, giggling and trying not to look in his direction.

Even Carl, Colonel Gray's batman, was smiling, looking in every direction except at Ben Raines.

"Assholes!" Ben said.

"Just like opinions, general," Denise said with a straight face.

"What's that?" Ben asked, looking at her.

"Everybody has one."

10

A runner from the communications van reached Ben, nearly out of breath. She handed Ben a folded piece of paper. "This just came in, sir. From General Jefferys."

Ben opened the paper. *Will hold long enough to allow civilians to leave area. Believe it is impossible to contain IPA troops for very long. Good luck.*

"Bad?" Ike asked.

Ben handed the paper to him. Ike read it and said, "Shit! It must be bad for Cec to send something like this. You want me to get my people together, Ben?"

Ben shook his head. "I don't know, Ike," he said with a sigh. "I think this message is coded. For Khamsin's benefit. I think Cec has something up his sleeve. I think he wants Khamsin to believe he's in panic."

Ike was thoughtful. "You may be right. He sure didn't ask for any help, did he?"

"No. And he wouldn't hesitate to ask. But I can't contact him about it without tipping his hand . . . if he's holding a good hand, that is."

"Just a few hours ago he was not worried at all," Ike mused aloud. "Ben, there is no way for Khamsin to have moved that many troops into position this soon. His troops are not concentrated; they're all over South Carolina."

"Very well." Ben made up his mind. "It's Cecil's show; we'll let him open and close the curtains as he sees fit. If he needs us, we're only a few hours away."

"I wonder if he's opened those sealed orders yet."

"I doubt it. He'd have said. All right, Ike. We've got two fronts, as usual. Let's start taking care of this one."

Emil Hite had been down for a year, but far from being out. The former used-car salesman from Chattanooga was also known as a con man from several other states, and for awhile he had even been known as Father Emil, earthbound emissary of the Great God Blomm.

It had been a pretty good scam for as long as it worked. Until those Ninth Order assholes had screwed it all up. And then those totally brutish mercenaries came charging in. And they *really* fucked things up.

But eventually they had left, leaving only a small number of Emil's former converts behind. But they were the hard-core Father Emil followers, totally loyal to him. And conditions being what they were, worldwide, it didn't take Emil long to put together another scam. One thing Emil could do, and do well, was talk very convincingly.

And he had talked enough to gather about two hundred new followers. Of course, he knew they were all yo-yos — some of them totally around the bend; but that didn't matter, not as long as they waited on him hand and foot and catered to his every need.

He had convinced his followers that the Great God Blomm, who had once sat by the side of the Almighty, had deserted them, allowing those brutish, repugnant types to enter their lives, as punishment.

Now Blomm was back, stronger than ever on the side of Father Emil and his flock. But, he cautioned his robed troops, "Don't expect miracles from me. I cannot deliver miracles. All I can do is tell you what Blomm tells me."

In other words, get off my ass and cool it with the demands for me to turn water into booze, and all that other hokey shit.

They believed it. Sure, they believed it. Made as much sense as some of those religions that were alive and kicking back when the world was normal—more or less.

Just to keep his followers guessing, Emil would occasionally fall on the ground and thrash around, speaking in tongues. Then he'd get up, brush himself off, and do his rendition of the Mashed Potatoes, the Funky Chicken, the Dog, and the Twist.

Hell, they loved it!

Silly shits!

And, Emil suspected, more than a few knew it was all a scam. He knew he was comic relief to many of the growing numbers. But he deliberately and very carefully kept those in the minority. They handled the tribute to Father Emil—and got more than their share of the pussy, too.

Emil had settled in North Louisiana, had him a real nice church (used to be a Baptist church) complete with a little band that could really cook with Christian rock and Roll. Emil had rewritten several hymns, putting them to the tunes of "Shake, Rattle, and roll," "Don't be Cruel," "Money, Honey," and "Pissin' In The Wind." To name just a few.

The flock really got down and boogied when Emil would pull his robe up past his knees, signal the band to start jammin', and Emil would start belting out in song.

Hot damn! but he loved to see those sisters strut their stuff, prancing up and down the aisles, shaking their money-makers and shouting in tongues.

But this new group was just a tad different from the last group Emil had formed. This time, he had vowed, no one was going to come along and fuck it up.

This time, everyone was armed. And well trained in the handling of the guns. And Emil and his enforcers — the ones who knew it was all pre-planned bullshit — saw to it that the farms were productive, the robe factories worked well, and everybody stayed in line.

All in all, Emil thought, it was working out fine.

If that fuckin' Ben Raines would just stay away.

Buddy stayed in deep cover, close to his Jeep, listening to the radio and thinking.

Now that he was away from his mother and could think without interruption, he was more than ever convinced the woman was stark, raving mad. And he was well aware of, and had been for some time, that the Old Man had deliberately let his mother think him dead for many years.

But why, only a couple of years ago, had the Old Man taken him to his mother? That puzzled Buddy.

And it just may be he'd never know.

The radio began crackling, and Buddy stopped his thinking to concentrate on the radio messages.

"Topeka One to Chanute. Come on, Chanute."

"Chanute here."

"Are you under attack, yet, Chanute?"

"Under *attack,* did you say?"

"Ten-four, Chanute."

"Hell, no. We're not under attack. What's going on, Topeka?"

"Stay alert, Chanute. Ben Raines and his people are about to pull something."

"Hell, they've been out there three/four days. They—"

A new voice took over the mike. A strong voice, with a heavy southern accent. "Do not question orders, Chanute. Just do as you are told. Is that understood?"

"Yes, sir!"

Ben knew that accented voice. He was sitting in his vehicle, Denise by his side, listening. And said aloud that the voice was familiar to him.

"An old friend?" she asked.

"I don't think so."

"An old enemy, then?"

"That would be more like it, I'm thinking. But from where, is the thing that puzzles me."

"It will come to you, general."

"Oh? You sound very sure of that, Denise. Are you all omniscient?"

"Possessing infinite knowledge, general? Oh, no. Are you surprised that I know the meaning of that large word?"

"Yes," Ben said truthfully, as was his way. "Most your age didn't have the time for much formal education."

"I had to teach myself after the bombs came. But then, I have always enjoying reading . . . even your rough, tough men's adventure books."

Ben had to smile. "Where did you find copies of those?"

"Oh, here and there."

106

"Uh-huh. Getting back to the mysterious voice we just heard? . . ."

"And why I think it will come to you? . . ." She trailed it off as he had done.

"Yes."

"Why . . . You're a god, aren't you?"

Ben glared at her, and then started laughing. He had a strong suspicion they were going to get along very well.

Ike approached the vehicle and said, "I'm pullin' out, Ben. I should be in position by late this afternoon, if all goes well."

Ben got out and stretched. Denise got out and stood a few feet away from the men, watching as Col. Dan Gray and Capt. Tina Raines joined the men.

"All teams ready?" Ben asked.

Sitting on Go.

"Not a whole hell of a lot left to say then," Ben told them.

Dan pulled a map out of his case and spread it on the hood of the vehicle.

Ike said, "Me and my gang will spread from right here at Marysville east to Sparks and work south from there."

"My teams will be spread from Elgin east to Baxter Springs," Tina said. "Our territory will be everything between the state line up to Highway Fifty-four."

"I'm taking everything from Fifty-four up to Interstate Thirty-five," Dan said.

"And I'm taking everything between Thirty-five and Seventy," Ben said. "And that included Topeka."

"You are taking the lion's share, general," Dan said, just as Dr. Chase joined the group.

"Of course, he is," Lamar said. "The old bastard still thinks he's a young buck."

Ike cleared his throat. "He's about the same age I

107

am, Doc."

"Well, that makes you a middle-aged fart, too, McGowan," Lamar popped right back. "You want me to maintain my field hospital right where we are, Ben?"

"For the time being, Lamar, I think that would be best. The LZ is secure and set up . . ." Ben paused, thoughtful. "But if Cec moves the big hospital? . . ."

"And he's probably doing that right now," Ike said. "Your emergency orders were to head for Alabama, Ben."

Ben looked at Lamar and raised one eyebrow in question.

Interesting gesture, Denise thought. From a very interesting man. Of course, even in the short time she'd been in camp, she had heard a lot of camp gossip about General Raines. About how he did love the ladies. Often.

Wouldn't hurt my feelings a bit, she silently mused.

"We can handle anything that comes our way, Ben," Lamar assured him. "But you know that we're practicing medicine on probably a World War Two level out here in the field. There might be a problem with whole blood; but we'll just have to wait and see about that."

"There is really a great hospital in Topeka," Denise said. "It's well staffed and well equipped, so I'm told."

All eyes swung toward her.

"I'm sorry. I did not mean to interrupt."

"You didn't," Ben said quickly. "That is very valuable intelligence. Anything you can think of, tell us."

She nodded her head. "I probably don't know that much."

"And you probably know more than you think you do," Dan said. "That is usually the case. What is the name of this facility?"

"The medical center."

"Location?"

She told him.

Ben smiled. "We'll try to keep it intact and take whatever medical supplies they might have stored, Lamar."

"I'm sure that will be an effort for you, Raines," Lamar said with a smile. "Not blowing things up."

"There was a man who stayed on the Potawatomi Reservation for a time," Denise said. "A very old man. In robes. He carried a great stick with him. A staff, I suppose you'd call it."

Ben felt a chill spread over him. Looking at the others, he knew they were experiencing the same sensation.

The Prophet.

That old figure that occasionally popped up — seemingly at the same time in many different places. Ben remembered the first time he had seen the man who called himself the Prophet.

Little Rock, a couple of years back, when Rosita had been by his side.

Looking at the others, Ben knew that they, too, were momentarily lost in memories.

"Heads up, general!" a Rebel called.

Ben and Rosita turned. Ben heard her sharp intake of breath.

"Dios mio!" she hissed.

A man was approaching them, angling across the street, stepping around the litter. It was the man in the dreams Rosita had been having. Bearded and robed and carrying a long staff.

The man stopped in the street, and Ben looked into the wildest eyes he had ever seen.

And the oldest, he thought.

"My God!" someone said in a whisper. "It's Moses."

A small team of Rebels started toward the man. He held up a warning hand. "Stay away, ye soldiers of a false god."

"It is Moses," a woman said, only half in jest.

Ben continued to stare at the man. And be stared at in return. Burning eyes, savage, but yet sad. Eyes filled with knowledge.

"I hope not," Ben said, and *his* statement was given only half in jest. The robed man was disturbing to Ben. "Are you all right?" Ben called. "We have food we'll share with you."

The robed man replied, "I want nothing from you." He stabbed his long staff against the broken concrete of the street. He swung his dark, piercing eyes to the Rebels gathered protectively around Ben, weapons at the ready. "Your worshipping of a false god is offensive." He turned and walked away.

Gunfire spun them around. Then the radio crackled with the news that a patrol had found a family unit of mutants and the great beasts had attacked them. The Rebels had been forced to kill them all. Ben and his patrol went to the building that had housed the mutants and were wondering what to do with the only survivor, a small mutant baby, savage and hideous looking.

"Here comes Nutsy!" a Rebel called into the basement.

"Who?" Ben asked, then realized the Rebel was referring to the old man in the robes.

The old man appeared at the shattered basement

door. "I am called the Prophet," he announced.

Ben said, "My name is—"

The Prophet waved him silent. "I know who you are." He pointed his staff at Ben. "Your life will be long and strife filled. You will sire many children, and in the end, none of your dreams will become reality. I have spoken with God, and He has sent me to tell you these things. You are as He to your people, and soon—in your measurement of time—many more will come to believe it. But recall His words: No false gods before Me." The old man's eyes seemed to burn into Ben's head. "It will not be your fault. But it will lie on your head."

The old man turned and walked back into the street.

The Rebels were silent for a moment until another Rebel stuck his head into the doorway.

"Sure is quiet in here," he said.

"What did you make of Nutsy?" someone asked him.

"Who?"

"The old guy with the beard and sandals and the robe and big stick."

The Rebel had seen no one answering to that description.

"Well, where the hell have you been?"

"I been sittin' right outside this door, in a Jeep! And there ain't been nobody wearin' robes or sandals and carryin' a big stick come out of this building. What the hell have you guys been doing—smokin' some old left-handed cigarettes?"

Later, Ben spoke with a Rebel sergeant, Buck Osgood, who had just pulled in from Arizona. Buck told Ben he had seen an old man who called himself the Prophet.

"When did you see him, Buck?"

111

"Ah, last week."

"In Arizona?"

"Yes, sir."

"The date?"

"Ah, the ninth, sir."

"Time, approximately?"

" 'Bout noon, I reckon."

"That's the same time and date I saw him," Ben told the young sergeant.

"I didn't know you were in Arizona then, sir."

"I wasn't, Buck," Ben said. "I was in Little Rock."

11

Ben brought Denise up to date on the old man called the Prophet. The others listened in silence.

The woman took the telling without any apparent disbelief or shock. "My people are not as skeptical or as frightened of spirits as your people, general," she told him. "Those from the other side often walk this earth years after their passing. Perhaps the old man is a messenger from God. Who can tell?"

"Is the old man still at the reservation?" Ben asked.

"Oh, no. One day he just vanished. No one has seen him since. Or if they have, they are keeping silent about it."

Ben nodded and put the old man called the Prophet out of his mind. "Let's roll, gang."

"We'll crush Ben Raines like a bug!" Big Louie said. "This time he's met his Waterloo."

"Uh-huh," Ashley drawled.

"Ashley, my good fellow," Big Louie said, leaning forward. "Don't you realize what this means?"

"I know that we've got one hell of a fight lookin' smack at us."

"Oh, pish-posh! You simply don't understand these military types, Ashley. They have no imagination. None at all. They go right by the book. They're totally predictable. I tell you, we are going to defeat Raines quite handily. And then, my good man, with that overblown legend rotting in the ground, the nation, the entire *nation,* will be ours for the plucking." He giggled. "And all those lovely young girls for the fucking!"

Ashley nodded his head. Might as well agree with the silly perverted bastard, he thought. Grown women intimidated Louie. So he used little girls. So he could intimidate them. Or young boys. It really didn't make that much difference to Louie. But this time, Louie was flat out wrong about the upcoming fight. The legend of Ben Raines might well be a bit overblown, but the man damn sure wasn't.

"So you think it's going to be a cakewalk, huh. Louie?"

"You forgot to say Your Majesty," Big Louie said.

The look in Ashley's eyes wiped the grin right off Louie's face. "I'm only joking, Ashley," Louie whined. "You know I don't demand that from you."

"You silly bastard!" Ashley hissed at him. "Do you have any idea how fuckin' ridiculous you look?" Before Big Louie could reply, Ashley said, "Sittin' up there on that goddamned throne; makin' people bow and scrape to you. You bear one thing in mind, you goofy fag: I put you up there, and I can jerk you down any damned time I please."

Big Louie pursed his lips, looking very much like a fat fish, and stamped his slipper-clad foot. "And you're forgetting that I saved your life, you ungrateful oaf!"

"Yes, Louie," Ashley replied wearily. "How can I ever forget? You keep constantly remindin' me."

"You'd have died if it hadn't of been for me, Ashley!" Louie screamed, slapping his hands against the arms of his great chair. "And this is the way you repay my bravery and kindness!"

Ashley at first looked irritated, then began laughing. "Bravery? You? Brave? You tossed a rubber inner tube to me when that damned boat sank in the Mississippi. Let's don't make any more of it than it really was."

"I nursed you back to health. Remember?" Louie asked coyly.

"Don't bat your eyes at me. I'm not one of your playmates, Louie."

"I would certainly be amenable to that, Ashley," Louie simpered.

"I can't think of anything more disgusting than that. Don't push your luck, Louie."

"Oh, Ashley. Don't let's quarrel."

"Stop simpering!" Louie was all twisted sexually, no one in their right mind would ever question that; but to take Louie lightly would be a fatal mistake. He might not be the bravest man in the world, but he was both dangerous and devious. He had killed many, many times; often for very little reason—that any sane person could see.

"You think I'm wrong about this Raines cretin, don't you, Ashley?"

"No." And Louie's face brightened. "I *know* you're wrong, Louie."

Louie looked crestfallen.

"And here is something else, Louie: You run your little kingdom. That's fine. But the military is under my command. They take orders from *me*." He watched Big Louie's face mottle with anger. "Go ahead and sull up, Louie. Won't do you a bit of good. Besides, Louie, you don't like combat. You might get your pecker shot off in combat."

Louie grimaced and crossed his legs. Daintily.

Just as the first teams were getting into position in Kansas, Gen. Cecil Jefferys was watching the first trucks begin rolling out of Base Camp One in North Georgia. Luck was on the Rebels' side on this night, for the moon was fat and full, and no other lights were necessary for the drivers to see their way.

Cecil stood by the side of the road, giving each vehicle a salute as they passed his position. These were the noncombatants pulling out: the old, the very young, the untrained, the wounded. And with their leaving, Cecil felt a weight slip from his shoulders.

"Give 'em hell, general!" a wounded Rebel called from the back of a truck.

"Will do," Cecil returned the call.

"See y'all in Alabama, general," another Rebel called.

Cecil waved.

The long, snakelike column rolled and rumbled its way west.

There would be a dozen convoys leaving that night, each one at least a mile long, leaving a half hour apart.

And so we do it again, Cecil thought, standing by the road, feeling the cool night wind from the passing trucks, cars, and Jeeps fan him, the breeze touched with the odor of gasoline and diesel, the smell of oil and rubber.

We tear it all down, all the refineries, the hospitals, the factories—and bug out. God, when will it end? he silently questioned. Are You up there, God? Are You listening? What are we doing wrong with our society? Why can't we just settle down in one spot and live in peace?

Cecil took off his beret and bowed his head. The moonlight touched the salt and pepper of his hair. There had been no gray in his hair when he and Ben and Ike had come together, to build the Tri-States. All of them young men not that many years back. Young men, of all races, creeds, nationalities, coming together to form a government, a country, a society.

And it had worked. A society free of bigotry and prejudice. A society with full employment; where no one went hungry; no one was denied medical care; where one could go to sleep at night with the doors unlocked and not be afraid; where the elderly were cared for with love and compassion.

It was almost perfect, Cecil thought, standing by the road with his beret in one hand and an M-16 in the other. Not perfect in the minds of those who lived outside our borders; but perfect for us who lived *inside* those borders. And isn't that the way it should be?

Cecil did not expect the heavens to open up and give him a reply. He had asked these questions many times before.

But he did long for an explanation as to why a decent society, which meets the satisfaction of all who live within its borders, can't exist free from outside pressures.

He had been waiting many years for that answer. And he was no closer to an explanation now than fifteen years ago.

He raised his head at the sound of boots on the gravel. Putting his beret back on his head, Cecil looked at Col. Joe Williams.

"Sons of bitches want a fight, huh, Joe?"

"Looks that way, general."

"Well, then . . . let's just give them that, Joe. A dirty, stinking, no-holds-barred run for the money."

Joe grinned in the night, waiting for Cecil to continue.

"No quarter, no mercy, no prisoners. Travel light, hit hard, then run like hell and circle around behind the cock-suckers!"

Joe and Cecil had been together for a long time. And Joe knew Cec never used profanity unless he was very angry. And the big ex-Green Beret was very angry.

Cecil motioned Joe to follow him, and the two men went into a building. There, Cecil spread a map of Georgia on a table. "They're coming at us from the south and the east, Joe. We're going to take casualties. But we've got to buy some time for those leaving for Alabama. So, in order to do that, we've got to create confusion, panic, and doubt. What's the latest intel on Khamsin's troops?"

"They aren't rushing toward us. They came across the river in a hurry, then for some reason, they slowed to a crawl. Many units even stopped their advance. I don't know why they did that. They sure as hell weren't meeting much resistance. From the east, they're about thirty-five miles inside Georgia. From the south, they've advanced just about that distance north of Interstate Twenty."

"Get on the horn. Tell Mark and Alvaro to start raising hell with the invaders. Hard, fast, deadly, and then run like hell."

"Yes, sir."

"Start mining the roads and blowing the bridges, Joe. Wherever our people can lay booby traps, do it. Make them very enticing. We've got tons of explosives. So let's don't skimp a bit. Start jamming their

118

communications. We've got a few people who speak Arabic; not well, but enough to do the job. Get them to start issuing false orders to the troops in the field. See if we can't get some of The Hot Wind's people running around in circles."

"Yes, sir."

"We've got supplies cached all over the northern part of the state, Joe. So our people can take off traveling light, except for ammo and grenades. Load 'em up, but don't overload them."

"Yes, sir."

"All right, Joe. You're in charge of the eastern section, I'll take the southern section. Let's start moving them out."

Cecil held out his hand and Joe shook it. "Watch your ass, old friend," Cecil said.

Joe squeezed Cecil's strong and thick upper arm. "Same to you, old friend."

Buddy gathered up his gear and packed the Jeep. He wanted to be ready when General McGowan and his people started forming up in this area. And from the radio transmissions he'd been monitoring, the forward recon teams were very close.

Buddy cleaned and oiled his weapons and checked his ammo pouches. That done, he fixed a cold supper and squatted by the dark outline of the Jeep, eating slowly as the sound of approaching vehicles grew louder. He remained very still in the night. He had chosen his position well, and knew that unless someone literally walked into the Jeep, the odds of his being discovered were slim. But, he cautioned himself, these were Raines's Rebels, and they were all professional soldiers, the recon teams picked and trained by the former SAS man, Col. Dan Gray.

They were the best in the world; even his mother would agree, reluctantly, with that.

Moving as silently as a cat, Buddy slipped full length on the ground, looking under the Jeep. He watched as the lead vehicle stopped and several people got out. In the moonlight, he could see tiger-stripe and lizard battle dress.

"It looks clean." The voice drifted to him.

"Yeah, but I don't like it," came the reply. "Down!"

The shapes vanished, hitting the ground.

They sensed my presence, Buddy thought. True warriors all. No wonder my father's Rebels are so feared and respected. I must be very careful; I must not be shot out of carelessness.

Buddy sensed more than heard movement to his right and to his left. And knew that he had been silently and effectively surrounded.

"If you're Raines's Rebels," he called softly. "I am your friend. If you are warlords' troops, not many will walk away from this place."

"And that includes you, too, partner." The voice came out of the darkness.

"But of course," Buddy said.

"You're pretty good, whoever you are. But you made one mistake."

"And that is?"

"You just ate. We smelled the food."

"Then that makes you even better than I first thought. I have some papers I took from some of Big Louie's men. After I killed them. Troop placements and so forth."

"That's nice."

The voice was much closer. Damn! Buddy thought. I didn't even hear or sense his coming nearer.

"What's your name?" another voice called.

"Buddy. And I have traveled far to reach Raines's Rebels. I wish to join you."

Buddy stiffened only slightly as he felt the cold muzzle of a rifle touch his neck. They move like ghosts, he thought. The Old Man warned me. He told me that while I was very good, I was not yet in the league of many of Ben Raines's Rebels.

"My name is Ben Raines Blackman," Buddy said.

A harsh burst of light flooded Buddy's face, blinding him to all but the beam.

"Jesus God!" a Rebel said. "He ain't lyin' about that, gang."

BOOK TWO

Sons of the Dark and Bloody ground.
O'Hara

1

"Forgive me for starin', boy," Ike said. "But the resemblance is kinda unnervin'."

"That is perfectly all right, sir," Buddy said. "I understand."

"Well, you got manners. Give your momma credit for that, at least."

Buddy's smile was thin. "Not my mother, general. Thank my grandfather for that. And he convinced me to leave my mother's Order."

"What if that crackpo—ah, your mother, finds out what he did?"

Buddy sighed. "She knows. I would imagine she had ordered him burned at the stake."

"Son," Ike said, leaning forward, "I know Ben would love to see you; love to welcome you into the Rebels . . ." He shook his head. "You mean, she would burn her own father at the stake?"

"Yes. She's quite insane. She is my mother, but I think the kindest thing anyone could do would be to put her out of her misery." Just please don't ask me to do it, he thought.

Again, Ike shook his head in disbelief at Sister

Voleta. But the boy seems genuine, he thought. "Well, son, as I was gonna say . . . puttin' your mother out of her misery is exactly what Ben plans on doin'. The very first chance he gets."

"Yes, I know," the young man said softly. "And so does my mother."

Ike nodded his head, then looked at the team leader who had brought the young man to him. "Not one word about who he is. Not a word. Get him outfitted and bring him back to me. He'll stay close to me. I want to see what he can do."

"General . . . if something were to happen to him? . . ."

"I plan on talkin' with the general in about a minute. Don't worry about it; the final word is up to Ben. Boy," he said, looking back at Buddy. "You go with Sergeant Rogers. You're now a buck-assed private in your daddy's Rebel army."

"Yes, sir."

Ike walked to his communications truck, telling the operator, "Go get a cup of coffee. Come back in about five minutes." He grinned. "Don't you dare leave me alone with all this mess for more than that. I'm liable to be talkin' with Mars."

When the operator was out of earshot, Ike lifted the mike and said, "This is the Shark. Get me the Eagle and put it all on scramble."

Ben put down the mike and stepped outside, motioning the radio operator to once more enter and take over.

Not much shook Ben Raines. Not much at all. But this shook him; shook him right down to his boots and toenails. So the rumors were not rumors at all, but fact. Ike had just told him that the young man

126

looked so much like Ben it was frightening. In Ike's words, "Man, it like to have scared the shit out of me!"

And Ike also said that he was going to test the boy in combat. No — not boy. Young man. He'd be in his early twenties by now.

Ben smiled. His son. Blood son. A buck-assed private, soldiering under one of the toughest men Ben had ever known.

Ike McGowan.

Well, Ben thought, Buddy had damn well better be tough, 'cause if there was any rabbit in him, Ike would sure discover it.

And, the thought once more came to Ben, the young man just might have been sent in here to kill me. His mother's hatred was so intense, that was something she would do — even if it meant her own son would die trying to accomplish it.

That was something Ben did not like to even think of. But he knew it was something that had to be weighed, and weighed very carefully. He had told Ike the same thing.

Ben was conscious of Denise coming up to him and stopping a few feet away. He glanced at her. "Yes?"

"This word, sir. All the troops are in position. They're settling down to get a few hours' sleep."

Ben nodded his head, then realized she could not see the gesture. "Very well. Wake me at four in the morning, please."

"Yes, sir. Sir? Would you like something to drink before going to bed? Some hot tea, perhaps?"

Ben again looked at her. Lovely in the moonlight. "Will you join me, Denise?"

"Why . . . yes, of course. That would be very nice."

"Fine." Ben smiled. "I'd like that very much."

Ike carefully went over the papers Buddy had given him. They were a godsend. If they were accurate, they would make the job much easier, for they showed the positions of every unit in Louie's army—or Ashley's army—whatever. And they showed where the units would fall back to in case of heavy enemy attack.

The person who had drawn them up was very, very good; almost brilliant. But it showed his, or her, lack of understanding when it came to guerrilla warfare.

The plan hinged on massive frontal attacks or rear assaults; classic battle plans. And that crap had all gone out the window during Southeast Asia.

Ike rang up Ben's CP and advised the officer in charge of the plans, telling him he was sending them over by runner immediately; just as soon as he had them copied.

"Would the general like to speak with General Raines?"

"Naw. He's probably asleep by now."

"Oh, no, sir. He's having tea with Miss Denise Vista."

Ike said his good nights, laughing. Same ol' Ben.

Tina and her teams had taken Highway 77 down to Arkansas City, on the border with Oklahoma, and then cut east on Highway 166. At the small and deserted town of Sedan, they began splitting up. One team would stay at Sedan until jump-off time; that team would head straight up Highway 99, clearing everything up to Highway 54, which was the beginning of Colonel Gray's territory.

There were two small towns between Sedan and Caney. Perhaps a half-dozen families were scratching out an existence in the two towns. They didn't know what to make of the Rebels.

"You folks don't look like none of Big Louie's people," a spokesman said.

"We're not," Tina informed him. "We're part of Raines's Rebels."

The crowd solemnly nodded their heads. They knew what that meant: All hell was about to break loose.

"Are you people armed?" Tina asked.

"No, ma'am. Louie's soldiers took our guns. Said we didn't need them. Said they'd protect us if it come to that."

"And you just handed them over?"

The man's smile was very sad. "When you're lookin' down the barrels of a hundred rifles, ma'am, you start figurin' real fast what's the best way to go. You know what I mean?"

"Yes," Tina said. "Yes, I do. You people just sit tight. We're going to clear this area of Big Louie and his crap. Then we'll return. My dad is going to put this country back on its feet. You want to be a part of that?"

The ragged group of men, women, and kids all began to grin. A woman said, "You just give us a chance, miss."

"You'll get your chance," Tina promised.

One team was left at Caney. At jump-off time, if all went as planned, they would travel up Highway 75, clearing the way of all Big Louie's people. They would stop at Altoona.

The teams traveled on eastward. Several hundred people were at Coffeyville, and not all of them were happy to see the Rebels. Those were the civilians who had joined forces with Big Louie. They liked the idea of having slaves and being able to torture and rape at their pleasure.

Just as Ben would have done, Tina turned that group of people over to the townspeople. The team that she left there did not interfere as the newly freed townspeople set about hanging those who had aligned themselves with Big Louie.

The Rebels moved eastward, stopping at the small towns near the border: Valeda, Edna, Bartlett — all deserted. Tina's team stayed at Chetopa while the remainder pushed on toward the junction of Highways 166 and 69.

The most easterly team would head north, stopping only when they reached Fort Scott. Tina's team would head north on Highway 59, securing the area and stopping about ten miles east of Chanute. Then three teams of Rebels would converge on Chanute, where a large force of Big Louie's people were dug in.

"Get a few hours' rest," Tina told her people. "We roll at four o'clock."

Col. Dan Gray and his teams barreled through the night, blasting the night air as they pushed eastward on Highway 54. They secured the towns of Rosalia, Reece, Eureka, Tonovay, and Neal. They hit some resistance at the town of Batesville and took a few minutes to clear that little town of Big Louie's crap, then rested for a short time.

Dan had left a team of Rebels at Tonovay. At jump-off time, that team would head straight north up Highway 57/99, securing everything up to Emporia.

At Yates Center, Dan dropped off another team; they had the task of clearing the thirty-eight miles up to Interstate 35.

Dan and his Rebels shoved on eastward, hitting a small pocket of resistance at Iola. The Rebels put them down hard, brutally, taking no prisoners. They returned the town to the survivors and armed them with the captured weapons. Dan told the survivors that this time they should hang on to their freedom.

Dan's people moved out east toward Fort Scott, seizing and securing all the little towns in their path.

At each major crossroads, Dan left a team. One would charge north up 169 from Iola, another up 59 from Moran, the last one up 69 from Fort Scott, breaking it off and cutting west just south of Kansas City.

Dan would lead the team that jumped off from Moran, to link up first with Ben at Ottawa.

Ike had left small teams of Rebels along the way as his people pushed north out of Manhattan, before his main force turned east at Marysville. The ex-navy Seal pushed his troops hard that night, making the crossing over to Sparks long before the pre-set jump-off mark. He had left teams at Beattie, Seneca, Fairview, Hiawatha, and finally, at Sparks. Ike would lead the team that would drive south out of Hiawatha, pushing all the way down to Lawrence.

It was only then, when Ike had the time to carefully mull over Ben's plan, that he realized what Ben was really doing. He sat in his Jeep and smiled grudgingly at the justice of it all.

Ben had said he was leaving lots of holes for Louie's people to run out of. Ben's commanders had accepted that. But now Ike knew that Ben had deliberately withheld the final truth: There would be only one hole for Louie's slave-masters to run for.

Ike grinned at the truth. Ben was using classic guerrilla tactics; he was effectively spiderwebbing the entire eastern sector of the state, closing off all holes except one. No matter where Big Louie's army ran, they would succeed only in running into teams of Rebels. If those troops of Big Louie ran from Tina, they would hit Dan's Rebels. If Louie's troops ran from Dan, they would run into Tina's people to the south, and Ben or Ike's troops to the north and west. If Louie's people tried to run from Ike's teams, they would hit Ben's teams to the south. If any of Louie's troops tried to run to the east, they would strike Rebels stretching from the Oklahoma border all the way up to Interstate 35, and from the Nebraska line all the way down to Leavenworth.

Ike leaned back and closed his gritty-feeling eyes. "That son of a gun!" he said. "He's givin' them one hell of an option." He laughed softly in the darkness.

"What do you mean, sir?" a platoon leader asked him.

"Ben Raines's type of justice," Ike said. "He's givin' Big Louie and his people between Interstates Seventy and Thirty-five a hole to run into." Again Ike laughed at the poetic justice of it all.

"I still don't understand, sir."

"They can either stand and fight us, or run to the only hole Ben's left them: Kansas City. Where they'll die from radiation or be killed by the human animals that live there. What a hell of an option Ben's left them."

"You think General Rains did that on purpose, sir?"

"Hell, yes, he did! Ben Raines is a mean bastard when you make him mad."

132

Denise lay in Ben's arms, her breasts pushing against Ben's bare chest. The cot was narrow, but neither one of them had expressed any misgiving about the slight discomfort.

As a matter of fact, they hadn't paid any attention to it at all. They'd been too busy.

Denise noticed, in the dim light, that Ben was smiling.

"Is sex amusing to you, general?"

"You will have to admit that the pleasure is fleeting and the position ridiculous," Ben said.

She laughed softly, her breath hot against Ben's neck. "But that is not what you were smiling about." It was not a question.

Then he told her what he had done.

She lay for a time, silent in his arms. Silent for so long Ben thought she must have fallen asleep.

Finally, she said, "It's a good punishment for what they have done."

And if anyone could be allowed to say that, Ben thought, this woman should have the right.

2

"We have met the enemy," the CO of Rebel patrol radioed back to Base Camp One. "Unfortunately, they ain't ours yet!"

Despite the situation, Cecil had to grin. The platoon leader, an ex-schoolteacher, could still find some humor.

"Ask him what he plans to do about it," Cecil told the radio operator.

The radio operator asked, then listened for a moment, a grin on his face. Looking up at Cecil, he said, "Jimmy says to tell you, sir, with all due respect, that he plans on haulin' his ass outta there."

Cecil laughed, then suddenly sobered, his brow wrinkling in thought. "Yes," he said aloud. "Yes, that might work." He began pacing the floor. "Ask Jimmy his location, please."

"Highway Seventeen, sir. 'Bout halfway between Royston and Vanna."

"Get in touch with Colonel Williams, or some of his patrols. Make damn sure it's all scrambled."

Joe's voice came out of the speaker after the first try. "I'm on One forty-five, general. Coming up on Royston. 'Bout eight miles out."

"Damn, but he's been hot-rodding it," Cecil muttered. He took the mike and said, "Joe, what do your forward recon people report?"

"Hundreds of troops, sir. They punched right through our people just south of Hartwell Lake and are pouring across."

"Hold your position, Joe," Cecil ordered. "Do not advance. Repeat: Do not advance at this time. Do you acknowledge?"

"But, sir. Jimmy and his people? . . ."

"Do you acknowledge my orders!"

"Yes, sir! Holding right here."

Cecil looked at the radio operator. "We had a full platoon just west of the river on Seventy-two, across from Calhoun Falls. Make contact with them, please."

Contact made, Cecil took the mike. "Is the bridge mined yet?"

"Yes, sir. The sixth vehicle that rolls over the switcher blows it. And it's all coming down, sir."

"Good. I want you to take your platoon and let the hammer down getting to the town of Bowman, or what's left of it. Set up an ambush site. Contact me when you're in position. I want you there fifteen minutes ago. Push it."

"Rolling, sir!"

"You listening to this, Joe?" Cecil asked.

"Ten-four, general. I'm reading your mind. If we time this just right, we can kick some ass."

"Right. Hang tight, Joe. Jimmy?"

"I'm listening, sir. Make it quick, general. I can damn near reach out and touch the bastards."

"Run, Jimmy!" Cecil ordered. "Run as if you're terrified. Run in panic. Grab some old weapons if you can find them and throw them away as you're running. Make the bastards think you're so afraid of them you're running in blind, panicked fear. Head

135

straight for Bowman. You copy this?"

"Pulling out now, sir."

"Joe? Let Khamsin's people cut south before you head after them. Then put them in a box and close the goddamned lid!"

"Yes, sir!"

"Bastards want to meet Allah," Cecil muttered, his face tight with anger. "Then I'll certainly give them a dandy chance."

The Ashley that now stood beside his Jeep did not at all resemble the man who had spoken to Big Louie the day before. His chin strap was buckled tight, the steel pot secure outside his helmet liner. He wore bloused jodhpurs and highly polished riding boots. Two pearl-handled and nickeled .45s rested in leather, one on each side. He wore a World War Two Ike jacket.

Patton had always been a favorite of Ashley's. He saw the movie about Patton dozens of times. Wore one cassette out. Ashley thought of himself as the reincarnation of Patton. Now he was going to prove that theory.

Ashley had always regretted that he'd never served in the military. But his daddy had told him he was needed at home, so he spread some money around and got his boy out of the draft. His daddy had said it would be unsightly for a man of Ashley's position to serve with rabble.

Ashley glanced at his watch. Four o'clock. And where was the much-legended and highly touted Ben Raines?

A man in full battle dress approached him. "Sir?"

Ashley turned. "What is it?"

"We can't make contact with any of our people

along the border, sir."

"How about Chanute?"

"Everything is quiet there, sir."

"Those two men north of here, and the couple who were killed . . . any idea who might have done that?"

"Not a clue, sir."

"Damn! How about any of our recon patrols? What do they report?"

"Nothing, sir."

"You mean they haven't seen anything?"

"No, sir. They just don't report. And we can't raise them by radio."

"Is everyone at their assigned positions?"

"Yes, sir."

"Very well. Stand by. You can't predict when or where Ben Raines is going to strike. The son of a bitch is unpredictable. I can't believe that none of our outposts are not reporting."

"Not a peep, sir."

One could say that Big Louie's men, who once manned the far outposts, enforcing Big Louie's harsh rule, were now just sort of—hanging around, so to speak; those whose throats hadn't been cut by various teams of Rebels.

As far as no outposts reporting to Ashley's CP in Topeka—they were unable to report. Those manning the outposts now sat in silence, wondering what in the hell was going on.

The Rebels had discovered their frequency early on and simply jammed it, preventing any radio contact at all.

Ben stepped out of his tent and looked up at the

137

starry skies. "Hey, Buck!" he called. "You ready to kick ass and take names?"

"Let's go give them hell, general!" the sergeant said.

"James?" Ben called.

"Here, Ben," James said.

"Let's do it."

"We have a large contingent of Rebels on the run!" a field commander radioed back to Khamsin's CP. "They are fleeing in blind panic, hurling their weapons to one side in their fearful retreat from the troops of The Hot Wind!"

Khamsin acknowledged the message and told the runner to wait. He poured them all coffee. They toasted, in what none of them realized was a most premature victory toast.

Khamsin's XO, Hamid, was smiling as broadly as Khamsin and the messenger.

"Tell our gallant troops to take as many prisoners as possible," Khamsin told the runner. "I am feeling most generous this day. Besides, I want to parade the so-called invincible Rebels in front of the civilians, to show them that nothing can stand when The Hot Wind blows!"

Col. Joe Williams lifted a leg and farted. His driver grinned and said, "I sure am glad we're movin', sir."

"That's what I think of that goddamned Hot Wind. Slow, now, slow. Let them stay well ahead of us."

The driver slowed the Jeep. Joe picked up the mike and said, "This is the Plug. Is the Bottle in place?"

"Bottle here, sir. In place. I can hear the Chicken headin' for the hen house now, sir. The Big Bad Wolf is hot on Chicken's heels."

"How far out, Bottle?"

"Maybe a mile and a half, Plug."

"Ten-four." He turned to his driver, at the same time raising his right arm high in the air, the fist closed. He pumped it up and down, signaling those behind him to come on. "Hammer down, Matt!"

In a very short time, Joe signaled his column to halt and dismount. The sounds of gunfire, hard and stuttering, drifted to them. Explosions ripped the early morning coolness. Screaming of the wounded shattered the dark as heavy machine gun fire staccatoed.

Joe positioned his people. "Stand or die!" he ordered. "No prisoners, no quarter, and no mercy."

His troops dug in, their faces grim, as they set the plug firmly into the neck of the bottle.

As the brigade of Khamsin's Islamic People's Army ran headlong into the dark ambush in the deserted town, one entire company was massacred before the others even realized what was going on. The screaming of the wounded and the frightened yelling of those caught in the hideous and heavy crossfires ripped the dark pre-dawn.

They had no place to run.

The small force of Rebels that had suckered them into the ambush had cut left and right upon entering the ruined town, falling into ambush positions. The killing fields of fire came at the IPA from three sides.

The commander ordered his troops to fall back, retreat, head north.

They did just that.

And ran headlong into the guns of Col. Joe Williams's Rebels. The Rebels raked the panicked troops of The Hot Wind with automatic weapons' fire, sending them jerking and screaming and death-dancing into that long sleep. Soon the littered streets of the old town were running thick and red with blood.

Close to a thousand men of The Hot Wind lay twisted in death on the dirty and littered street. The near-deafening cacophony of gunfire abruptly ceased. To the uninitiated, the silence would have seemed far too loud.

A few of The Hot Wind's troops begged for mercy from the Rebels.

But the Rebels were in no mood to offer mercy toward those who had started this little dance. Colonel Williams settled that point with one blunt statement.

"Finish them!"

Single shots rang out in the night.

"Strip the bodies of weapons, ammo, grenades, and boots," came the orders from down the line.

The Rebels never left nothing behind that might be of some use to someone later on. The orders of Ben Raines.

"Booby-trap some of the bodies," Joe ordered. "We can send a few more of the bastards to hell when they come snooping around to inspect the awesome forces of The Hot Shit!"

Joe's smile was grim, but filled with a soldier's satisfaction. "We stung them, people. But they'll be a lot more cautious after this." He motioned for his radio operator to come over. "Get General Jefferys on the horn. Tell him I'm blowing all bridges from Augusta north to the mountains."

He hesitated for only a second. "Yes, sir."

That had not been an easy decision for anyone to make, and the radio operator, as well as all the other

Rebels listening, knew it. Considering the times, once those vital links were gone, they would, in all probability, be gone forever. Millions of dollars of state-to-state links destroyed.

Joe was very conscious of Rebel eyes on him in the gunsmoke-filled and bloody pre-dawn. And as was the Rebel way, he said, "I'm open for suggestions, people."

To a person, the Rebels shook their heads. They might not like the idea of destroying those bridges, but the decision was necessary. Anything to buy them a little more time. It had to be.

Without the bridges, Khamsin's IPA would have to detour a hundred miles or more to get into Rebel-controlled territory. And the Rebels were just aching for the IPA to meet them in the mountains — something all knew that Khamsin would not allow, for his recon teams who had been sent into the mountains never returned. They had disappeared into the foggy mountains and misty hollows without a trace.

And without the bridges, the IPA would be forced to use the remaining bridges far south of Rebel-held country. Time. Precious time for the Rebels.

"General Jefferys says to blow the bridges, colonel," a runner informed Joe. "And may future generations forgive us."

"They're all over the damn place, sir!" Ashley was informed by a breathless aide. Breathless and pale, Ashley noted.

"Who is all over the damn place, man? And get 'hold of yourself."

"Rebels, sir! They seized towns from the Oklahoma line clear up to Nebraska. We just got a message in from Chanute. Had to be transmitted by

CB radio, using relay points. We got another message in, same way, from just east of Emporia. Them guys there is lookin' smack at Ben Raines and his people. Like to have scared the shit outta them ol' boys when dawn come and there they was."

"You mean no one heard them settin' up or comin' in?" Ashley yelled.

"No, sir. Ain't nobody heared nothin'."

Ashley thought hard for a moment. "All right. Listen to me. Carefully. These are my orders: Everybody between Interstate Seventy and Highway Fifty-four, pull back. Set up defense lines along Highway Seventy-five. We'll form a line so solid that no one can break through. Raines wants a head-to-head fight, all right, by God, let's give it to him. Order everyone out of the southern sectors of the state. Have them pull back to Yates Center and then spread east to Fort Scott. Order everyone in the northern section of the state to drop south to Interstate Seventy and stretch from Topeka to the hot zone edge. We've got just as many troops as Ben Raines has Rebels. So let's give them a fight. Tell the men to take as many women and kids and old fuckers prisoners as they can. If Raines wants us, he'll have to fire into lines of civilians. That'll stop the son of a bitch! He won't hurt them. Go, man, go."

"They're pulling back, sir," Denise said, reading the message just delivered from communications. "Big Louie's troops appear to be forting up behind Highways Fifty-four to the south, Seventy-five to the west, and Seventy to the north. Field commanders awaiting your orders. There's more."

"The silly shit," Ben muttered. "He didn't have enough sense to see that we were spread so thin he

142

could have bunched his people up and punched right through us at damn near any point." He looked at Denise. "Tell all teams to push hard toward their objectives, but to halt just outside of those boundaries you just named. No one goes in or comes out. I've got a hunch what he's planning; I've seen it before, and it isn't very pretty."

But she was right in step with him. "He's used women and kids and the elderly before, general," she said. "As shields for his troops."

"Yes. That's what I'm afraid of."

"And? . . ."

Ben shook his head. "I don't know, Denise. We'll just have to wait and see. What else was in that message?"

"General McGowan captured some of Louie's people. They told him that Ashley's hatred for you goes all the way back to Louisiana. Back before the Great War."

"Strange," Ben said. "But I still cannot place this Ashley person. Should be a very interesting encounter. When we do meet."

3

Mark and Alvaro sent sappers from their contingent in the Oconee Forest racing eastward across Interstate 20 to Augusta. They carried enough explosives to destroy twenty bridges. They had four bridges to blow: the I-20 bridge, the Highway 25 bridge, the 1-78 bridge, and the bridge that ran Highway 28 into Augusta. At the junction of I-20 and State 232, the teams shook hands and split up. They would regroup that night at the deserted town of Wrens, just south of the old Fort Gordon Military Reservation. If all groups were not there by 2000 hours, those not present were on their own. Guerrilla warfare is not for the faint at heart.

Col. Joe Williams had sent teams of his Rebels north and south, loaded down with high explosives. After they blew their assigned bridges, they were to set up observation posts on the Georgia side of the river.

Cecil Jefferys had ordered his teams to destroy the northernmost bridges linking South Carolina and Georgia. The only bridge that was to be spared — Cecil just could not bring himself to destroy it — was the I-85 bridge. But it was to be heavily mined and guarded from the Georgia side.

Cecil knew, without any doubts, thanks to many intercepted messages from the IPA, that Khamsin did not want to mix it up with the Rebels in the mountains; Khamsin did not want to stick his nose anywhere near the mountains — and that was not just because of the Rebels.

The mountains were filled with tough, single-minded folks, people whose basic nature, even in the best of times, was to shoot first and ask questions later. Their names were synonymous with legended feuds. The Rebels had made an easy truce with the mountain people, simply because, in many ways, their own philosophy of living was much the same: You mind your own business and I'll mind mine; but if you come fucking around, with intentions to harm me or mine, I'll kill you!

Khamsin sat in his office and stared at the radio message that lay on his wide and polished desk. The copied message had succeeded in souring Khamsin's stomach and ruining his entire morning.

Second brigade wiped out in ambush with Rebels. No survivors. Do we pursue?

How? Khamsin silently pondered the awful question. How could such a tiny force of Rebels wipe out an entire brigade?

He sighed heavily. He looked at his coffee cup. The thought of drinking more of the bitter brew was totally repugnant to him. He turned in his leather chair and gazed out the window, his thoughts revengeful and savage. The commander of the Second Brigade had been with Khamsin for many years. He had been such a fine terrorist—and also a deeply religious man. Khamsin had spread his rug and prayed with the man many times.

Such a fine and honorable man. Now he was dead at the hands of savages.

"You'll pay for this, Ben Raines," Khamsin swore, his voice low. "I swear that you will. You will never be rid of me. I will follow you to the smoking gates of hell and beyond to have my revenge."

Khamsin buzzed for an aide. "Contact all troops in Georgia and order them to stop their advance. Do not pursue the Rebels."

Khamsin's XO, Hamid, entered the room and took a seat.

Khamsin said, "We have a foothold in Georgia. And that is good. We know that the black general, Jefferys, has ordered his troops north of Interstate Eighty-five . . . that may or may not be accurate information. But I would wager that the black man has ordered recon and sappers into the area between Interstates Eighty-five and Twenty; probably to engage in guerrilla warfare with our people. And I would expect him to start destroying all bridges linking the two states—"

An aide knocked softly on the door.

"Come!" Khamsin said.

"General, the bridge at Calhoun Falls is gone. We lost several hundred men and many trucks. The Rebels on the other side shot those who tried to swim to safety."

Khamsin slammed a hand down on the desk. "Savages!" he hissed. "They are savages. There is not

146

one ounce of honor in the entire filthy lot of them."

But a lot of dedicated and highly professional soldiers, the XO thought. He kept that thought to himself, however.

Khamsin nodded at the young aide and the man left, closing the door behind him.

Hamid said, "We have three places left to us to cross, general. And the first bridge south of Augusta is said to be mined."

Khamsin waved him silent. "I know. I know all that. And I also know that if I were General Jefferys, I would have teams of Rebels on the western side of those bridges. Just a small team could block the bridges for a very long time. We could quite easily get men across the river in boats, but heavy equipment is yet another matter. Jefferys would like us to try an approach through the mountains. I have no doubt that, in time, we could cut through. But at what cost of lives?"

Hamid said nothing. He had personally led a patrol into the mountains. The dark and foggy roads and misty, forbidding, green dripping terrain had filled him with uneasiness. He could feel eyes on him at all times; hostile eyes, watching, waiting. And it would take but a single stick of dynamite to bring down part of any mountain on his force. Hamid had turned back after only a few hours into the mountains.

"All right," Khamsin said with a sigh. "For the present, we hold what we have taken. Order our people to dig in hard and deep. Make no further advances. I'll leave at dawn tomorrow to begin an inspection of the southern bridges. We can't move effectively, but then, nether can the Rebels. But time is on our side. We can afford to wait, Hamid. We can only grow stronger, while the Rebels can only grow

147

weaker."

Hamid nodded his head. But he was thinking, I wonder about that. I really wonder.

Cecil had taken five hundred troops and moved to the south. Colonel Williams had taken five hundred troops and spread out along the eastern border.

"What a thin brave line," Cecil said aloud. "If Khamsin ever discovers just how thin . . . "

He trailed that off into silence.

"Beg pardon, sir?" Cecil's driver asked.

"Just talking to myself," Cecil said. He noticed a rusted, battered, and shot-up road sign. "Is that trash still in Athens, Harrison?"

"Yes, sir. A bunch of losers, they seem to me, sir. They've turned the place into kind of a trash-can fort. Field reports say the bunch seemed to have no direction, no goals, no nothing. I agree with that assessment."

"You've seen these people?"

"Yes, sir. When I was working recon. Before I got hit."

Cecil knew the young man had very nearly lost his life due to a mine. The mine had broken his legs. He walked with a limp and always would. He had been taken off of field duty and assigned as Cecil's driver.

"Bring me up to date, Harrison. How many people in Athens?"

"Oh, five or six hundred. But they're a sorry lot, sir."

"Maybe they just haven't had the right person to point out a few facts of life to them."

"What do you mean, sir?"

"Get on the horn, Harrison. Tell the point to take us into Athens. I have an idea. It might go sour, but

148

if it works, we'll be a bit stronger."

"What the hell is that nigger doin' out there?" Jake asked.

Jake — no last name — was the unofficial leader of the ragged and dirty bunch of drifters and misfits who now inhabited the ruins of Athens, Georgia. Jake was big and rough and mean and ran his little kingdom by brute force, crippling or killing anyone who dared defy him. Some of the residents stayed on willingly; others stayed because they felt they had no other place to go, and the closed city did afford some degree of safety. Others stayed because they were scared of Jake and his enforcers.

"General Jefferys," someone told Jake. "Ben Raines second in command. I'd go easy with this one, Jake."

"Oh, yeah! Well, that's a pretty fancy title for a coon," Jake said, eyeballing Cecil over the barricaded end of the street. "I thank I'll jist snatch that funny-lookin' hat offen his head and then I'll be a general." Jake laughed, exposing yellowed and rotten teeth.

His breath would have stopped a blowfly in midair.

"Jake . . . " his buddy tried to warn him off.

"Jist cool it," Jake said. I've done a good job of runnin' thangs so far, ain't I?"

His friend nodded his head.

"So's how about you just shet up and let me handle this nigger."

His friend again nodded his head, eyeballing the Rebels who lined the street. It's been pretty good while it lasted, he thought. But now it's time to haul ass.

He walked slowly away. He knew that when Ben Raines's people come to town, they ain't totin' Christmas presents.

Cecil stood a few yards in front of the barricade that blocked entrance to the small city. Jake had not blocked the bypass loop running around the city, only the exits leading into the city proper.

The sight of Jake was nothing new to Cecil or to his Rebels. They had all seen little two-bit dictators many times in their travels across the devastated land that was once called the United States of America.

The Jakes of the world were all the same. Only the names and physical descriptions varied from place to place. The Jakes of the world had been losers when the world was whole, rebelling against all authority, bulling their way through life, intimidating those who would allow it, sucking up to those who were stronger, more powerful, richer, possessing some degree of influence. One could, unfortunately, find them in any two-bit redneck honky-tonk in any state—when there were states, that is. And honky-tonks. Only the rednecks remained. Unfortunately.

The Jakes of the world were easy to spot when the nation was whole, Cecil thought, looking at Jake. Just as easy to spot now.

Cecil walked up to the barricades and stopped. Jake stepped forward, shoving his face about six inches from Cecil's. Cecil grimaced at the man's body odor and foul breath.

Rebels with weapons at the ready stood left and right of the barricade. And Cecil had to smile as the Rebel behind the Jeep-mounted .50 caliber machine gun jacked a round into the weapon and swung the muzzle toward the crowd of unshaven and stinking men and women on Jake's side of the barricade.

The crowd backed up. Jake almost swallowed his chaw.

"Whut the hale do you want, boy?" Jake mush-mouthed.

"Perhaps actions will speak much louder than words," Cecil said.

"Haw?"

Cecil reached over the barricade and slapped Jake across the mouth.

Jake did swallow his chaw.

Jake coughed and hacked and spat and choked and finally managed to find his voice. "You gawddamn nigger! You cain't do 'at to me! Why, I'll—"

Cecil backhanded him, then took a half step closer and hit Jake in the mouth with a hard straight right. Jake sat down in the street, blood and tobacco juice leaking from his busted mouth.

Some of Jake's enforcers looked as though they would very much like to do something. But they weren't all that certain just exactly what they could do. Considering the reputation of the Rebels.

"Remove the barricades," Cecil ordered.

Rebels ripped down the makeshift barricades.

Cecil stepped forward and kicked Jake in the mouth with a jump boot. Big Jake lay on the street, unconscious, his mouth leaking blood. His people stood with their mouths open, staring in disbelief. They were, to a person, armed, but not one among them made a move to lift a weapon.

Oh, they wanted to. They wanted to shoot this big black bastard so badly they had to grit their teeth hard to fight back the feeling.

But they stood as one, looking down the barrels of automatic weapons. They knew, to a person, that if any one of them made just one funny little move, there would be a bloodbath; and the blood would be theirs. Even though they outnumbered the Rebels, the Rebels looked so hard, so professional, so lean and mean.

Cecil said, "Now that I have your attention, I'm going to tell you all a story. A southern cop told it to me, about fifteen years ago. Just before the Great War. And you will listen to me. In silence."

The sullen crowd looked at Cecil. In silence.

"This cop was a very fair man, an educated man, and I like to think that he was representative of a good many southern cops in that. But some of his views were controversial back then, and they made me angry for a time . . . until I had the time to think them through, calmly and rationally.

"This cop told me that he believed with all his heart that there were, always had been, and always would be, classes of people. Yes, and he used the term nigger at the bottom of the black scale. And in the same breath, he said redneck and white trash.

"That balanced it out some, but it still made me very angry—at the time.

"This cop told me that niggers and white trash were exactly the same; the only difference being the pigmentation of skin. He said the two groups were ignorant, and proud of it. They wore their ignorance as a badge of honor. And that they were dangerous. Dangerous because even when given the opportunity to improve themselves, most would reject it, scoffing at it.

"He told me there was only one way to handle those groups of people, and that was by and with brute force. Because that's all they understood. They did not, and could not, comprehend compassion; they took it as a sign of weakness and held compassionate people in contempt.

"Just about the same kind of contempt I hold for most of you losers."

The crowd stood in silence and glared at him. Then about half of the crowd dropped their eyes, not meeting Cecil's hard gaze.

"This cop went on to say that he had found a very practical method of handling white trash and niggers. Practical, but brutal. Every time they screwed up, he'd just beat the shit out of them. He said on his beat, that averaged about once a month. And it took anywhere from six months to a year for the light of understanding to start shining in that murky cesspool they called a brain. He said that when those particular types of people get tired of wiping the blood out of their eyes and going to first the hospital and then to the jail, ninety-five percent of them will then begin to realize that there are social and moral codes, and rules and regulations and laws that they have to follow and obey just like other folks.

"Well," Cecil said, "I was a lot younger then, and a lot more idealistic. And I thought that police officer's philosophy was just awful! Then I began to ride with him on his patrol. He was a deputy sheriff. He'd point out people to me. 'See that punk over there, Cec?' he'd say. Then he'd tell me what that particular person had done. Horrible, terrible things. But there he was, walking the streets, a free man, thanks to our judicial system. He pointed out people and told me what they had done. And pointed out that they showed no signs of remorse. Ever. Some of the things he told me made me sick at my stomach.

"How many of you people fall into the category I just named?"

The crowd was dead silent.

"Uh-huh," Cecil said. "More than a few of you, I'd imagine. Well, then. I guess I'm just going to have to put that cop's philosophy to work here, with you people. Anyone have anything to say about that?"

"Yeah," a man called. "I think you're nuts!"

The Rebels began smiling; a few in the crowd, not

really understanding what was about to go down, smiled nervously.

"I don't think I'm going to like this very much," said a man from out of the crowd.

"I think," Cecil said, his voice carrying firm to them all, "that you are right."

4

"What will my father do if this Big Louie or Ashley person decides to use old people and women and children for shields?" Buddy asked.

"I don't know," Ike said. "I'd hate to have to make that decision."

"What would you do?" the young man persisted.

Ike was silent for a time. Then he looked at Buddy. "Freedom sometimes comes with a high price tag, boy."

Then Ike walked away, leaving Buddy to sit by himself in the shade of a truck. Buddy had noticed, since joining the Rebels, that unless Ike was with him, he was usually alone.

It wasn't that the other men and women were unfriendly—for that was not the case at all. The others would answer his questions, greet him, all the small social amenities; but they did not include him in their small groups, sitting and chatting of little things. And for a short time, that bothered Buddy. Then he began to understand it.

The others did not know where Buddy stood in the

scheme of things. Only that he was, without a doubt, and without begin told, Gen. Ben Raines's son. And that alone made him someone special. And until they found out a bit more about him, Buddy was going to have to settle for his own company.

Buddy looked around him and spotted that very pretty young woman who was part of Ike's personal team. Rising, Buddy walked over to her.

She smiled up at him. "Buddy. Getting a little jumpy about the upcoming fight?"

"No," he replied honestly. "I've been in firefights before. This one shouldn't be different from the others. May I sit down?"

"Sure."

He sat on the ground beside her. "You know my name, but I don't know yours."

"Judy." She inspected the young man with her blue eyes. No doubt about it, she thought. He's just about the best-looking guy in camp.

Buddy was aware that he was being given the once-over. He endured it silently.

Judy took in the muscular arms and shoulders. The thick wrists. The big chest and trim waist. She let her eyes linger on his face. A strong, square-jawed face. Eyes that gave away very little of his inner feelings. Looking into those eyes, Judy felt a mixture of strange emotions. The stronger emotion was that she was looking into the eyes of General Raines. And the face. This was what General Raines would have looked like as a young man.

Buddy had been given tiger-stripe battle clothes, but he chose not to wear the black beret of the Rebels. He wore only a dark red bandana tied around his forehead, over the mass of dark curly hair.

He isn't just good-looking, Judy thought. He's sensational-looking.

"You haven't seen your father yet?" she asked. There were other emotions she was experiencing as she looked at Buddy. She tried to ignore them. She failed miserably.

"Not yet. I would imagine he's allowing General McGowan to test me; to see if I'm worthy of being a Rebel. I can't fault him for that."

Judy wasn't about to comment on any of the general's decisions; if, indeed, that was what Ben Raines was doing. "I guess you've wondered why people are kind of ignoring you?"

"Yes. I have given that some thought."

"And? . . . "

"They're unsure of me. And a bit leary of me. I don't blame them. Then, too, I am the son of Ben Raines." He smiled. "The general's bastard son."

"That doesn't bother you? That . . . last statement?"

Buddy shook his head. "No. A child cannot chose its father. I had nothing to do with it. He will either accept me, or order me to leave."

"You talk like an educated person. I wish I had more education. I was entering my first year of college in the Tri-States when the government declared war on us. Hasn't been much time for studying since then. Except the study of war, that is."

"That is probably a good thing to study, considering the times. But the Old Man, my grandfather, saw to it that I was educated, and educated well. He shielded me from my mother and her insanity for years. He was the one who convinced me to leave, and to seek out my father."

Judy touched his strong arm. "I think there has been enough of this standing away from you, Buddy. Come on." She tugged at him. "Let's go meet the others."

157

And for the first time, Buddy felt he was being accepted.

"Guy's nuts!" a man said.

Cecil laughed at the voice. "Nuts? Oh, I might well be slightly mad. I think that anyone who pursues the dreams of putting this nation back together again might be suffering from a humpty-dumpty syndrome. But it's certainly better than what you people are doing—which is absolutely nothing."

"Our right," a woman called. "Ain't it?"

"No," Cecil said. "I don't believe it is. I don't think anyone has the right to just sit back and watch a once-productive country sink further into a terrible morass."

"A whut?" a man called.

"A morass, you ignorant bastard!" Cecil replied, a definite edge to his voice. Cecil had never had much patience with people who voluntarily chose to wallow in ignorance. "All right!" he shouted. "Enough talk. The draft has now officially been reinstated."

"The whut?" the same voice asked.

"The draft! Surely you know what that means?"

"You mean, lak bein' forced to join up with some army and play soldier boy?"

"And girl," a woman Rebel called, smiling as she spoke.

"That's your ass, honey!" a woman shouted from out of the crowd.

"Who said that?" the woman officer said, stepping forward to stand beside Cecil.

The civilian woman suddenly decided to play the army game: stay low and don't call any attention yourself. The crowd became silent and sullen.

"Lieutenant Mackey," Cecil said to the woman by

his side.

"Yes, sir."

"You're in charge of this . . . new contingent of Rebels. See to it that they are given quick physicals, long soapy baths, haircuts, and issued field clothing."

"Yes, sir."

"Now, you wait just a goddamn minute!" a man said, stepping from the crowd. He carried a rifle and very quickly placed the weapon on the ground as the .50 caliber machine gun was swung in his direction. "Don't get no itchy finger, man," he pleaded. "I ain't hostile none a-tal." He looked at Cecil. "General, you cain't just come in here and draft us! That ain't right none a bit. You ain't got the authority to do that!"

"Big black sucker shore looks like to me he's a-gonna do 'er though," said a voice from out of the crowd.

Cecil's eyes found the man who had just spoken. He waggled a finger at the man and his mouth. "Come over here."

His eyes downcast, the man reluctantly walked out of the crowd and up to Cecil.

"What's your name?" Cecil asked.

"Billy Bob Manning."

"Well, Mr. Billy Bob. Let me assure you that I am not a 'big black sucker.' "

"No, sir. I reckon you shore ain't."

"My name is Gen. Cecil Jefferys."

"Okay."

"Yes, sir!"

"Yes, sir!"

"How old are you, Billy Bob?"

"Forty-two . . . sir."

"You've seen service time?"

"Shore . . . Yes, sir!"

159

"What branch?"

"Marine Corps, sir."

"Then you certainly should understand military discipline and bearing and courtesy."

"I'm afraid I shore do, sir," Billy Bob answered mournfully.

"Billy Bob?"

"Yes, sir?"

"You are back in the military," Cecil informed him.

"Lord have mercy," Billy Bob said, adding, "sir!"

"Be-bop-a-lula and shake rattle and roll to you, too," Emil Hite said, concluding the religious services for that day. He managed to walk to the front of the church without tripping over the hem of his robe. He smiled at each of his followers as they trooped out.

Late summer, and hotter than the hinges of hell in North Louisiana.

One of Emil's "deacons" motioned for him to walk around to the side of the church.

"God, what is it?" Emil bitched, wiping away the sweat. "This robe is burning me slap up."

"Some of your, ah, flock is getting antsy, Brother Emil. They would like some sort of miracle to prove that you haven not lost contact, again, with the Great God Blomm."

Emil stared at him. "Brother Matthew, have you lost your fucking mind? The only miracle I've performed lately is getting a hard-on last night. I thought we went all over this crap before. I — don't — do — miracles!"

"Can't be helped, Emil baby. There's a new kid on the block."

160

"Now what does that mean?"

"Francis Freneau and his Joyful Followers of Life are camped just across the Boeuf River."

"Who?"

"Francis Freneau and—"

Emil waved him silent. "I heard you awready! What kind of scam is he running?"

" 'Bout the same kind you are," Brother Matthew said drily. "Only difference is, his is a lot more sophisticated."

"I resent the hell out of that!"

"It's true. Francis wears a white robe . . . all the time. And it's clean . . . all the time. He had about a half-dozen real cute chicks running ahead of him, wherever he goes, sprinkling flowers and grass and that stuff in his path. It's really neat. And Francis has this little bell with him."

"So I'll get a cowbell. Big deal! And some of these broads we got around here need to run some. Lose some lard. In case you haven't noticed, some of them are really draggin' a lot of ass."

"No, no, no, Emil. This Francis Freneau really speaks from the Bible. The folks dig it."

"Well, what the hell do you think I'm speaking from . . . most of the time? *Gone With The Wind?*"

"You gonna be gone with the wind if you don't spruce up your act, Emil. I'm tellin' you. You're losing converts. Didn't you notice a few people missing this morning?"

"Hell, I never pay any attention to that crap. I just figured they were drunk or something. Listen!" He held up a finger. "What in the hell is that god-awful sound?"

Matthew listened. "Sounds like a lost calf bellowing for its mother, don't it?"

"I know what that is," Emil said. "Bagpipes. Bagpipes and . . . tambourines. Last time I heard bag-pipes I was at this broad's house in Knoxville. We stayed drunk for a week. Woke up, I thought I was havin' the d.t.'s. Turned out to be some old movie on TV. *Gunga Din,* or something like that."

A fat man in a robe rushed up to Emil and clapped his hands while he did a little jig. "Oh, Brother Emil — come quickly! Francis Freneau and his Joyful Followers of Life have come to visit. Isn't that just *grand!*"

"Yeah," Emil said sourly. "Just friggin' wonder-ful."

The happy messenger went tripping off, clapping his hands and singing, stopping occasionally to do a little jig, his sandals kicking up dust as he danced.

Then Brother Emil got a glimpse of Francis Freneau and felt a little sick at his stomach.

"Guy looks like Arnold Schwarzenegger in drag. I'm in trouble, Matthew."

"I tried to tell you, Emil. You know who he is, don't you?"

"Well . . . he does look sort of familiar." Emil shrugged. "Another con artist, like me, I guess. What else?"

"Yeah. But this one used to be a magician."

Emil looked harder. Damn! but he looked familiar. Emil felt weak kneed. He could just see this hand-some guy taking *all* his flock with him. Emil knew that most of his followers were on the unstable side anyway. So if this muscular son of a bitch started pulling cucumbers out of his ears and proclaiming himself to be King Tut, most of Emil's flock would split.

"A miracle," Emil said. "I gotta come up with a miracle. Either I do that, or I'm back hoein' the weeds outta greens and butter beans for something to eat." Francis sure did look familiar, though.

"Yeah," Matthew said. "And don't forget us, Emil. If you go down, we go with you."

"Then come up with something, Brother Matthew. Don't just stand there with your face hanging out . . . *think!*"

Ben was sitting in the shade of a truck, deep in thought. His recon teams had reported Louie's thugs were rounding up many women and kids and elderly people. The recon teams had managed to intercede in some of the gatherings-up, but were spread too thin to save many. Ben just did not know what to do.

"Uneasy is the head that wears the crown, Ben?" Dr. Chase said, walking up.

Ben looked up and tried a smile. "I guess so, Lamar. I'm damned if I do and damned if I don't, no matter which way I turn this time."

"Well, you want a sounding board to bounce some thoughts off of, Ben?"

"It might help. Pull up a piece of ground and make yourself comfortable."

The doctor sat down beside Ben, plucked a blade of grass and stuck it in his mouth. Finally, he said, "Can we just bypass this fight, Ben?"

"I gave that some serious thought. But what comes after that, Lamar?"

Chase knew what Ben meant; but he knew that Ben wanted to say it. "What do you mean, Ben?"

"We back away from this fight, Lamar, because of the taking and using of women and kids and elderly for hostages, where does it end? The news will surely spread all over this shattered nation. We'll be putting every woman, every child, and every elderly person still alive in jeopardy."

Lamar nodded his head. "I agree, Ben. But I don't have to like it."

"Neither do I, buddy."

"So? And?"

"I try to arrange a meeting with this Big Louie and Ashley. Whoever the hell Ashley is."

"Good luck," the doctor said.

Big Louie waved a sheet of paper under the nose of Ashley and giggled. "Gen. Ben Raines wishes a meeting with me." He did not mention that Ben wanted to see Ashley as well. "A messenger delivered this only moments ago." He looked at Ashley's battle dress and giggled. "And you say that I look funny? George C. Scott, you ain't."

Ashley ignored that. "This meeting—where is he suggesting it take place?"

"On neutral ground. He will be on one side of Interstate Thirty-five—the west side. And I, and my entourage, shall be on the other side. We shall meet in the median. I've ordered my purple robe cleaned and ironed. I wonder, though, should I wear my white pumps or my black ones?"

Ashley stared at Big Louie, disbelief in his eyes. Here was a chance to kill Ben Raines, by ambush, and this fool was concerned only about his goddamned shoes.

"Now listen to me, Louie. We've just been handed a fantastic opportunity."

"Oh, I know!" Louie gushed. "At last I get to meet Ben Raines. Do you know that some consider the man to be a god?"

"Louie, goddammit, stop simpering for a moment and listen to me. We can kill Ben Raines, and it'll be easy."

"Kill Ben Raines!" Louie shrieked, horrified. "Why, I have no intention of killing Ben Raines. I'm gong to offer him a chance to join us. What do you think about that?"

Ashley stared hard at Big Louie. There was a very strange, odd light in the man's eyes; a glint that had not been there a couple of days ago. A bit of spittle oozed out of one corner of Louie's mouth. Louie started humming a little ditty.

Then it came to Ashley.

Big Louie had gone off the deep end.

Never too stable—at least in the years that Ashley had known him—Big Louie had finally tiptoed over into yo-yo land.

And a plan, springing like a large dangerous panther in the night, leaped into Ashley's brain. The plan cat-footed about in the man's head.

Why not? he thought. It'll work. Kill two birds with one stone, as the saying goes.

"Why, Louie, Your Majesty," Ashley said with a smile. "I think it would be grand for you to meet with Ben Raines and offer him a chance to join with us. Yes, indeed, Louie. A lovely idea. I'm sorry that I didn't think of it."

Big Louie leaned forward and touched Ashley's shoulder with a soft and perfumed hand.

Ashley fought to suppress a shudder.

"My dear boy," Louie said. "I thought of it because it is my duty to do so. It is my obligation to the masses inferior to me. After all, I am the king, you know."

"Yes, Your Majesty," Ashley said, bowing. "Of course. May I take my leave now?"

"Yes, yes, yes!" Louie waved a hand. "Run along and play soldier boy. I have royal arrangements to mull over. I'll call you when I have them completed."

Ashley backed out, bowing as he went. In the hall, he looked at one of his bodyguards. "He's flipped out." He jerked a thumb toward the Royal Room, as Louie called it. "Come on. We've got a lot of work to do."

5

"He agreed to it," Ben said. Colonel Gray, Ike, and Tina had been called back to Ben's CP. Dr. Chase was busy with his doctors, tending to the needs of those civilians the Rebel teams had managed to wrest from the hands of Big Louie's men.

"Bet on one thing, Ben," Ike said. "It's a trap of some sort."

"No doubt. But probably from the mind of this Ashley person. Not from Big Louie."

"Why do you say that, Dad?" Tina asked.

No one had yet brought up the subject of Buddy. Ben had not mentioned it, and until he did, no one else was going to say anything about it.

"Listen to this," Ben said, lifting the letter, which had been handed to a forward recon team, by a bearer under a white flag.

Tina sniffed at the paper. "Smells like expensive perfume."

"Chanel," Dan said. "From a *man?*"

"Quiet," Ben said. "Listen: *To his Majesty, the supreme general of forces, Ben Raines . . .*"

Ike swallowed a bit of chewing tobacco and began coughing.

167

"Serves you right for sticking that dreadful mess in your mouth," Dan said, smiling. "Do continue, general. Pardon this oaf's interruption." He whacked Ike on the back a couple of times.

When the laughter had subsided, Ben read on: *I, King Louie The First, do hereby accept your kind offer of a meeting. I am so looking forward to it. Being men of like mind* . . . Ben rolled his eyes at that. *I am certain we can reach some understanding which shall enable us to work out this small difficulty without the use of force. Do give some serious thought to joining me and together, we can sit side by side on the throne of greatness and certainly rule the world.*

"That fellow," Dan said, pointing to the letter, "is certainly bonkers!"

"At least," Ben agreed.

"When is the meeting?" Tina asked.

Ben looked at the letter. "Tomorrow, at noon. At the Osage City exit, just off the Kansas Turnpike."

"Just up the road," Ike said. "Still no clue as to who this Ashley person is, Ben?"

Ben shook his head. "No." He cut his eyes to Tina. "Met your half-brother yet?"

The question caught her off balance. "Ah, why, no, Dad, I haven't."

Ben smiled. "There are no secrets in any army, Ike. That much has not changed."

"Sure hasn't," Ike said. "But hell, Ben. He looks just like you."

Ben nodded his head. "Go see him, Tina. I want him at the meeting tomorrow at noon."

"Dad? . . ."

"Do I have to make that an order, girl?" Ben asked, cutting his hawklike eyes at her.

"No, sir!"

Ben smiled and the young woman returned the smile. "Report to me at least two hours before the meeting. I want your opinion of him."

A mischievous look passed over the woman's pretty face. She stepped forward and kissed Ben on his tanned cheek, tweaking him under the chin. "Yes, Daddy," she cooed, then ran out of the CP before Ben could catch her.

After the laughter had died down, Ben cleared his throat and, red faced, said, "Now you both see why nepotism is such a lousy idea."

"*Yes, Daddy!*" Ike and Dan shouted in unison.

Together, they ran out of the CP, with Ben throwing his spare boots at them. One of the boots just missed Denise, who was bringing Ben a message from one of the recon units.

"Be careful in there, love!" Dan called over his shoulder. "Big Daddy is a bit testy today."

Giggling like a pair of kids, the ex-SAS man and ex-Seal ran out of sight, straight to the hospital, to tell Dr. Chase what had just gone down.

Shaking her head, Denise entered the CP, after picking up Ben's boots from the ground. Ben glared at her.

"You could hire that face out to frighten little children, general," she told him.

Ben growled at her.

"Shall I call Dr. Chase to have you checked for rabies?" she asked innocently.

Ben glared for a moment more, then smiled. He walked to the door and told his guards, "I do not wish to be disturbed."

"Yes, sir."

Ben closed the door and picked the woman up in

169

his arms and carried her to the bedroom, laying her gently on the bed.

"Do all generals behave like this?" she asked.

Grinning as he unbuttoned his shirt, Ben said, "If they get the chance."

"Give me your left, left, left, right, left!" Lieutenant Mackey called out the cadence.

After the group had been bathed and inspected and curried and given physicals, the force had been culled down considerably. Out of the initial six hundred men and women, three hundred had been deemed physically fit to be a most unwilling unit of the Rebels.

And at this, the first full half day's training, the entire new unit was playing alligator.

Their ass was dragging out their tracks.

"Company . . . halt!" Lieutenant Mackey shouted the welcome words.

The men and women slumped to the ground, too tired to even try to seek some shade from the merciless heat.

"Piss-poor-looking bunch," Cecil said to Lieutenant Mackey, a grin on his face.

"I sure won't argue with that, general," Mackey said, also grinning.

A medic approached them. "Jake wants to see you, general."

"Oh? I gather, then, his jaw is not broken?"

"No, sir. Just bent a little." All laughed at the old army joke. The medic said, "He did lose a couple of teeth, though."

"I imagine that Jake is a bit upset, is he not, son?"

The medic laughed aloud. "Yes, sir. He says just

any ol' time you feel lucky, he wants to challenge you to a fight for leadership."

Cecil smiled. He knew all about that. He remembered those from his days as a Green Beret. "Oh? Is that right?"

"Yes, sir. And he demands the right to let his followers know that."

Cecil nodded his head. "Very well. Harrison?" he called, looking around for his driver.

"Here, sir."

"Will you please bring this Jake person to the parade ground?"

The parade ground was an old high school football field.

"Right away, sir."

Jake was escorted to the parade ground, a Rebel on both sides of him. He looked at what were once his people, sprawled in near exhaustion on the field. His eyes found the remainder of his people—the culls—that Cecil had ordered placed in the stands. Jake looked at Cecil. Jake's jaw was slightly swollen, and one lip was cut, but when he spoke, his words were clear.

"I'm a-gonna whup your ass, spade!"

"Really?"

"Yeah. 'At air's a purdee fact, boy."

"And what do you think that will accomplish . . . should you be instrumental in succeeding in that highly unlikely bit of braggadocio?"

"Haw?"

"What will it prove?" Cecil said with a sigh.

"Hit'll prove whut ever'body else awready know. That I'm the better man."

Cecil smiled. "Surely, God must have had a sense of humor."

171

"Haw?"

"Nothing, you cretin. Very well. How do you want this fight?"

A sly look crept into Jake's eyes. "You really gonna fight me, boy?"

"Oh, yes. Most assuredly."

"You dumb ass! I never knowed a nigger in my life that had no sense."

"Surely a startling revelation is just around the corner, Jake."

"Whutever 'at means."

Cecil started to tell him. He decided that actions would speak louder than words.

Cecil stepped back and removed his web belt, laying it to one side. He looked at his Rebels, now all gathered around. "No interference, people. If Jake wins, we pull out. If Jake loses, he joins the group and takes orders just like any other buck-ass private." He cut his eyes to Jake. "Is that amenable to you, Jake?"

"Haw?"

"Is 'at awrat with chew?" Cecil mush-mouthed. He could not contain a small smile.

Somewhere in the ranks of the newly drafted members, a woman's laughter reached out, taunting. "You should be able to understand that, Jake!" she called.

Jake's face mottled and flushed with anger. "Yeah, I understand hit, awrat. You ready to fight, boy?" he asked Cecil.

"Oh, quite!" Cecil responded cheerfully.

Jake danced a bit, balled his big hands into fists, and stepped forward, tossing out a quick testing fist.

Cecil stepped inside the punch and planted one on Jake's chin, staggering the bigger and stronger and

172

younger man.

Cecil stepped to one side, dodging another of Jake's punches.

Jake snapped a left, catching Cecil on the shoulder. The punch stung, and Cec knew he would never be able to stand up and slug it out, toe to toe, with the man. At least, not yet. That point was further emphasized when Jake popped Cecil on the side of the head with a left hook. The blow brought stars into Cec's vision, and little birdies chirped.

Cecil sidestepped and brought his elbows in close, his fists up, protecting his face and belly and dancing a bit until his head cleared. Then he heard Jake's breathing. He smiled. If he could keep Jake moving and swinging, all the while protecting himself, he could wear the bigger man down and then beat the shit out of him.

Although Jake was younger and stronger, he was very much out of shape.

"You stand still and fight, you black son of a bitch!" Jake yelled, the frustration evident in his voice.

Just to let him know that he hadn't forgotten him, Cec popped Jake flush on the mouth with a short left. Jake's head snapped back, and the blood flew from newly busted lips.

Cec danced back, his head clear of little birdies, keeping Jake moving. "You know what they say, Jake!" Cecil taunted him. "We got rhythm!"

"You nigger ape!" Jake hissed, panting for breath. He stepped in, wanting to mix it up, nose to nose.

Knowing he was taking a terrible chance, Cec gave the man his wish, for a couple of short, hard blows. Cecil hit him with a right to the stomach and a hard left to the jaw.

173

Cec stepped in close and brought his right fist up in a vicious uppercut. Jake's teeth slammed together.

Jake's knees buckled for just a couple of seconds, and his eyes glazed over, blood pouring from his busted mouth.

That was all Cec was looking for. He stepped in and began battering the man, smashing him with combinations of lefts and rights. Cecil's big hard fists turned the man's face into bloody pulp. Both of Jake's eyes were swollen and closing, blood dripping from his mouth; the big man was staggering.

"Give it up, Jake," Cec panted. "You're finished. Don't make me kill you."

"Ain't no goddamn nigger gonna do 'at," Jake hissed at him, the words whistling through broken teeth.

Jake swung at Cec and Cec stepped to one side, grabbed the man's wrist and forearm, and tossed him over his hip. Jake landed hard on the ground, on his butt, the breath whooshing out of him.

Cec knew he should end it right there simply by kicking the man in the head. But he didn't want it like that. Even though he had been shown otherwise hundreds of times down through the long years, he wanted to prove that cop wrong. Just one time.

Cecil waited until Jake had crawled to his feet, standing there, swaying. Cec stood, his fists raised, waiting.

"You're not an animal, Jake. You're a human being, with a brain that can think and reason and learn. Come on, Jake. Help me prove that cop wrong."

"Whut cop?" Jake panted the words. "I hate cops as much as I do niggers. Especially coon cops. Whut'd you thank about that, black boy?"

174

"Actually," Cec said, "I've always thought that a misnomer, since I am more cinnamon colored than black."

"You smart-assed coon!"

"Oh, come on, Jake! Join us. Fight for the side of reason and right and freedom."

Jake's grin was bloody and savage and unrepenting. "I'm rat. My daddy was rat. And his daddy was rat."

"Right about what, Jake?"

Jake swung a feeble fist and Cec brushed it away, shoving the man back down to the dirt. Jake sat hard.

"Ever'thang I know," Jake mumbled. "Goddamn teachers tried to teach me otherwise, but I knowed better. I knowed they was wrong and my daddy was rat."

Jake sat on the ground, unable, or so it seemed, to get to his feet.

Cec knew he was taking a terrible chance with Jake; that he should end it. But unlike Ben, Cecil still clung to the faint hope that there was good in even the worst of men.

Although at times that belief was sorely tested.

"One thang for shore," Jake said. "The only good nigger is a dead one!" He came off the ground fast, and Cec knew the man had been faking it, gathering his strength.

Jake tried to grab Cec in a bear hug, his arms around Cecil's waist. Cec twisted, breaking the hold, at the same time hammering on the man's neck and kidneys with his fists. Jake's hold slipped away, and Cec slung him to the ground. Jake slid on his face, his blood marking his trail.

Proved right again, Mr. Deputy Sheriff, Cecil

thought. Someday maybe I'll get it through my head.

Jake crawled to his feet, a very tough and very pure redneck. White trash clear through, but he still refused to give up. He raised his fists and lumbered toward Cec.

Cecil planted his booted feet and started his punch chest high, twisting his body. He put everything he had left in the punch: a solid straight right, with no detours and no curves. The fist caught Jake flush in the mouth. Jake's feet flew out from under him; he was out cold before he hit the ground.

Cecil stood over the beaten and bloody man, shaking his aching right hand. Ben was right, he thought. It's in the home. There is living proof of it. But how in the hell do we combat what is taught in the home? Or is that a moot point now?' Surrounded by the devastation of war.

Cec sighed. He had fought Jake with his fists only because he had wanted to. Not because he had to. Cec was well schooled in the art of hand-to-hand combat. He could have ended it very quickly by using any number of martial arts movements, and he knew most of them. But he also knew that a certain class of people would not have been impressed by that victory. They would have accused him of "not fighting fair."

Or some such shit as that!

Cecil walked to the front of the very quiet group of men and women resting on the parade field. He faced them, trying to make eye contact with as many of them as possible. Many would not meet his stare.

"Get on your goddamned feet!" Cecil roared.

The crowd quickly rose from the ground.

"You do not sit in my presence," Cecil informed them. "Unless I give the orders to do so. Is that

176

understood?"

The crowd collectively muttered its response. Everybody but one. His voice rang out loud and clear, in Marine Corps boot camp remembrance. "Yes, sir!" the ex-Marine shouted.

"I can't hear all of you!" Cecil shouted.

"Yes, sir!" they said.

"I still can't hear you!"

"*Yes, sir!*" the crowd roared.

"That's much better." Cecil smiled. "Now, is there any doubt in anybody's mind as to just exactly who is running this outfit?"

"*No, sir!*"

"That's good." Cecil's eyes found the ex-Marine. "Step out here."

The man quick-timed to face Cecil. "Yes, sir!"

"What is your last name, Billy Bob?"

"Manning, sir."

"Well, Mr. Manning, you are now a Top Kick in Ben Raines's Rebel army," he informed the astonished man. "You will act accordingly. It's going to be up to you to appoint platoon sergeants and squad leaders. I shouldn't have to tell an ex-Marine to make your choices wisely. It's going to be a big company, Sergeant Manning. You think you can handle it?"

"Yes, sir. No sweat, general."

"Fine. Tell me this: Why did you stay with Jake?"

"I . . . don't know, general." Manning's reply was softly given. "I left two/three times. But alone, out there . . ." He jerked his thumb. "It's tough. I think after you talk to some of these people, you'll find that we were planning a revolt against Jake and his men. It just got to be more than a lot of us could take."

Manning shook his head. "There isn't any *law*

anywhere. And people need law and order, don't they?"

"Yes, they do, Sergeant Manning. They certainly do. All right, Master Sergeant Manning. The company is all yours. Run them through a few minutes of PT; don't let them stiffen up; and then march them down to that creek." He pointed. "For a bath. Then get them back up here for chow."

"Yes, sir."

"Billy? What would you suggest I do with Jake?"

"If I was you, sir?"

"Yes."

"I'd shoot him. He'll never forget or forgive, sir. And he'll never be no part of this outfit. He's gonna hate you for the rest of his life. He'll be schemin' and plannin' on a way to kill you. Don't never trust him, general."

Cecil nodded his head. "Thank you, Billy. See to your command."

"Yes, sir."

Billy turned to leave, and then stopped, turning around, looking at Cecil. "General? The near three hundred you and your people culled out? They was the bad ones."

"Oh?"

"Yes, sir. I've knowed most of them ol' boys and gals for most of their lives. They never was any good. Drunks, dishonorable discharges from the service, thieves, back-stabbers, womanizers, game poachers, outlaws, two-timers . . . you name it. What you've got here, in this bunch . . ." He jerked a thumb at the lines of men and women, standing at ease. "Is not a bad bunch of people. Damn near every one of them was a decent, hard-working man or woman." A curious look crept into his eyes. "What puzzles me is

178

this: How'd you and your Rebels know which ones to cull and which ones to keep?"

Two faces came to Cecil's mind. That deputy sheriff and the face of Ben Raines. Both of them thought alike on one particular subject. "We've had a lot of practice, sergeant. Down through the years. And I had a good teacher in the subject of human behavior."

"Oh? Who was that, sir?"

"Ben Raines."

6

He was pointed out to Tina, and as she drew nearer to the young man, she had to smile. This, then, was what her adopted father had looked like as a young man.

Buddy glanced up as the officer approached him. He stood up. New to this, he didn't know whether to salute or not.

"Relax," Tina told him. "I'm your sister, Tina Raines."

Buddy smiled and held out his hand. She shook it. Brother and sister stood for a moment, looking at each other.

"The general adopted me, long years ago," Tina said, clearing up any doubts that might be lingering in Buddy's mind. "When I was just a little girl."

"Where is the general?"

"Getting ready for a meeting tomorrow. I . . . don't think he's quite ready, yet, to meet you. It was quite a shock for him."

Buddy smiled. "Yes, I bet it was. He send you up to check on me?"

"Yes. And to bring you to meet him tomorrow morning."

"Well . . . what do I call you? Captain? What?"

"Tina will do. Or sis," she added, smiling.

The young man and young woman put their arms around each other. Both of them began to softly weep.

"Sounds good to me, Ashley," his men told him. "It'll be an easy shot from this spot." He punched a dirty finger at the map spread out on a table.

"With Ben Raines out of the picture," Ashley said, "the Rebels will be completely demoralized and frozen in their tracks. They won't know what to do. I want all of our troops ready to go at my command. The women and kids and old people in front of the point teams. Just as soon as Ben and Big Louie go down, move out and hit the bastards with everything we've got. Remember this: The first strike is going to be the most important one. And once we start, we cannot, we must not, stop our momentum. All right, men, move out and get your snipers in position. Good luck to you all."

The field commanders moved out quickly. Night was fast approaching, and the men had to be briefed and the gunmen in position before dawn. All the field commanders of Big Louie's army were smiling, one thought uppermost in their minds: It would be such a relief to get that idiot Louie dead and in the ground.

Why Ashley had put up with the silly prick was something that none could understand.

If they could pull this off, the entire United States could easily be theirs for the taking.

And Ashley had promised them all the women they

181

could ever crave.

When the command post had emptied, Ashley sat down and propped his highly polished boots—shined by a slave, certainly not by Ashley—up on a table. He smiled, thinking that he really wished he could be the one to line up Ben Raines in the cross hairs of the scope and pull the trigger. He would like to see the expression on Ben Raines's face as the bullet struck him in the center of the chest, exploding his heart.

And forever stilling that bastard!

"God, I hate you, Raines!" Ashley muttered. "I despise you with all my heart."

For a few hot moments, Ashley let the hate wash over him, enjoying the venomous sensation. The moment he had dreamed of for years was now only hours away.

And Ashley could hardly wait.

What would be appropriate for the body? Strip it naked and hang it up by meat hooks? That might be nice. He'd have to give that some more thought.

That would certainly draw some attention.

Ashley sat with the hate bubbling within him. He remembered, recalling with startling accuracy, each detail of the humiliating beating he had received at the hands of Ben Raines so many years in the past. But the memory still burned as hotly in his brain, the flames of reminiscence blazing just as intensely as they did twenty years back.

The days he'd spent in the hospital, thanks to Ben Raines, the looks he'd received from the nurses—trashy little bitches; half of them niggers. Disgusting.

And his reputation as quite a good fighter had plummeted after that. Ben Raines had used all that tricky stuff on him. Man didn't fight fair. But what could one expect from a damned Midwesterner?

And for a time, Ashley let misty memories take

him winging back in time; back to when life had been so good, and he and his mommy and daddy and sister had lived the good life. No matter that there had been poverty and hunger all around them. They had all inherited the money; it was theirs, to spend it on whatever one damn well pleased.

Then the awfulness of the bombs that carried the deadly germs spreading all over the land.

And Ashley had lost everything. Everything.

He had, for the first time, been on his own. He had to learn survival. But he'd gone too far with it, and became an outlaw. What the hell? No law to speak of. Except the law of the fittest. And Ashley became fit.

It wasn't until about a year after the Great War that Ashley learned what finally became of his sister. But by then, he was well on his way toward becoming a warlord, and his sis was doing quite well—no point in upsetting any applecarts.

So he had never seen her again.

But he kept up with her. And when the government finally moved against Ben Raines and his damnable Tri-States, Ben Raines had sent out his Zero Squads; something that no one thought he would ever do.

And his sister had been killed. By that goddamned lowlife son of a bitch Ben Raines.

And Ashley's hate had only intensified after that.

Sitting, thinking, Ashley wondered, since he'd later found out that his sis had traveled with Ben Raines for a time, if Ben had ever screwed his sis.

Surely not. That thought was just too disgusting to ponder. Besides, sis had been much too much the lady to ever allow someone of Ben Raines's ilk to get into her pants.

A couple of years after his sis had been killed, Ashley had teamed up with Big Louie, adding his own small army of thugs and outlaws to Big Louie's troops. And for a time, they all had it pretty damned easy. Ashley had all the pussy he could stand; servants to wait on him, catering to his every whim.

Of course, he had to put up with Big Louie; but that was not that difficult. Just let the fool simper and have his perverted pleasures and Louie was happy, thinking that he was running the show. That gave Ashley ample time to subvert Louie's army, weeding out those who were truly loyal to the fool.

Then Ben Raines just had to come along, tilting at windmills like the damned idealistic bastard that he was.

But maybe, Ashley thought, leaning back, his hands behind his head, just maybe Ben had come along at a most opportune time.

Ashley smiled. He firmly believed that if Ben Raines were to die, the Rebels would disintegrate, falling apart without Raines's leadership.

Oh, sure. Ashley had heard all those silly rumors about Ben Raines being some sort of god. How ridiculous! He was a god, all right. A goddamned meddling asshole. Ben Raines was pure flesh and blood just like anyone else. But if the Rebels even remotely believed that garbage, the sight of their wonderful god being shot dead before their eyes would be so demoralizing to them that their ranks would crumble. And then Ashley would have had his revenge and be rid of the do-gooder bastard Raines once and for all.

Damn! but that thought was so good it was almost as good as sex.

He felt himself gaining an erection. He rubbed his crotch and thought about all those cute little girlies he had stashed away, willing to do anything to serve him.

And some of them just barely into their teen years. Hot little bitches!

He stood up, his hardness a throbbing painful pleasure, and exited out the back door, heading for his house. He'd think about killing Ben Raines while getting a blow job from that cute little blonde. That would make sex even better.

"I've been frightened of a few things in my life, Tina," Buddy admitted. "But I will freely admit to you, that at this moment, I am scared half to death."

She laughed at him. "Why, Buddy?"

Buddy turned and pointed. "Because of that."

The tall figure of Ben Raines stood out, leaning against the fender of a Jeep. Ben was having a cup of tea and smoking a hand-rolled cigarette.

"He's just a man, Buddy. Your father. And there is no doubt of that. You two look enough alike to be scary."

Tina did not tell Buddy that she had already met with Ben a couple of hours before.

Ben turned his head, looking at the pair.

"Here it comes," Buddy muttered.

Tina laughed at him. Together, they walked toward Ben. And then the father and the son who had never seen one another were only a couple of feet apart.

Father and son stared at one another. Tina stepped to one side, to stand beside the man she called her Uncle Ike. She felt the same affection for him as she did for the man she called her Uncle Cec.

"You want some hot tea, boy?" Ben asked, his voice gruff.

Buddy was afraid the man would hear his knees knocking; and he was certain that they were. He opened his mouth to speak. But nothing came out except an unintelligible squeak.

Buddy felt like a fool.

Ben smiled. "Early morning is when my voice does that. That's why a long time ago, I started using honey in my coffee instead of sugar. Honey smooths out the throat."

Buddy found his voice. "Yes, sir. I'll remember that. If I ever find any coffee, that is," he added.

Ben laughed. "Save some for me when you do. About that hot tea? . . ."

"Oh, yes, sir. That would be very nice. Sir," he added.

Almost before the words were out of his mouth, a cup of steaming tea was placed on the hood of the Jeep.

Ben waited until the younger man had sugared and stirred the tea before saying, "How did you leave your mother?"

"Quite insane, sir."

"Her army?"

"Numbers, sir?"

Ben nodded.

"Several thousand, sir. A very large group of motorcyclists had just joined prior to my leaving. I believe that they had been a part of Sam Hartline's army before that."

"Grizzy, Sonny Boy, Skinhead, Popeye, and Plano among them?"

"Yes, sir. That's the bunch."

"Then your mother has taken up with scum," Ben said flatly.

"Yes, sir. I know. Most of the people who follow her are nothing more than savages."

Ben looked at Buddy's weapon. The old Thompson looked to be in fine shape. "Interesting weapon you carry, boy."

The son met the father's steady gaze. "I find that it does the job, sir."

"Yes. I agree." Ben looked at his watch; plenty of time. "Tell me about yourself, Buddy."

And for five full minutes, Buddy told Ben of his past—as far back as he could remember—and about his grandfather raising him, shielding him, letting his mother think him to be dead.

He concluded by telling Ben of his belief that his mother probably ordered the Old Man burned at the stake.

Ben stared at him, then shook his head. "Her own father?"

"Yes, sir. But he would go to his death singing Christian songs. He was dying of the cancer."

"Then he is a brave man."

"Was, sir."

"You know that someday I'm going to have to fight your mother and her army?"

"Yes, sir. I know. And so does she. The people she has gathered about her might well be savages, but they have professional soldiers, ex-mercenaries, training them. She will be hard to handle. And I don't mean to be disrespectful in saying that."

"I'm glad to have that word, Buddy. What would you do if I should order you to take part in the action against her?"

"I would go. I would not want to; but I would follow your orders."

"And if I ordered you to kill your mother?"

"I don't believe I could kill my own mother, sir. I know she is evil, and that she deserves to die, but not by my hand. Not unless she was trying to kill me. And even then . . . I just don't know."

Ben smiled. "You just saved your life, son."

"Beg pardon, sir?"

"If you'd said anything else, I would have had you tossed out of my sight. I'd have known you were lying."

"I spoke the truth, sir."

"Yes, I believe you. I'm not a very emotional man, Buddy. Never have been. Perhaps that is a fault of mine. I don't know. What I'm trying to say is . . ." He blinked away a slight mist in his eyes and cleared his throat.

Buddy put a strong young hand on his father's shoulder. The two men looked at each other just as the sun broke through the overcast skies that had put a pall on most of the morning. The sun bathed the countryside in all of God's brilliance.

"I'm glad to be with you, Father," Buddy said. "I only hope that I never do anything to make you feel ashamed of me."

Ben nodded his head and smiled. He did not trust his voice just yet. He put his right hand on his son's shoulder and squeezed.

Boy was as solid as a damned rock!

"Come on, boy," the father said. "Let's get some lunch."

"Ah . . . sir?"

"Yes?"

"Do you object if Tina and, ah, someone else joins us?"

"Of course not. Who is the someone else?"

"A young lady from General McGowan's command. She befriended me when the others were reluctant to do so."

"Handsome scoundrel takes after his father in more ways than one," Tina said, smiling. "Half a day in camp and he's got the best-looking woman cornered."

"Pay no attention to your sister, boy," Ben told

188

him. "She exaggerates at times."

And the family, plus one, walked off to have lunch.

Francis Freneau didn't pull any cucumbers out of his ears, but what he did was just as bad. He sang religious songs with such a pure, sweet, fine tenor voice he damn near had Emil weeping; most of the others were blubbering and snorting with joy.

And then Emil recognized him.

"I knew it!" Emil said. "I knew I'd seen that sucker somewheres before."

He leaned over and whispered in Brother Matthew's ear. "I know that son of a bitch! That's Stanley Ledbetter. He had a finance company in Chattanooga until the state put him out of business; he was runnin' two sets of books. Then he popped up in Atlanta, selling phony stocks and bonds out of a boiler room. He just got out the state with his ass intact, the cops right on his tail. Then he got him a face lift out in California and was working the schools with a two-bit magic act. Among other things, he got busted for screwin' the little chickies and was about to stand trial when the bombs came."

"Hush up," Matthew said, awe in his voice. "Ain't his singin' beautiful?"

Emil whacked Brother Matthew on the side of his head with his fist. "Goddammit, Matthew, listen to me!"

"Ooww!" Brother Matthew said, holding the side of his head. "Shit, Brother Emil, that hurt!"

"Then pay attention, you dumb ass! I *know* that guy calls himself Francis Freneau."

"So what?"

"He's a fraud!"

189

The look Emil received from Brother Matthew was not a pleasant one. "And you ain't?"

"That's neither here nor there you dummy! You and a few others got a pretty cushy job with me, working this scam. You think Ledbetter is gonna keep you on?"

The two of them were joined by a few more of Emil's Enforcers.

"Ledbetter?" Brother Carl asked.

"Yeah. Stanley Ledbetter."

Brother Matthew thought about that for a moment. He finally nodded his head in agreement. "We gotta come up with a spectacular miracle, Brother Emil. That's the only thing that's gonna save our asses."

Emil's face brightened. "You got something in mind?"

"No."

"Wonderful," Emil said. "I'm surrounded by yo-yos."

"We can always shoot the son of a bitch," Brother Carl suggested.

"No, no!" Emil said. "I am opposed to violence. Unless it just absolutely has to be. It'd be so much better if I could best him at his own game."

"How?" Brother Roger asked.

"If I knew that, you dummy, I wouldn't be standing here listening to Stanley Ledbetter bellowing songs!"

"How come he's got all them good-lookin' chickies and we get stuck with the dogs?" Brother Carl asked, a wistful note in the question. His eyes were on a shapely brunette standing beside Francis Freneau, her eyes glazed over in reverence as Francis crooned.

Of course, the joint she'd just toked on might have had a little bit to do with it.

" 'Cause he's got a dick like a donkey," Emil said. "He was into porno flicks for a couple of years. You could use that thing of his for a flagpole; I'm telling you." Emil started smiling and humming and snapping his fingers.

The others waited in silence. They knew that when Emil started behaving like this, an idea was forming in his head.

Either that, or he'd gotten off into the mushrooms again.

"I wonder if the other guys with him are all hung like Stanley?" Emil asked.

"According to Sister Linda they sure are," Brother Carl said.

"You mean, some of my flock have already begun to betray me?" Emil said.

"They been slippin' crost the Boeuf River for more than a week, now," Brother Roger said. "We was afraid to tell you, Brother Emil."

"Echoes of Gethsemane!" Emil moaned. "The Judas bitches have shown their true colors."

"Naw," Brother Matthew said. "They're just lookin' for a better screw, is all."

"Cretin!" Emil glared at him. "Never mind. I have a plan. I'll be gone for a few days. I'll be in Monroe, looking for . . . something. I might have to go as far as Shreveport to find it. I don't know. You'll come with me, Brother Carl."

"What are we looking for, Brother Emil?"

Emil smiled. "That will be my secret for a time."

"Are you going to find a miracle, Brother Emil?" Brother Roger asked.

"I better," Emil said grimly.

"Our people are being forced to fall back," Khamsin was informed. "The Rebels have booby-trapped nearly everything that can be wired to explode. Our hospitals are rapidly filling up with the wounded and maimed."

"How are you getting them across the river?"

"We're not. That would take too long. We're setting up field hospitals south of Interstate Twenty."

"Have the Rebels tried to storm the hospitals?"

"No, sir. They have not. They are not known for doing that."

"How noble of them," Khamsin said bitterly. He turned in his chair to gaze out the window. The bitterness in his soul had manifested itself in his mouth. His tongue held the taste of copper.

"Disgusting!" Khamsin said. "We have conquered half the known world, and are halted in our tracks by a band of rag-tag Americans. Disgusting!" he repeated.

Khamsin knew perfectly well that his forces outnumbered the Rebels by at least twenty-five to one; yet his forces, since the start of the invasion, had known only defeat. It was humiliating and appalling. Khamsin had conquered almost the whole of South Carolina with ease. Then Ben Raines and his Rebels had stepped into the picture, and that ease had turned to agony.

And what was worse, Khamsin did not know how to stop the tide of defeat. Little two-bit units of Rebels were stopping his superior and most elite forces at every crossroads. Out-gunned and out-manned, the Rebels were drawing blood at every encounter, and then the shadowy bastards just seemed to melt into the landscape. And woe be unto any who attempted to follow the Rebels. For almost every time that happened, those who followed were never seen again.

Hamid wanted to say to Khamsin: We have the state of South Carolina. Let's be content with it. Live here and grow stronger before we try General Raines.

But Hamid did not say that. He kept his mouth shut. The Hot Wind gave the final orders. Hamid carried them out.

Khamsin sighed heavily and turned in his chair. "Reinforce my orders, Hamid. No advance. And . . ." Once more he sighed, the unspoken words sour on his tongue. "Order all units to pull back south of Interstate Twenty. And tell them to be careful in doing so. Touch nothing; it might blow up. Do not, *do not* engage the enemy unless a confrontation is forced upon them. We're going to have to rethink our plans."

"Yes, sir." Hamid quietly left the room, leaving Khamsin alone with his bitter thoughts.

Hamid silently cursed the day the IPA landed on these hostile shores.

"Good jumpin' Christ!" Ike said, looking through binoculars, eastward across the Kansas Turnpike. "I don't believe what I'm seein'. But there it is. Whatever the hell 'it' is."

He lowered his binoculars and laughed.

Ben lifted his binoculars, looked, blinked, lowered the field glasses and rubbed his eyes. He lifted the glasses to his eyes and looked again. "That's got to be Big Louie."

Tina lifted her field glasses and took a look. She quickly lowered the binoculars and turned away, giggling.

Dan peered through his lenses and said, "My word! It looks like a purple blob. General, do you see anyone that you recognize?"

"Not a soul. If this Ashley person is there, I sure don't know him, or remember him."

"You don't suppose they are one and the same?" Ike questioned. "Big Louie and Ashley?"

"I certainly would never forget a sight like *that*," Ben said.

"One wouldn't think so," Dan muttered, then he too turned away to hide his laughter.

"Oh, yoo-hoo!" Louie called, standing across the four lanes of concrete. He was resplendent in his purple robe and white patent-leather pumps.

"I want to hear Dad say, 'Yoo-hoo,' " Tina said.

The entire line of Rebels closest to Ben all began laughing.

Buddy turned away so the general would not see him laughing.

"Very funny," Ben said, eyeballing his kids and his field commanders, all of whom were either laughing or red faced trying to suppress laughter.

"I say, general," Dan said. "I have this lovely pink sash I was saving to give to a lady back at Base Camp One. But considering the gravity of this momentous meeting, I could loan it to you. You'd look perfectly precious with it tied about your waist."

That did it. Everyone started laughing.

Ben took the ribbing with a smile on his face. When the laughter had subsided, he asked, "What do you hear from the Scouts, Ike?"

"Nothing, Ben. They've been searching the other side through long lenses since dawn. If anyone's over there, they're well hidden."

"I say!" Big Louie called, waving a hand. "Are you there, Supreme Commander Raines?"

"Yes!" Ben shouted. "Right here . . . Louie."

"Is the terrain firm?" Louie called. "If not, I'll have some of my bearers carry me across for the

194

meeting."

Ben sighed. "Just think," he said. "All I ever wanted was to write books."

"Do you want me to have some Rebels tote you across, Ben?" Ike asked.

"Ike!"

"Just a suggestion, supreme commander."

"Jesus," Ben muttered. "I don't believe you'll have to utilize bearers, Louie!" Ben shouted. "The sun has dried the ground fairly well."

"Oh, good!" Louie shrieked. "Shall we begin our trek toward an everlasting place in history, general?"

"By all means, Louie. Here I come."

"What for me! Wait for me! One, two, three, *go*!" Louie stepped out on the concrete.

One man was with him, his entourage left behind.

"Come on, boy," Ben said to Buddy. "Let's assure your place in history, too."

"Yes, sir."

Father and son began the walk across the lanes of hot concrete. Big Louie was carefully mincing his way toward them.

"Has it occurred to you, Father, that this might be some sort of setup?"

"It has occurred to me, boy."

"We're certainly going to be wide open out here."

"That we are. Any suggestions?"

"If shooting starts, head for the low place in the area between the lanes."

"The median."

"Sir?"

Ben thought hard for a few seconds. Buddy was probably about six or seven when the Great War came. He had probably never heard the term "median" before. "It's called the median."

"Oh. I knew that, of course, from reading highway

195

signs. But why is it called that?"

"Because median means middle."

"I see. Well, if shooting starts, we head for the median. That will give us the best protection from gunfire coming from the east."

"Good thinking." Ben smiled.

"Thank you, sir. Although I would imagine that had already occurred to you."

Buddy noted Ben's smile.

Louie had stopped on the shoulder of the north-bound lane.

"Why is he stopping there?" Buddy whispered.

"So he can command the higher ground," his father told him. "That way, he can look down at us."

"Ah! He really believes himself to be a king, doesn't he?"

"It would appear that way. But that's good, Buddy. Let him have the high ground. He presents the better target. If it is a setup, he just might take lead intended for us."

"Unless we are all the intended targets," Buddy said.

And that was something that Ben had not thought of. He glanced at his son. "Why would you say that, boy? And slow down; give us a few more seconds to reach him."

"Well, the man is obviously a fool. Perhaps the real power behind the throne is weary of him. And this way he, or she, we really don't know, do we, could not only get rid of Louie, but the immediate enemy as well. And that's you, Father."

"Very good, Buddy. Excellent. Head's up, son."

"Yes, sir."

"My dear General Raines!" Louie gushed. "At last, two of the world's great leaders come together to forge our places in the still-to-be-written history of

196

this devastated land."

"Louie," Ben said.

"And who is this handsome lad with you, General Raines?"

"My son, Buddy."

"Oh my, you are a magnificent specimen, aren't you?" Louie eyeballed Buddy.

"A good enough specimen to have killed four of your followers north of here," Buddy said.

"Oh?" Louie's voice softened. "Don't you feel that was a bit overly dramatic . . . putting two of their heads up on poles?"

Ben looked at his son. Buddy hadn't told him about this.

"It got your attention, didn't it?"

"Yes, it did, Master Buddy. Oh, my, yes, indeed."

"I thought it might. But you came to speak to my father, not to me."

"Yes. Thank you for reminding me, young man."

"What's on your mind, Louie?" Ben opened the dance.

"A man of few words, eh, general? Very well. You and I joining forces. That's it as succinctly as I can put it."

"I don't think our philosophies will work well together, Louie. I don't believe in slavery—among other things."

Louie waved his hand. "Very minor details that can be worked out at a later date, my dear General Raines. The important thing is that we cease this little war between us, before it gets completely out of hand. Don't you agree, sir?"

"That's easily accomplished, Louie. You just disband your army and turn loose the slaves and the women and kids and old people you've taken for hostages, and then we'll talk."

"Oh, my! Has Ashley been a naughty boy again? I wish he would consult me before he goes off on these little tears of his."

Ben's eyes caught the glint of sunlight off of metal or glass. In the tall grass on the side of that overpass. Might be a sniper up there, he thought.

"So you didn't know that Ashley did that, Louie?"

Ben shifted as he spoke, with Buddy following his motion. Now Louie was almost directly between Ben and Buddy and the overpass.

Louie sniffed daintily. "I never become involved in such mundane matters."

"Oh, I see," Ben replied. "You're that sure of Ashley, are you?"

"I'm sure of this: Ashley hates you and has for years. Why, would you believe that he wanted you killed during this meeting?"

"What a naughty, naughty boy!" Ben said.

Buddy looked at him, oddly.

"What does he hate me, Louie?"

"Oh . . . I don't *know!* Some silly little schoolboy matter of eons ago." He waved his hand. "Forget about Ashley. You're talking to *me.*"

"Sorry, Louie. But I like to be liked by everybody."

This time, Buddy's look was not just odd as he glanced at his father. It was downright astonished!

Ben looked at him and winked.

"Well, what about it, Louie?" Ben said.

Louie's lips grew pouty. "Ultimatums, general? That's not a very nice way to begin a relationship."

"Sorry, but that's the way it is. Take it or leave it."

Louie stamped his pump-clad foot. "You're just not being a very nice man!"

"That's the breaks, king."

Louie began jumping up and down in the middle of the highway, waving his arms and shrieking to high heaven. His actions startled the man with him.

The sound of the rifle booming reached them just as the slug tore through Louie, exploding the heart.

The man with Louie turned in panic, stepping to one side, that movement putting him directly in front of Ben.

The rifle cracked again. The slug hit the man's battle harness. More rifles boomed and spat just as Ben and Buddy hit the earth of the median.

"Smoke!" Ike shouted, his voice reaching Ben and Buddy. "Give them cover smoke."

An explosion momentarily deafened Ben and Buddy, just as the man who had been with Louie seemed to disintegrate before their eyes.

Then something smacked Ben on the back of his head, dropping him into darkness.

7

"The IPA has stopped all forward movement," Colonel Williams radioed to Cecil. "At least from this side."

"That's what my scouts have reported, too," Cecil radioed back. "What do you make of it?"

In Khamsin's communications complex, his radio people were struggling to understand the messages, but they were unable to unscramble the transmissions.

Finally, one of them threw his headset to the table. "It's no use," he said. "We can't unscramble it."

"General," Joe radioed. "My guess is that we're fighting the type of war this Hot Wind can't fathom. And that's surprising to me, since he was a noted terrorist back in the '80s. I just don't know what to make of it."

He's unsure of himself, Joe. He thought that he could come in here and just walk all over us. But that uncertainty won't last long. Khamsin may well be the world's biggest asshole, but he's no dummy. So we've got to keep him off balance."

"How, sir?"

"By doing what is not expected of us and by keeping up those tactics. Joe, start sending out false transmissions by walkie-talkie between your units about us planning a major invasion into South Carolina. His listening posts on the other side of the river will pick up those walkie-talkies. We're going to start infiltrating troops into South Carolina between Augusta and Savannah, and also through the mountain passes of the Sumter National Forest. Got it?"

"Yes, sir."

"I'll radio back to Base Camp One and have all the spotter planes we can put up into the air flying all over the place. We'll start sending ground troops into the areas by day, and moving them back out at night. Lots of rattling and banging tanks and APCs and trucks during the move-in. No noise coming back out at night. Got it?"

Joe laughed. "I got it, general. If we can pull this off, we'll have that son of a bitch running up and down the state until his tongue hangs out."

"That's the idea, Joe. Good luck to you."

"Luck to you, sir."

Cecil turned to the operator. "Any word from General Raines?"

"Nothing, sir. I think we're being jammed from the west. What do you reckon is going on out there?"

"I wish I knew. I really wish I knew."

Ben opened his eyes and blinked a couple of times. His vision cleared and he could see a group of people gathered around him.

Ike grinned down at him. "Good thing your head is so hard, Ben."

Groaning, Ben tried to sit up. Hands pushed him back down. "You just keep your ass right where it is, Raines," Dr. Chase told him. "You took a pretty good lick on the noggin; so just lie still for a time."

"What happened?" Ben asked. Jesus! but his head hurt.

"Near as we can figure," Ike said, "that guy wearing the battle harness took a slug into his ammo belt. Slug must have hit a grenade. It exploded his ammo and all the grenades around him. Literally blew him apart. Piece of shrapnel conked you on the noggin."

"Big Louie?"

"Dead. Must have been a setup all the way."

"That poor sad foolish man," Ben said. "He was crazy."

"Yeah. Well, his troubles are over now," Dr. Chase said.

Ike said, "I ordered our people in and to hit them hard."

"The civilian hostages?" Ben asked.

Ike's eyes clouded briefly. "They're gonna take some hard hits, Ben."

"One of us had to make that decision. Where's Buddy?"

"He's all right, Dad," Tina said. "He took some shrapnel in his back, but his wounds are minor. Judy is taking care of him."

"Yeah," Ben said, smiling. "I just bet she is. We have any word from Cecil as yet?"

"Not a peep, Ben," Ike told him. "I think Khamsin's western people have found our frequencies and are blocking them. Not much we can do about that."

"Let's clean it up here and then get the hell moving east. That goddamned Ashley wanted a fight. All right. Give it to him."

"Yes, sir!" Ike said.

Lines of profanity rolled through Ashley's brain, coming so hard and fast his tongue would not have handled them had he attempted to verbalize the filth.

And it was all directed at Ben Raines.

Ashley's field commanders, all of them, even the top soldier, Colonel West, reported that the squeeze was on from Raines's Rebels. And they were squeezing hard.

Ashley could not understand how the Rebels seemed to know the exact location of everyone of his companies.

Was that goddamn Ben Raines some sort of mystic?

Ashley sighed in frustration. How could that damned fool with the rifle have missed Ben Raines? An easy shot like that. Incredible.

The only good thing to have come out of the whole affair was that Big Louie was dead. At least that much to the good had been accomplished.

But had it been worth it?

Ashley still hadn't made up his mind about that.

He wasn't even certain that to continue fighting was worth the effort. For Ashley knew, deep in his heart, that eventually Ben Raines was going to win.

The only bright spot in the whole ugly mess was that Ashley's troops were holding the Rebels outside of the areas claimed when Ashley ordered the pullback. Of course, that wasn't necessarily due to their bravery. One of his listening posts had intercepted a transmission that brought it all home to Ashley and his men: Ben Raines was going to push them back into Kansas City.

That was Raines's plan. And that bit of news had been quite enough to drive some steel into the backbone of his men. Nothing like a little directed fear to turn cowards into fighting heroes.

Again, Ashley sighed, wishing there was some way he could get out of all of this and still save face. But he couldn't come up with anything.

He leaned back in his chair, deep in thought. No one really knew exactly what Kansas City was like. Or really, what it was like from Fort Smith all the way up to Kansas City. That narrow corridor had taken both germ and so-called clean nuclear hits during the Great War. And that zone had been declared hot by the government.

Back when there was a government, that is. Back before the rats and fleas and deadly germs had threatened to wipe out civilization entirely.

For a time, Little Rock had been ruled unsafe; but that had proved to be false information. And a dozen areas between Fort Smith and Kansas City had also proved out to be safe.

But Kansas City proper, and for about thirty to forty miles in any direction extending out from it, and the dozens of tiny towns along a two hundred and fifty miles strip running north to south—No one really know. And damn few had the courage to even venture into those areas. And fewer still ever came out.

But reports that had filtered back from those areas all held one bit of like information: There were some strange creatures roaming about, both animal and human. Or sub-animal and subhuman would be more like it, probably. Ashley didn't know for sure; he'd never been into those areas.

But he had seen some of the creatures that had been shot and carried back out. They were not pleasant to look at.

Those writers, directors, actors, and makeup people who had put together the science fiction movies had pretty well pegged it right with their descriptions of what might follow after a nuclear war. God-awful-looking men and women and young people, some with no hair, others with chalk-white eyes; some with hideous burns on their bodies, others grotesquely misshapen. But they all shared this in common, for whatever reason: They hid from the light and came out only at night, to scavenge for food.

All in all, those areas contained some hideous forms of life, and if Ben Raines thought he was going to drive Ashley and his troops into those areas—the man had best rethink his plan. For to a person, male or female, Ashley's people had said, loudly and clearly, that they would rather die than be driven or pushed back into those unknown fear-producing areas.

Even though no one among them actually knew much about the people who lived there.

But they did know that Ben Raines's Rebels were not in the habit of taking prisoners.

So what choice did that leave any of Ashley's people?

None. None at all. Stand or die. That's all that Raines had left any of them.

All right, then. So be it.

With a sigh of resignation, Ashley stood up, put on his helmet, picked up his M-16, and walked outside. He motioned for an aide to come to him.

"Yes, sir?"

"Where is the force of Rebels commanded directly by Ben Raines?"

"At the junction of Highway Seventy-five and Interstate Thirty-five, sir. Colonel West's troops are looking them square in the face. And I'm glad it's West and not me," he added.

Ashley's smile was thin. But he knew what the man meant: Colonel West and his men were the best Ashley had. His own people were not even in the same ballpark.

And he also know that Colonel West did not particularly care for him. What the hell was the matter with these professional soldiers, anyway?

Damn high and mighty bunch of moralistic assholes.

But he knew, with a sinking feeling, that if West and his bunch could not contain Raines, it would all be over very quickly, for his own people would fold up like a house of cards.

Ashley said, "The dividing line is Highway Seventy-five?"

"Yes, sir."

"And in the other areas, our people are holding?"

"Yes, sir," the man said, smiling grimly. "They don't have much choice in the matter, do they, sir?"

The look Ashley gave the man was sharp, but he did not chastise him. For after all, the aide was correct. They had absolutely no choice in the matter. None at all.

"You ever been in or close to the Hot Zone?" Ashley asked him.

"Close to it, sir. I sure as hell wouldn't want to go in there."

Ashley nodded his head. "It's that bad, is it?"

The aide was silent for a moment, his brow furrowed, remembering.

When he spoke, his voice was soft. "It's awful, sir. Them so-called clean bombs that the Russians used did save the cities; I mean, the buildings and all that, but they sure screwed up any survivors. Really fouled up their minds and bodies. I've seen some of them. I don't never want to see no more of them. Not ever. I guess no one really knew what them bombs was gonna do, huh, sir?"

"I suppose so. But those . . . people, for want of a

better word, they can still produce? I've heard they can have offspring?"

"Oh, yes, sir. I've seen some of the kids. Some of them kids is teenagers, now. They're some better lookin' than their parents, some of them, and some of them is worser lookin'. Them real ugly ones have a . . . well, culture that's set apart from the others."

"A culture? What exactly do you mean?"

"It's kinda hard to explain, sir. Since I ain't really never been that up-close to none of them. And what I know is just secondhand information."

"Do try," Ashley urged.

"Well, they get along, sort of, so I'm told. But they don't live together, none of them, like no family should. As soon as the kids is old enough to get by on their own, the parents drive them off. Kinda like animals, you know?"

"Ummm. How many of these people would you guess live in the Hot Zone?"

"God, sir. I don't have no idea. Hundreds of them. Maybe thousands of them. It's that way in all the pockets of the country that was declared hot by the government. Ain't nobody been in them areas in . . . well, since the bombs came. Near'bouts fifteen years ago."

"I see," Ashley said. At least this conversation was taking his mind off the immediate and clear danger known as Ben Raines. "Yes. But Kansas City, unlike a few other cites on the continent, is not still dangerous, right?"

The aide thought for a moment. "You mean, sir, like in hot from radiation from the bombs that was fired?"

"Precisely."

"No, sir. Only a couple of cities here in America took hits from regular atomic bombs. And them areas is gonna be hot forever, I reckon. But these . . . people, I don't know what to call them. I think they're called the Night People. Yes, sir. That's it. The Night People, they don't bother no one, unless you wander into the areas they've claimed for their own. Then they'll kill you, or use you for slaves, or something a hell of a lot worser than that."

Ashley thought he knew what was meant by that last bit. He sat down on the steps and motioned the man to sit with him. "I've heard rumors about this for years; I always dismissed it as claptrap. But, then, it's *true!*"

"Oh, yes, sir. It's sure enough true, all right."

"Then the rumors, facts, now, I suppose, that used to come out of those areas, that talk about these Night People having some sort of program to breed out the sickness . . . that's true? And that's the 'worser' that you mentioned?"

"Yes, sir. As far as I know, sir. But there again, no one knows for sure. I doubt if Ben Raines even knows."

The look the man received from Ashley told him it was time to shut his mouth.

That was further emphasized when Ashley abruptly stood up and walked away without even a second glance.

But Ashley was not angry with the man for throwing Ben Raines's name at him. He hardly even noticed that. Ashley's mind was working fast and furious on a plan to keep from being pushed back into the ugly embrace of the Night People.

"They're holding us, Ben," Ike radioed to Ben. "And you're facing the top soldier of the bunch. A Colonel West. I know about him. He's a good soldier."

"I just spoke with Dan and Tina; they're reporting the same thing. Fear seems to be the great motivator, Ike. Ashley's men must have heard some radio chatter about us driving them back into the hot areas."

"Orders, Ben?"

"What do you think, Ike?"

"Well, Ben, Big Louie is dead. All the Indian reservations have been returned to the tribes. If we push on, we'll win, no doubt about that, but a lot of innocent people are going to get killed in the process before we get to Ashley. You wanna try to talk with him, Ben?"

"I can try. Dan? Tina? Are you monitoring this?"

They were.

"Suggestions?" Ben asked.

"I think we need to get to Base Camp One, general," Dan said. "We're going to be confronted with two-bit warlords like Ashley forever, it seems, but Khamsin needs to be dealt with right now."

"All right," Ben said to his field commanders. "We've seized enough weapons from Ashley's people to rearm the citizens. All we can do is hope that they'll keep their freedom this time. Hold your positions and cease all actions immediately. I'll try to make contact with Ashley."

Ben didn't tell any of them of the plan he'd been mulling over.

He wasn't sure Ashley would go for it.

"Misfits," Billy Bob said, disgust in his voice as he spoke to his company of Rebels. "That's what Jake called us just before he pulled out. You people feel like misfits?"

"Misfits!" a woman yelled. "Hell, no. Jake took all

209

the misfits with him."

The company growled their displeasure at being called misfits.

"I know that I'm sure as hell no misfit," Billy Bob said. "I feel better than I have in years. I feel like I finally got some purpose, some direction in my life. But I tell y'all what. Let's just keep the name of misfit. By God, we'll wear it proudly. Let's be the best damn bunch of fighters in all of Ben Raines's Rebel army. How about it?"

"Ben Raines's Misfits!" a man called. "That sounds damn good to me. That's us, then. The Misfits!"

The company roared their approval over their new name.

Billy Bob stood back and laughed with them.

The Misfits had been formed.

Billy Bob looked over at Cecil and Lieutenant Mackey and winked.

"It's working, sir," Lieutenant Mackey said to Cecil. "They're beginning to take some pride in themselves. You give me two months and I'll have the best damn unit in the Rebels."

"I'll give you a week," Cecil replied. "And that is going to be stretching it, lieutenant."

Mackey looked at the general as if he'd lost his mind. "A *week!*"

"Five working days, lieutenant. Then you and your company go on the line. Khamsin is not going to fall for our ruse much longer. He'll put it all together. Believe it. Think you can do it, lieutenant?"

She sighed and shook her head. She caught Billy Bob's eye and motioned him over.

"Yes, ma'am?"

She informed him of Cecil's orders.

Billy Bob almost swallowed his chew of tobacco.

210

Cecil smiled at the man's antics.

"Good God Amighty!" Billy Bob blurted.

"What can we accomplish in five days, Sergeant Manning?" Mackey asked.

Billy moved his chaw over to another spot in his mouth and said, "Well, we ain't gonna have no spit and polish parade ground types by then. But I figure they'll be pretty much of a unit. Y'all are forgettin' this: They all got combat experience of one sort or another. It's just that they ain't never had it in no regular outfit. But we can work it out. Can I make a suggestion, general?"

"Certainly, sergeant."

"Them that take to the M-16 let 'em have it. But them that would rather have their .3030 or .308 or what-have-you, let 'em be. That's the weapon they're familiar with and that's the one they'll perform best with. We got good reloading equipment here, and we've been doing it for a long time. How about it, general?"

Cecil thought about that for a moment. It would certainly be a strangely armed unit, but what the hell, it was a strange bunch to begin with.

No doubt about that. None at all.

"I like it," Mackey said.

"All right, Sergeant Manning," Cecil said. "We can provide .223 and .308 ammo. A lot of our people prefer the M-14. But the .33 and .243 and .270 ammo is another story. That's going to be up to you people. And it's going to take a lot of ammunition; I don't want anyone to be caught short and endanger the life of someone else. What do you say . . . can you do it?"

Billy Bob grinned. "We can do it, sir. You just watch us go."

"Well, get going then, sergeant. Time's a-wasting!"

Jake had taken his rejects and culls and left the area. But not under his own power. The man had been so thoroughly beaten by Cecil that he was unable to walk. His followers had placed the big man in the bed of a pickup truck after lining the bed with old mattresses for his comfort. And the fleas.

Cecil had seen him off amid threats and much profanity from Jake.

Cecil's Rebels and the new Misfits had stood by, listening to Jake.

"You ain't done with me yet, coon," Jake told Cecil. "You gonna regret the day you come into my territory and started shootin' off your big fat mouth. It ain't over. I promise you that."

Cecil stood a few feet from the truck and let Jake vent his rage.

"You can have all them pussies and candy-asses you picked, nigger," Jake verbally boiled. "I'm glad to be rid of them. And I'll tell you this: The next time we meet, you bush-ape, I'm gonna spit on your grave."

"Yes, I saw that movie a long time ago, Jake."

"Haw?"

"Never mind. Are you all through, Jake? Running that ignorant mouth?"

"Ifn I wasn't all busted up inside, you burr-head," Jake blustered, "I'd git up outta this truck and kick your ass!"

"You just won't learn, will you, Jake?" Cecil said.

"I got learnin'! And you ain't got no right to call me ignorant."

"Whatever 'learnin' you have, Jake, it was wasted on you."

212

"Haw?"

"You're a fool, Jake. Ben Raines is right and that deputy sheriff was right. People of your ilk will never change. You're ignorant and you're proud of it. I've offered you a chance to do something decent for once in your life. You refused it. To hell with you, Jake."

Jake lay on the mattresses and glowered at Cecil through eyes that were swollen almost shut. The man's mouth was puffy and his jaw swollen. "Why should I change, nigger? I've done pretty well the way I is."

"And you really believe that, Jake?"

"Hale, yes, I do!"

Shaking his head in disgust, Cecil stepped away from the truck and faced the company of men and women who had chosen the name of Misfits. "Any of you people want to go with Jake?" he questioned.

No one moved from the ranks. Not one person even changed expression. Only Billy Bob Manning smiled.

Jake painfully raised himself up on one elbow to glare at the rows of men and women. "You're be sorry," he said. "And that's what you is . . . Sorry! Cowards and trash. I'm plumb ashamed I ever called any of you friend. But they'll come a day when ever' one of you will regret what you've done. No one turns his ass to Big Jake lak y'all done and gits away with it. You'll see. I promise you that."

Cecil again faced Jake. "Hear me now, Jake. And pay close attention to me. Against the judgement of a lot of people, I'm letting you leave. But I have this bit of advice for you: Find you a little piece of ground and plant a garden. Live very quietly and peacefully. Maintain a very low profile. Give up your plans of ever setting up another warlord state. And

213

do everything that I've told you many many miles from here. For I warn you now: If I ever see you again, I'll kill you, Jake."

Under the bruises of his face, Jake flushed. "Big talk, coon. But I don't think you got the balls to kill me."

Cecil laughed at him. "That makes you a bigger fool than I first thought, Jake. You think I'm joking. Believe me, I am not. I don't have much of a sense of humor when it comes to rednecks and white trash, or people of my own color who think like you do. I have offered you a chance to join us. To fight with us, and not against us. You've all chosen to turn down my offer. All right. So be it. Now get out!"

There was something in Cecil's voice that caused Jake to remain silent. Cecil's eyes were flat and cold, hard looking. But Jake's eyes burned with a wild hate that would never fade.

And Cecil knew in his heart that someday, perhaps very soon, he would have to kill Jake.

Jake waved his hand, and the driver tried to crank the pickup. It would not start. The driver ground the battery down to nothing. Jake lay in the back and cussed.

"Get a mule," Cecil ordered. "Get it in harness and pull this wreck out of here."

No one could find a mule. Cecil looked at the sullen men and women who chose to follow Jake. "Push it out of here," he ordered.

Pushing and sweating and cussing, a group of men got the pickup rolling while Jake lay in the back, shouting orders and profanity.

"You made an enemy, general," Billy Bob said to Cecil.

"Yes, I know, sergeant. And I'm ashamed to say that I believe I did it deliberately."

214

"Yes, sir."

Cecil glanced at the sergeant. He couldn't tell if the man was merely extending military courtesy or agreeing with him.

"You should have shot him, general," Billy Bob said. "But I reckon you know that you're gonna have to kill him someday."

"Yes. I know that, too, sergeant."

Just as Jake's pickup truck rounded a corner, Cecil watched as the man lifted his right fist and extended his middle finger to him.

Quite unlike Cecil, he smiled and returned the gesture.

8

Denise stepped into Ben's CP. "Ashley is on the radio, general. Says he wants to talk to you."

"That was quick," Ben said, looking up. "Must not take Ashley very long to look at a horseshoe."

"Beg pardon, sir?"

Ben smiled and shook his head. "Old joke, Denise." He stood up and motioned her out ahead of him. Together, they walked to the radio shack.

The young woman behind the maze of equipment handed Ben the mike. "He's on the horn, sir."

Ben pressed the key. "Ashley. What can I do for you?"

"You wanted to talk to me, Raines?" said the voice from out of the speaker. "Not the other way around. What's on your mind?"

Ben listened to the voice. It was just vaguely familiar to him. But still he could not place it. "I'd like to put an end to the fighting, Ashley. How about you?"

"I'm listening, Raines."

Was that a note of relief in Ashley's voice? Ben thought so.

"Are you familiar with a Libyan named Khamsin?"

"I've heard the name. What about him?"

216

Ben took a deep breath, then keyed the mike. "We're both in trouble if he gets a firmer toehold in American. Are you in agreement with that?"

Silence on the other end. Then Ashley said, "Yeah. I'll agree with that." What the hell was Raines getting at?

"I've got a proposition for you, Ashley. Give it some thought, if you will."

"Lay it on me, Raines."

"I'll level with you, Ashley. I've got about three thousand troops with me. You've got just a bit less than that. So listen to me. How about us putting hostilities aside and head east, link up to fight this Libyan. How about it, Ashley?"

The offer was so totally unexpected, it caught Ashley completely off balance. He sat in stunned silence for a long moment. He was almost giddy from relief, but didn't want to appear too anxious. Finally, he said, "You're fucking *serious!*"

"Yes, I am, Ashley."

"But I just tried to kill you, Raines! What kind of crap are you pulling?"

"No crap, Ashley. I'm on the level. Are you familiar with the old saying about politics making for strange bedfellows?"

"Yeah," Ashley said slowly. "And the same could be said for war, right, Raines?"

"That's about it."

"And if I take you up on this offer? And we kick this Libyan's ass. What then?"

"Ashley, I honestly don't know. We're going to have to talk about that."

In his own radio room, the mike off, Ashley grunted, thinking: The son of a bitch is honest, if nothing else. He leaned back in his chair, his mind working hard. He knew Raines was totally correct about the Libyan. Crazy ex-terrorist had kicked ass all over the world before coming to the shattered land that was once called the United States of America.

And another thought came to Ashley's mind: United we stand.

"Well," he muttered, "it's a way out of this box I'm in. I can always split the scene once out of here."

He keyed the mike. "Raines? How do you know I won't turn on you? Maybe join up with the Libyan?"

"I don't."

Ashley sighed, recalling his daddy's words: A man who has no honor has nothing, son. Of course, Ashley remembered, his daddy underpaid the help and was a fucking crook. "Well, Raines," he said, the mike open, "I wouldn't do that. For the simple reason that I don't trust that rag-head any more than I do you."

"I understand."

"And something else, Raines: You have to know that I hate your goddamned guts!"

"I think you've made that abundantly clear, Ashley." His reply was very dry.

"And if I take you up on this deal, Raines, I don't want to see your goddamned ugly face. Ever! I might just decide to hell with it and shoot you on the spot. Is that understood?"

"Perfectly clear, Ashley. But would you object to clearing up one little matter?"

Ashley laughed, knowing what was coming. "What is it, Raines?"

"*Why* do you hate me?"

Ashley chuckled. The son of a bitch really didn't remember him. Good. "Don't you just love a mystery, Raines. Let's just say this: You whipped my ass once. But you'll never do it again. Enough about that. We've got a problem with logistics."

218

"We can work that out. You want me to take care of it?"

"Suits me."

"How about your men, Ashley?"

"What about them?"

"Will they fight?"

Ashley paused for a moment. "All right, Raines. You seem to be leveling with me, so I'll give it to you straight. First Battalion is commanded by Colonel West. They're solid professional—all the way. That's what he and his men do for a living. Fight other folk's wars. Second Battalion is average. Third Battalion is the pits. That answer your question?"

"I appreciate your honesty, Ashley."

"Fine. Just don't put any of them into a position of having to take orders from some damned nigger."

"I'll certainly keep that in mind. I'll be back in touch with you first thing in the morning. That all right with you?"

Another pause from Ashley. "Yeah. Fine. If I'm gone, Colonel West will be in charge."

Ashley signed off.

Ben laid the mike aside and looked up at Denise.

"You're a man of many surprises, general."

"Not really," Ben said with a smile. "There is always the chance that Khamsin's men will kill Ashley. If that's the case, then I won't have to do it."

She laughed aloud. "How about a devious man, general?"

"I've sure as hell been called worse."

"It was a good move, Ben," Ike said. "I didn't even think of doing anything like that."

Ben smiled.

Tina looked at him curiously. "Why are you smil-

219

ing, Dad?"

"He had no choice in the matter, people. He knew damn well he didn't have a snowball's chance in hell of winning this fight. All I did was give him an out."

"And a chance to save face," Dan added. "A fine move, general."

"Don't compliment him too much," Dr. Chase said. "It'll go to his head."

When the laughter had died down, Ben said, "But I still don't know who the man is. The voice is somewhat familiar. But I just can't put a face to it."

"You think this might all be a game to him, general?" Dan asked.

Ben shrugged. "I hope not. But he'll damn sure find out when his troops face Khamsin that it's not a very funny joke. If this Ashley actually leads his troops."

Ike nodded his head in agreement. "Yeah. I've thought along those same lines, Ben."

Dan said, "I've seen some of Ashley's troops who were solid professional. Others that were good for no more than cannon fodder."

"Does anybody have any additional information on this Ashley person?" Ben asked.

"About your height, Dad," Tina said. "A bit heavier. Just about the same age."

"Comes from the Deep South," Chase said. "What kind of accent did you detect while speaking with him, Ben?"

"Louisiana or Mississippi, I'd guess."

"Great fan of Patton," Ike said. "But unlike Patton, not a very good solider. From what we're able to learn from questioning both civilians and captured troops, Ashley is pretty much of a showboat. Pearl-handled forty-fives, shiny helmet, riding britches . . . the whole nine yards. A very cruel man, from what I

220

can gather."

"Have to be cruel, or crazy, or both, to hook up with Big Louie and then plot to kill him. Right?" Ben stood up. "Have all hostilities ceased?"

"Not a shot being fired, Ben," Ike said.

"Good." Ben held up a piece of paper. "According to this communiqúe I was just handed, a few minutes ago, Ashley has put Colonel West in charge. Now whether that means Ashley has pulled out, I don't know. I'm to meet with Colonel West in Topeka in a few hours." He glanced at Ike. "How did Buddy perform?"

"Top soldier, Ben. Very smart. Cautious, but not too. His grandfather must have been quite a soldier. He sure taught the boy some good moves."

"How are the troops accepting him?"

"Fine and dandy, Ben. They all seem to like him and most look to him for orders." Ike smiled and braced himself. He had a strong hunch what might be coming at him from Ben.

He was right.

Ben glanced sharply at his friend. "You give him any rank?"

"Nope. But he's your son, Ben. You know damn well that a lot of Rebels—hell, most of them—are going to look at Buddy in a different light."

Ben nodded his head. "Yeah. Okay. Sure, you're right." To Dan: "Have you observed him, Dan?"

"Yes, sir. He's a natural leader and natural soldier. No matter what group he joins, they all seem to instinctively defer to him. He doesn't ask for that; it just happens. You've got the same quality about you. He is quite fortunate that he inherited it. And from what I've been able to hear and observe, he conducts himself admirably."

"Quite a glowing recommendation, Dan," Ben

221

said, his tone very, very dry.

"Thank you, sir," the transplanted Englishman said with a straight face. "I thought it read well myself."

Ben glared at him. It bounced right off of Dan.

"Buddy will damn well earn any rank," Ben said. "Just like anybody else."

"Oh, quite right, general," Dan said.

"Pip, pip, and all that," Ike said.

Ben took a step toward Ike, and Tina stepped between them. "Dad, the Rebels are putting the leadership role on Buddy. He isn't asking for it. It's like Dan said; he is a natural. And a lot of Rebels want to follow him."

"And? So?" Ben demanded, considerable heat in his voice.

"Aw, *shit,* Ben!" Ike flared. "The kid deserves a team. He's that good. Buddy is as good as any soldier I've ever seen. Even as good as a lot of Seals," he added, a wicked glint in his eyes.

Dr. Chase laughed and rubbed his hands together. "This is going to get good here any minute."

Ben ignored the doctor. "If I decide to give Buddy any rank, Ike, that will be solely my decision to make."

Dan backed up, pulling Tina back with him, getting them both out of the way.

"American special troops can be quite boorish," he said to her. "Don't you know?"

"Oh, quite," she said, grinning. She knew that Ben and Ike occasionally had to clear the air between them. But they both knew the other's capabilities when it came to gutter fighting, and no blows had ever been landed.

Yet.

"That's your ass, Ben." Ike stood his ground. "That would be solely *my* decision to make."

"What the hell do you mean?" Ben roared.

"You assigned Buddy to me, oh great supreme commander, General Poo-bah! And if I decide to give him a team, that is my decision to make. And it's already done been decided. I gave him a recon team this morning and told him to have at it."

"Without consulting me!" Ben yelled.

"I don't need to consult you!" Ike returned the yell. "I give folks grade all the goddamn time."

"Well, Buddy is not just anybody! Or have you forgotten that?"

"No, I ain't forgot jack-shit! I don't give a good goddamn if he's your son or the great-great grandson of Cochise. If he can do the job, that's all that counts."

Dan, Tina, and Dr. Chase stood smiling. They'd seen this little drama unfold many times in the past. Denise sat on a camp stool and remained very still, not knowing what to make of all this shouting between the generals.

"I'm surprised you didn't give the kid a fucking division, *General* McGowan!"

"Well, by God, *General* Raines, I just might do that someday. Thanks for the suggestion. But for the time being, I gave him a platoon to ramrod, and he's doin' a damn fine job of it, too. Now if you don't like it, shove it up your tush!"

Chase burst out laughing.

Both Ike and Ben gave the doctor hard looks.

Dr. Chase said, "Both of you are behaving like children."

"Who the hell asked you!" Ike yelled, beating Ben to the words.

"I think a cup of tea would be nice right about now," Dan suggested.

"You know what you can do with your tea?" Ike

223

told him.

"Drink it, perferably," Dan replied.

"That ain't exactly what I had in mind," Ike told him.

"All right!" Chase put an end to the bickering. He glared first at Ben, then at Ike. "I've a good mind to exercise my authority as chief medical officer and relieve both of you of command and put your asses in the hospital for observation. And you both, by God, know that I can and will do just that."

"That might not be a bad idea, doctor," Tina said, smiling. "They are showing signs of stress, wouldn't you agree?"

"What the hell do I have going here?" Ben said. "A revolt?"

Denise stood up. "May I please say something?"

Everybody looked at her. She had sat so quietly, they had forgotten she was among them.

"A voice of reason would certainly be welcome here," Dr. Chase said.

"Of course, you may say something, my dear," Dan told her. "But don't be too alarmed. They've been doing this for years."

"Well," Denise said. "It seems to me that you, General Raines, are concerned more with saving face than you are the welfare of your son. It might reflect badly on you if Buddy should fail in his leadership role. And you, General McGowan, should have informed General Raines of what you planned to do. As for Buddy, I thought that field promotions went on all the time, in any army. That's all I have to say. Now if you'll excuse me, I have to make some preparations for the trip to Topeka. Thank you for allowing me to speak." She turned and walked outside.

Chase jerked a thumb toward the departing

Denise. "I like her. Nothing like a bit of reason amid chaos." He turned and followed Denise outside.

"Come, my dear." Dan took Tina's arm. He looked at Ben and Ike. "Ta-ta, all!" he said cheerfully.

Ben rode in an open Jeep up the Kansas Turnpike toward Topeka, Denise driving. Out of pure spite, Ike had assigned Buddy and his team as point for Ben.

Ben pointed at the Jeep a few hundred yards ahead of them on the cracked old turnpike. "Doesn't that boy know how to wear a beret?" he bitched, referring to Buddy's headgear: a dark red bandana. He looked at Denise. "What's so damn funny?" he asked, noting her smile.

"You. You act like a big ol' bear with a sore paw. You're so proud of Buddy you're about to bust. But the only way you can show it is to sull up and act ticky."

"Ticky? I am behaving *ticky?*"

"Uh-huh."

Ben grunted.

She laughed aloud.

Ben smiled, his mood lifting. "Ike and I have to clear the air every now and then, Denise. Don't worry about us. I just don't want Buddy to fall flat on his face, that's all."

"I think, Ben, that if Buddy gets in over his head, he's the type who will admit it and call for help."

"Yeah, I think so, too. He is a good-looking kid, isn't he?"

Her laughter rang out in the open air of late summer. "Yes, Daddy."

"General Raines," the man said, holding out his

hand. "I'm Colonel West."

Ben shook the offered hand. He inspected the man. In his late forties, Ben guessed. Stocky and appearing in good physical shape. Very competent looking. "Might as well get right to the point, colonel. Clear the air."

The legendary Ben Raines, West thought. Big mean-looking bastard. Be interesting serving under him. "Yes, sir. I expect there will be some changes made."

"A few, for sure. But nothing you can't work with. Where is Ashley?"

"Pulled out, sir. Left last night. Took his personal company with him." He did not say he was glad to see the pompous bastard leave.

Ben smiled. "Ashley appears to be a very elusive type."

"And he hates your guts, general," West told him bluntly.

"For reasons I have yet to fully understand. How about you, colonel?"

"How do I feel about you?"

"Yes. Let's be perfectly honest with each other. Our lives might well depend on it."

"All right. Let's put it this way, General Raines. I don't like niggers, I don't like spics, I don't like Jews, I don't like Indians. I think white people are the superior race; all others are inferior. But I'm smart enough to know that there are exceptions to every rule. And I have respect for those exceptions."

"Gen. Cecil Jefferys?"

"One of those exceptions I mentioned. I have the utmost respect for him. I would certainly take his orders."

"That's good to know. You probably will be taking orders from him. Go on, colonel."

226

"I don't believe that inferiors should be mistreated."

"But you endorsed the slavery that went on here."

West shrugged. "I took no part in that. Although I certainly knew it was going on."

Ben smiled. "Just following orders, Colonel West?"

"That's one way of putting it, General Raines."

"Go on."

"I didn't like everything that Ashley did; and I sure as hell didn't like *anything* that fag Louie did. But for me and my men, it was the best game in town. So to speak. General, I'll come right up front and say that I don't believe that I could ever live under your rules; the way you and your Rebels believe. But for this operation, I'll take orders and carry them through to the best of my ability."

"Thank you, colonel. That is certainly clearing the air, all right. But let's get it all said. Anything else?"

"Yes, sir. I am a professional soldier. I've been a soldier since I was seventeen. Thirty years, sir. I think we're about the same age. Give or take a few years. Ashley might well be a borderline nut case, but he's a good organizer. He needed an army, I needed a job. That's all there is to that."

"I appreciate your candor, colonel. I didn't believe Louie or Ashley were calling all the shots."

West smiled. "Louie was a poor, pitiful fool, general. Ashley is a piss-poor soldier. But like I said, he's a good organizer; a good manager. I let Ashley think he was calling the shots—and to his credit, he did call a few—but First Battalion is all mine. They are the top soldiers. Solid professionals. Second and Third Battalions are, well . . . " He moved his right hand, palm down, from side to side.

Iffy.

"I get the picture, colonel. All right. Of the Second and Third, which is the best?"

"Second," he answered quickly. "The Third is a bunch of losers."

Ashley had been honest, Ben thought. "Go on, colonel."

"The only reason Second and Third fought as well as they did was out of pure fear, general. They didn't want to get pushed back into Kansas City." He smiled. "Neither did I."

"The Hot Zone?"

"It's called that, general. But that's a misnomer. The area is not hot. And my compliments on a damned fine field plan, general. Eventually, you would have broken through my lines and the Second and Third would have folded up."

Ben nodded his head. "That's all behind us, colonel. You say Kansas City is not hot?"

"Not as far as radiation goes, general. I guess those so-called 'clean bombs' the Russkies came up with really worked." He smiled a smile that only another soldier would have understood. "Real shame that none of them got to see it."

Ben returned the rough smile. Despite what the man represented, he found himself liking this Colonel West. He made no excuses for what he was.

"The reason I might be staring, colonel, is this: You don't speak or conduct yourself like a man who could condone the burning alive of another human being. Feel free to correct me if I'm wrong in that assessment, Colonel West."

West grimaced and shook his head. "Barbaric, general. Good God, don't put me in that category. Neither I nor my men had anything to do with that. Oh, we *knew* about it; we can't be excused for that. Or forgiven, if there is a God. I am a soldier, general.

A mercenary, if you wish, but still a soldier. Certainly the universal soldier. I'm not ashamed of it. Ashley and Louie offered good food and gear, comfortable surroundings for me and my men. And since the collapse of the government, money is useless. So it's the small amenities that now count." West grinned. "And, General Raines, speaking of that, I believe you did a bit of merc work yourself, did you not, before becoming a writer?"

Ben threw back his head and laughed aloud at that. "I sure did, colonel. I sure did. Come on, Colonel West. I want to meet your men. As philosophies go, we might be far apart. But as soldiers, we think alike. You'd better watch me, colonel. I'm awfully persuasive. I just might have you coming over to my way of thinking, voluntarily, if you're not careful."

Colonel West grinned. "Don't count on it, general. Personally, I find myself liking you as a man, as a leader of troops. But I do not believe in the mixing of races."

"Oh, we're going to have a good time, colonel!" Ben said. "I can just see it. I do love a spirited debate."

9

The Misfits had been issued Rebel uniforms, brought in from the North. And much to Cecil's and Lieutenant Mackey's delight and surprise, the Misfits were beginning to look and act like a military unit. They had a long way to go, of course, but they were getting there.

"It's a miracle," Lieutenant Mackey said.

"They just needed some direction in their lives," Cecil said. Maybe that deputy sheriff was only half right, Cecil thought, clinging to part of his dream.

He said as much aloud.

Mackey looked at him. "You're forgetting about Big Jake, aren't you, sir?"

"Thanks for bringing me back to reality, lieutenant. No, I haven't forgotten about that cretin. But we salvaged this much, didn't we?" He pointed at the Misfits.

"They weren't human filth to start with, sir."

Cecil sighed. "I suppose not."

Since no one in the Rebel Army, from command to private, gave a flying flip for any type of close-order drill, that was not stressed. What was being taught, in the hot, exhausting days, stretching fourteen to sixteen hours at a time, was teamwork, the care of weapons, stealth, guerrilla tactics — as much as could be taught in five days — and pride.

And Billy Bob and Lieutenant Mackey drove themselves just as hard as they drove the Misfits.

And they found themselves getting a bit closer than sergeant and lieutenant should. But since that was not against the rules in the Rebel army, they just let nature take its course.

And May, Lieutenant Mackey's nickname — she refused to tell anyone her real name — as Cecil said to her once, "Had a real nice shine to her, now."

Since Lieutenant Mackey never really knew how to take General Jefferys, she kept her mouth shut. The general had sort of a weird sense of humor.

But he cleared that up on the fourth day of training. "Hadn't you better tell Billy Bob that your mother was half black, May?"

Now May knew what Cecil had meant when he chose the word "shine."

"He knows," she said.

Cecil smiled and needled her. "And you mean to tell me that Georgia Cracker doesn't *care?*"

"Said he didn't. He said there wasn't a Georgia anymore. No Mason-Dixon line. No American flag. No nothing, except for people. He said it was way past time to bury the hate, and anyone who still carried it."

"Well," Cecil said. "That Cracker is quite a philosopher, isn't he?" Putting the needle to her.

"General," May said, standing up straight and looking Cecil smack in the eyes.

"Yes, lieutenant?"

"Don't you ever call Billy a Cracker again!"

Cecil smiled. "All right, May. I surely won't."

Cecil walked off, whistling "Love Is A Many Splendored Thing."

Billy Bob had slipped easily back into his former role as a Marine Corps sergeant. And the man was proving to be invaluable. And not just with May. The Misfits, to a person, all liked him and, so far, at least, he had experienced no discipline problems.

Jake, so it seemed, had taken his pack of losers and dropped out of sight. But Cecil had a gut feeling that Jake had not gone far and they would meet again.

Khamsin's men were being kept busy running up and down the South Carolina side of the river, reinforcing units here, pulling people out of position there, all due to the seemingly never-ending talk of Cecil's upcoming "invasion."

The Rebels had intercepted several radio messages between Khamsin and his field commanders, and Khamsin, to put it mildly, was highly pissed-off. "Son of a bitch!" Khamsin shouted, although the use of profanity was forbidden in the teachings of his religion. Terrorism was all right, but profanity was not. "I'm beginning to believe, Hamid," he said, calming himself, "that there never was any invasion planned."

"What do you mean, sir?"

"It's a trick on the Rebels' part. They're buying time and that's all they're doing. There is no impending invasion." He spun around to face the window of his office. He could scarcely conceal his rage. "The black general has made fools of us, Hamid. And I won't soon forget or forgive that." He turned slowly to look at Hamid. "But why did he want a little more time?"

"Waiting for reinforcements, perhaps?"

"Perhaps. But if that is the case, why is he shifting the location of his base camp? And we know from recent fly-bys, what was called Base Camp One is now nearly deserted; everything is being moved west."

"Then he has something else in mind," Hamid said. Hamid's speculations posed no threat to Mohammed the Prophet.

"What?" Khamsin asked.

"I don't know, sir."

Khamsin cursed again, silently.

"But our recon teams reported that he is training a group of people in the city of Athens."

"They saw this with their own eyes?"

"No, sir. They captured a civilian woman and tortured the information out of her, then killed her." Torture was all right, too. Sort of like bombing abortion clinics for God and fucking for virginity. "A warlord named Jake something-or-the-other had lived there for a year or so. This General Jefferys came in, whipped the warlord . . ."

Khamsin waved the man silent. He was thoughtful for a moment. "Wait, wait!" he said. "I don't understand something here. What do you mean, Hamid . . . he *whipped* the warlord? Whipped him how?"

"With his fists, sir."

"A *general* fought a person with his fists!"

"Yes, sir."

"How crude. Go on, Hamid."

"The woman told our recon team that Jake challenged General Jefferys to a fight, some sort of winner-take-all affair. One would have to assume that type of thing is quite common in this primitive land, even before the Great War. Then, with several hundred people watching, the general beat this Jake person unconscious with his fists. Then General Jefferys threw out about half of the inhabitants; they left with this Jake. These people have such strange names. The others were formed into a new unit of the Rebel army."

"To be used as what?"

Hamid lifted his shoulders. "That, I do not know, sir."

Khamsin smiled. "Conditions are becoming desperate for General Jefferys, Hamid. That is surely the reason for his taking on of green troops." He walked to a large wall map and stared at it for a long moment. "What do our teams report about Atlanta?"

"A place to avoid at all costs, sir. It is inhabited by what are called the Night People."

Khamsin nodded his head. He knew about those people. "The survivors and the offspring of the bombings. The same in Europe and South America as here. Then it's true; they're moving into the cities across the land?"

"Yes, sir."

"Very well. Advise our field patrols to stay away from the larger cities. Those people are surely unclean. We'll have to deal with them, of course, but not now. One step at a time for us. Hamid, start moving our people into Georgia, using the southern route. Bring them up and form them along Interstate Twenty, east to west."

"How many troops, sir?"

Khamsin stared at the map for so long Hamid thought he had forgotten his being there. Khamsin turned and announced dramatically, "All of them, Hamid. We are going to take Georgia!"

"Found it!" Emil yelled, holding up a small box.

"What is it, Brother Emil?" Brother Carl cried happily. Whatever pleased Emil surely pleased the Great God Blomm. So everything was just hunky-dory.

"A miracle, Brother Carl." They were standing in the rubble and litter of what had once been a fine hospital in Monroe, Louisiana. In what used to be the nut wing.

Brother Carl looked at the box. *That's* a miracle, Brother Emil. You could have fooled me. It looks like a box!"

Emil looked at Brother Carl. The guy was as loyal as a cocker spaniel and a damn good bodyguard, but a little bit short when it came to brains. "Our great and magnificent Blomm instructed me to come to this place. I am acting on Blomm's orders, Carl. And this package and its contents are to be our secret. When it's time for me to inform the others, Brother Matthew and Brother Roger, Blomm will let me know. Is that understood?"

"Oh, yes, sir, Brother Emil. I gotcha."

Emil glanced out a broken window. Still about an hour before full dark. He didn't want to get caught inside the city limits at night. For even in the small cities, that group of misshapen and deformed and totally weird bunch known as the Night People had gathered. Why they chose the cities was still a mystery to Emil; but he knew firsthand, having almost been captured by them, that you damn sure didn't want to get trapped inside the cities after dark.

235

For that's when the Night People came out to prowl.

Emil bounced the package from hand to hand and smiled. Stanley Ledbetter aka Francis Freneau, was about to discover that when it came to running scams, he was up against a master of the trade.

Emil chuckled softly.

"What's in the box, Brother Emil?" Brother Carl said, hopping up and down. "Huh? Huh? Come on, tell me, *please!* You know I get the hives when I get nervous."

"It's a drug, Carl. The Great God Blomm told me where to find it."

"A miracle drug, huh?"

"Sort of, Carl."

"Does it make you feel good?"

"It ain't gonna make Francis Freneau feel worth a shit."

"I don't understand, Brother Emil. Does it cure the hives?"

"No, Carl. It's a drug that doctors used to give . . . certain people. It reduces the sex drive."

"Huh?"

"It means," Emil said with a sigh, "that if you was to take some of this stuff, you wouldn't be able to get a hard-on."

"Ohh!" Brother Carl said, grabbing at his crotch. "Why would anybody want to take something like that?"

"I don't think anybody ever took any of this stuff voluntarily," Emil patiently explained. He looked at the expiration date on the box. Out of date, naturally, but that was no big deal. He'd just triple the dosage. And then he'd see what Francis could do with a limber fire hose.

Nothing, he thought, smiling. He could just sit there and look at that donkey dick.

"You're so smart, Brother Emil," Brother Carl said. "I don't know what I'd do without you to guide me."

Emil smiled. "Carl, stick with me, kid, and we'll soon have all the . . ." Nuts and fruitcakes and cult followers and banana cream pies ". . . world at our feet. When word of this miracle gets around, we'll have it made, Brother Carl."

"Oohhh!" Brother Carl gushed all over Emil.

Emil patiently brushed the spittle off the sleeve of his robe.

Carl tugged at the robe after taking a look outside. "let's get out of here, Brother Emil. We don't wanna get caught here after dark."

Emil nodded. He knew that a large hospital complex would be an ideal spot for the Night People to hole up in during the daylight hours. They were probably the ones who trashed the place, looking for medicines. Poor misshapen and twisted bastards would take anything in hopes of relieving their condition. But Emil knew the only thing that would help them was death.

Emil put the package into his knapsack and slipped it over his shoulders, adjusting the straps. He picked up his rifle.

"Let's split, Brother Emil."

Both of them breathed a sigh of relief as they walked out of the hospital and into the sunlight of late summer. Both of them held their weapons at the ready, fingers just off the trigger. They walked to Emil's car, a twenty-five-year-old black limousine. They got in and locked all the doors. Emil cranked it up and checked the gas gauge.

"Crap, Brother Carl. We're almost out of gas."

Carl looked out the dusty window and shuddered. Dusk was no more than fifteen or twenty minutes away. "And we used all the gas we had in the can, Brother Emil."

"We'll try that old station up there," Emil said, pointing.

But the storage tanks were dry.

"What are we gonna do, Brother Emil?" Carl asked.

"Don't panic," Emil said. "There are lots of stations in this burg."

"But we ain't got much time 'fore dark!"

There was panic in Brother Carl's voice. And for good reason. He knew what happened to people who were taken by the Night People.

"Steady, Brother Carl." Emil tried to calm the man's fear. "Blomm is with us."

Emil believed that about as much as he did in sweet potatos lining up and doing the can-can.

They pulled into another station, the limo just about running on fumes. The storage tanks were empty.

The fuel needle indicated they were slap out of gas.

And the shadows were creeping around them, and with the shadows, hooded figures could be seen.

"They're out there, Brother Emil!" Carl whispered.

"I see them, Carl," Emil replied. His heart was beating so fast and so hard he thought it might burst.

"Get us a miracle, Brother Emil," Carl urged. "You can do it. Call on Blomm."

Poor simple bastard, Emil thought. Well, Carl's saved my ass more than once. Now it's time for me to save his.

"Stand by me, Carl," Emil heard himself saying.

"I'll get us out of this mess."

Carl was too frightened to even reply.

Emil and Carl sat in the limo and watched as the hooded figures drew closer.

Emil pissed in his underwear.

Emil lowered his window and stuck the muzzle of his automatic rifle outside. "You come any closer and I'll blow your asses off!" he shouted.

The line of hooded figures stopped their advance. Several of them huddled together, their voices low in the dusk; too low for Emil to hear what they were whispering about.

"Back off, I say!" Emil shouted. What the hell? he thought. Might as well give it a try. "I am the earthbound spiritual messenger of the Great God Bloom. I command you all in his name to carry your asses on outta here!"

"That's tellin' 'em, Brother Emil," Carl whispered. "Blomm'll strike 'em down."

For the umpteenth time since he started his present scam, Emil wished to hell he had thought of something else. Blomm was getting a bit wearing. Not to mention hard in keeping up a good front.

"We come with peace and love in our hearts," said a female voice out of the gathering purple shadows. "We mean no harm to anyone."

"Yeah?" Emil shouted. "That's what Kong said to what's-her-name, too. Drop them hoods so I can see your faces!"

The line of robed and hooded people pushed back their hoods. Emil lowered the muzzle of his rifle and clicked it to safety. The men and women were unblemished. The men handsome, the women beautiful.

They were not the Night People. Those creeps

could haunt graveyards. And probably did.

"What's your problem?" Emil asked. "Don't you have no better sense than to prowl around cities in the night?"

"Our bus broke down," a woman said. "The old engine finally gave up the good fight. There are but six of us."

Emil counted. There were six of them. He could have sworn there were sixty. Fear in the night can play tricks on a person.

"If you are going east, would you be so kind as to give us a lift?" the spokeswoman requested. "We are not going far."

"You got any gas?"

"Plenty of fuel, neighbor. We'll give you gas for a ride."

"I'm only goin' about forty-five miles," Emil said.

"That would be wonderful," the woman said. "That would put us precisely at our destination. You're so kind. The night can be fearful, can it not?"

"Bet your ass," Emil muttered. He looked at the woman. And speaking of ass—

"Okay," Emil said. "Let's get you all loaded up and this buggy gassed up."

They worked quickly, for full night was upon them. Emil noticed that all the newcomers, despite their talk of peace and love, were heavily armed. But in this day and time, only a fool wasn't.

With the softness of the chickie pushing against him, Emil cranked the limo, now with a full tank of gas, the luggage on the rack on top. It headed out into the night.

"See the Night People, over there!" Carl said, pointing.

"Screw 'em," Emil said, driving past the dark

240

outline of what had once been a shopping mall. He was soon on the highway.

Everyone breathed a long, collective sigh of relief.

"It could have become very ugly back there," a man spoke from the back seat. "The Night People are organizing, all over the land. They have a system of radio hookups that stretch all over the lower forty-eight. They will soon be a force to reckon with, I am afraid."

"They hate and despise everyone who is not like them," the chickie beside Emil said. "And where once they were to be pitied, now they have turned savage and hateful. They are becoming increasingly dangerous."

"Blomm will protect us, won't he, Brother Emil?" Carl asked.

"The Good Book says the Lord helps those who help themselves," Emil stated. Or something like that. Pretty profound, anyways.

"Blomm?" the chickie by Emil said. "I don't think I've ever heard of Blomm."

"Nor I, Sister Susie," a man spoke from the back seat. "We worshipped with Brother Fladstool out in California for a time; but then the Russian and his troops came along and we had to flee for our lives. Remember, Sister Susie?"

"Oh, yes, Brother William. It was after that we went to Arizona and for a time worshipped with the Reverend Mugwan, and his Sun, Moon, and Stars Church. But we became dissatisfied with East Indian mystics and are now looking for something more gentle."

"Wonderful!" Emil cried, almost losing control of the limo as Sister Susie's softness pressed against him. He had a hard-on that was throbbing like a bass

241

drum. "I know just the place for you to settle."

"Oh, wonderful, Emil!" Sister Susie cried, clapping her soft little hands together. "I'm so glad we'll all be together."

"Oh, we'll be close, all right," Emil promised. Bet your ass on that, chickie.

She put her hand on Emil's thigh. "Tell me, Emil, how long have you been with Francis Freneau and his Joyful Followers of Life?"

A back tire on the limo blew out with a bang!

10

Colonel West and his three battalions of troops took the northern route. They cut up to Highway 36 at St. Joseph, Missouri and then followed that due east. Ben and his troops cut south of Kansas City, then gradually began working their way east, taking the southernmost route of the two armies.

Before they left, Colonel West told Ben, "Louie is rumored to have some old ICBMs fully functional, general."

Ben almost choked on his tea. "Nukes?"

"That's what Ashley thought. That's why he was always so secure. He was even going to use them against you."

Colonel West was smiling.

"Why are you smiling, colonel?"

"You know anything about guided missiles, general?"

"No."

"Well, on these, sir, you don't just push a button and the birds fly. It takes a sequence of events to launch. Here's the way it might work: Your PAR, the

Perimeter Acquisition Radar, would gather initial trajectory data on targets and then transmit that to the Fire Coordination Center. The FCC would then select the most appropriate missile site to respond, and then transmit the collected data to the MDC, the Missile Direction Center located at that site."

"Good God!" Ben said.

"Oh, there's more, sir. Believe me. It is not and cannot be a one-man show. Besides, I looked at one of the missiles. They aren't ICBMs. They're Spartan."

"Shorter range."

"Yes, sir. And this particular Spartan was designed to explode in the exoatmosphere."

"Outside the atmosphere."

"Hopefully."

"What do you mean, colonel?"

"Well, sir, these birds haven't been checked in years. And Louie was a genius. I've heard that he monkeyed with the guidance system on some of them. Maybe he did, maybe he didn't. I just don't know."

Ben thought for a moment. "Is it possible, colonel, for Louie to have . . . hell, rewired the system?"

"To make it a one-man show?"

"Yes."

West sighed. "It's possible, general. I think. And that screwball just might have done it."

"Any idea which direction they were programmed to fly?"

"No, sir."

"But you don't believe they're nuclear, right?"

"No, sir. I do not believe they are."

"Would they blow up by themselves?"

"It's possible, sir. You see, general, the firing sequence is almost entirely automated through the Data Processing System. *But,* Louie could have found a way to hook into or bypass that, because they're all capable of having manual intervention at any point deemed necessary."

"Deemed necessary by . . . whom?"

"Maybe by Louie."

"God help us all!"

"That's it, people!" Cecil shouted at Mackey and Billy. "Both of you, over here."

Leaving the Misfits to grab five on the field, Mackey and Billy trotted to Cecil's side. "What's up, general?" Lt. Mackey asked.

"We're moving out. Khamsin's people are crossing the river, using the bridges just north of Savannah. His first teams are racing toward Interstate Twenty, to beef up those already there."

"Where do you want us, sir?" Mackey asked.

"Right here," Cecil said, punching a spot on the map laid on the hood of a pickup. "You'll be about fifteen miles east of Atlanta."

"Why there, sir?" Mackey asked.

"Because it is close to Atlanta, May. And Khamsin's people, so our reports indicate, are avoiding Atlanta. The chances of your Misfits mixing it up with a stronger force are lessened there."

"The Night People?" May asked.

Cecil nodded his head in silent agreement.

"What's that, sir?" Billy asked. "What's the Night People?"

"You haven't heard of them?" Cecil asked.

245

"No, sir. But then, that's easy to explain. None of us have left this immediate area in more than a year and a half."

May explained about the Night People.

Billy listened and chewed his chaw slowly. "That might account for the strange radio transmissions we intercepted ever' now and then. Wild, crazy talk."

"Frequency, sergeant?" Cecil asked.

"High band, sir. Just about off the scale."

"I'll order a listening team to start monitoring the high band," Cecil said, as much to himself as to Billy and May. He looked at May. "We're getting reports from all over the country about these Night People banding together, always in the cities. They could be a problem in the future."

A runner came panting up. "Sir! A forward recon team from General Raines just radioed in. They must be east of Khamsin's jamming team. General Raines is on the way, sir. And he's linked up with a Colonel West; that's that mercenary. West has three battalions with him. Contact says to look for a man named Ashley; he'll have about a company of men with him. He's friendly and will be working with us to fight Khamsin."

"What's Ben's location?" Cecil asked.

"Still a couple of hundred miles west of the Big Muddy, sir."

Cecil thanked the runner and dismissed him. "It'll take Ben a good five or six days to get here, the roads being what they are. We're going to have a tough go of it until Ben gets here."

"And spread pretty thin," Mackey said.

"Razor thin," Cecil agreed. "So let's be damn sure we're razor sharp." Cecil shook hands with May and

246

Billy Bob. "Move out, people. And good luck."

Cecil walked to his communications vehicle. "Get me Colonel Williams," he ordered.

Joe on the horn, Cecil said, "How's it looking, Joe?"

"Quiet here, general. Too damn quiet. My scouts report a lot of troop movement across the river. All heading south. Is the big push on?"

"Looks that way, Joe. You're certain there is no movement north?"

"Not unless the IPA is goin' way inland and then cuttin' north."

"I don't think they want to try the mountain route, Joe. All reports indicate they're coming across at Savannah." Cecil thought for a moment, then made his decision, and silently prayed it was the right one.

"Joe, leave a team guarding the I-Eighty-five bridge and start the rest of your people heading south. Link up with me in Athens."

"Moving out now, sir."

Cecil walked back to his vehicle and began studying his map. He felt, for several reasons, that Khamsin would not put many troops west of Atlanta. For one, the area between Atlanta and the Alabama line had turned wild, filled with thugs and outlaws and warlords. Khamsin would not want to mix it up with them; not just yet. Another reason was that he would surely know that Ben was on the move, and he would not want his people to get caught in a box, with Cecil's Rebels to the east, and Ben's people coming hard from the west.

Smiling, he closed the map case and once more walked to communications. "Get me Mark and Alvaro."

"Mark? Scramble this. The push is on from Khamsin. Get your people up and moving. Move them south of Interstate Twenty, slip into the woods just east of Sinclair Lake. Slide in there and stay low and quiet. I'm going to pull my people into the area you're leaving. Got all that?"

"Yes, sir. What's the drill on this move?"

"Khamsin's people will want to punch a hole in the center of our lines. Fine. We'll let them think they're doing that. I'll fall back and let them think the line is broken. As soon as they pour across the highway, you and your bunch plug the hole. I'll keep falling back and split my bunch, putting those troops of the IPA who have crossed the line in a squeeze. if we have any kind of luck at all, we can destroy a battalion."

"Yes, sir!"

"Ben is on the way, Mark. We've got to hold until he gets here." Cecil brought the man up to date on Ben and Colonel West.

"Move out, Mark."

Cecil looked at the woman behind the maze of electronic equipment. "Pull everybody north of Interstate Twenty. Everybody. I can't risk losing a single person in guerrilla action."

"Yes, sir." She reached for the mike and began transmitting in code.

Cecil looked toward the west. "It's gonna be close, Ben. Real close."

"I'm being forced to detour, general," Colonel West radioed to Ben's column. "We've got some bridges out on Thirty-six. I'm cutting south to Interstate Seventy."

248

"Try to avoid St. Louis, colonel. Some very strange people are now inhabitating the nation's cities."

"Ten-four to that, general. I'm looking at a map now. I can't figure out where to cross the Muddy."

Ben checked his map. "Try either the northern or southern loop, colonel. You might have to cross at Alton."

"Ten-four, general. I'll get back to you."

Ben looked at Buddy. "As many bridges as possible have to be saved, Buddy. Roads can be patched up and maintained. But once the big bridges are gone, they will not be rebuilt; not in our lifetimes."

"Yes, sir."

"Haven't seen you since we pulled out of Kansas, boy. Everything going all right?"

"Fine, sir. General McGowan reassigned me to your column."

"How considerate of him," Ben said drily.

"Yes, sir."

Ben looked the young man over for any sign of rank. He could find none. "Exactly, boy, what is your position in this army?"

"Sort of a roaming recon team, sir. I don't have any rank."

"Is that your idea, or Ike's?"

"Sort of a mutual agreement, sir."

"I see. Doesn't that present some difficulty in your giving orders?"

"No, sir. I have experienced no problems as yet."

Ben was conscious of Tina and Dan standing close, smiling. Denise was sitting behind the wheel of the Jeep, looking straight ahead, but smiling.

"Big goddamn joke," Ben groused. He glared at Buddy. "Well . . . go roam and recon, boy."

"My team is doing that, sir," Buddy responded. "Sergeant Major Riverson assigned me as your bodyguard."

"I am just delighted that everyone is so concerned with my welfare."

"Yes," Buddy agreed, straight-faced. "It must be quite an honor to be so well-thought-of."

Ben stared at the young man. But he couldn't tell if Buddy was putting him on, or not.

"Let's roll!" Ben ordered. He looked at Buddy. "You take the lead, boy," he said to a very startled Buddy. "I'll ride with Dan for an hour or so."

"Sir! . . ." Buddy opened his mouth to protest. Then closed it as Ben cut him off.

"I'm putting you in charge of the column, boy. What's the matter. Don't you think you can handle it?"

Buddy's face tightened. "I can handle it, sir."

"Then get to it," Ben said gruffly. "If you hit a snag, holler. I'll be a couple of miles back with Colonel Gray."

Buddy turned away.

"Boy!" Ben said.

Buddy slowly turned around. "Yes, sir?"

"I got something I might as well get said. Now is as good a time as any, I suppose."

Buddy braced himself. He knew it had really irritated his father when General Ike had given him a team. Now he felt sure his father was going to make a fool of him by taking that team away from him, or something worse.

But he had come here to be with and to serve his father. So whatever his father decided, he would accept it.

Suddenly, Ben smiled and extended his hand. "Welcome home . . . Captain Raines."

11

"I can drive my own vehicle," Buddy bitched to Denise. She had insisted upon driving him.

"No, sir," she said. "General Raines signaled for me to drive you."

Buddy nodded his head. He wasn't about to argue that. "You're leaving behind any family, Denise?"

"A few cousins. My immediate family was killed fighting Ashley and Big Louie."

Before he could reply, the radio in the Jeep crackled. "Recon One to Eagle."

Buddy looked at the radio. "That's your call, Buddy," Denise said. "You're in charge, now."

"I'm not the *Eagle!*" Buddy protested.

"Recon One to Eagle. Come in, Eagle."

"Take the call." Ben's voice popped out of the speaker. "Little Eagle."

Denise laughed aloud.

Buddy reddened and then laughed. "All right, Father," he said. "I can play games, too."

He picked up the mike and said, "This is Little Eagle, go ahead."

There were a few seconds' pause before the recon team responded. "Little Eagle, the highway is blocked your side of Norwood. Outlaws. They're

252

demanding a tariff to pass. Orders?"

"Stand by," Buddy said, then consulted his map. Or rather, his father's map. The point of the column was about five miles from Norwood. He picked up the mike. "This is . . . Captain Raines. My team up front. On the double."

In the center of the column, Ben sat with Dan, both men listening. Ike had walked up to join them.

"You just gonna sit there, Ben?" Ike asked.

"Yep. It's Buddy's show."

"You're a hard bastard, you know that, Ben?"

"What would you do, Ike, if that were your son up front?"

Ike mumbled something under his breath.

"What was that, Ike?" Ben asking, smiling. "I couldn't quite catch it."

"I said I'd probably let him handle it!"

"Just wanted to be sure, Ike."

Buddy had ordered Denise out of the Jeep. She refused. "I'm your driver, captain."

Buddy thought he might know just a tad how his father felt at times. "Fine, Denise. Let's go."

They stopped a few hundred yards from the blocked highway. Buddy had sent two squads left and right, out of sight of the men behind the barricade.

"There is a bullhorn on the floorboards, back seat," Denise told him.

"Thank you." Buddy got the bullhorn and stepped out of the Jeep.

Lifting the bullhorn to his lips, Buddy pulled the trigger and said, "You men behind the blockade. What do you want?"

"This here's a toll road, boy," a man shouted back. "You don't pay, you don't pass."

"We can always backtrack, captain," Denise said.

"Nobody owns the highway system," Buddy told

253

her. Lifting the horn to his lips, Buddy said, "I have three thousand troops behind me."

"You a goddamn lie!" the man shouted.

"And there are troops all around you," Buddy informed the man.

"Another goddamn lie, boy!"

"You do not own this road!" Buddy shouted through the bullhorn.

"I took it from them goddamn McCoys, and now I own it. So fuck you, soldier boy, or whatever the hell you is!"

"Troops left and right!" Buddy shouted. "Clear the road!"

The quiet morning stillness was shattered by the violent sounds of gunfire. The men standing behind the blockade were knocked backward to the roadbed, their blood soaking into the highway as two dozen M-16s and M-14s rattled and spat death.

When the gunfire ceased, Buddy said, "Mop up and post guards on both sides of the road." He walked back to the Jeep and lifted the mike to his lips. "This is Little Eagle. C Company, first and second platoons, up to my position, pronto."

Ike looked at Ben. "Ain't you gonna get on that horn and ask him what went down, Ben?"

"Nope."

"Ain't you the least bit curious about what happened?"

"Yep."

"Ben Raines, you are a plumb exasperatin' asshole! Anybody ever tell you that?"

"Yep."

When the first and second platoons from Charlie Company arrived at Buddy's position, he told them to range east, up the highway, securing the way east for the column.

"How secure, captain?" a platoon sergeant asked.

Buddy looked at the man. "Whoever you encounter will either be our friends, or they will be dead. Is that understood, sergeant?"

The Rebel grinned. "Yes, *sir!*"

He was not quite out of Buddy's hearing range when the sergeant said, "We don't have to worry none about him, people. That's Ben Raines all over again. Let's roll!"

Buddy walked back to his Jeep and picked up the mike. "This is Little Eagle to Old Eagle," he said with a smile. "You may advance now, Father. I have secured the area."

Dan was laughing so hard he fell out of the Jeep. Ike and Tina were roaring, tears running down their faces.

Ben sat quietly, shaking his head and smiling. When the laughter died away, he said, "I sure set myself up for that one, didn't I?"

And a few miles outside of Topeka, the clock that Big Louie had set before his fateful meeting with Ben Raines started clicking.

Louie might well have been crazy, but he was not stupid. He had known for some time of Ashley's deceit and subversion. Louie wanted to leave something for the masses to remember him by in case this meeting with Ben Raines turned out to be a trap and he did not survive.

He had entered the silo and worked for more than an hour, resetting and reprogramming the firing and guidance systems. But Louie was going to be just a bit short and south of his goal of dropping one in on Khamsin in South Carolina. Besides, while Louie had been brilliant in some areas, he was quite stupid in others. This type of missile was not built to explode on land contact.

But no matter. It would certainly help a fellow that Louie would have loved.

Far away. In Louisiana. When the clock finally reached its firing point.

BOOK THREE

Don't look back. Somebody might be gaining on you.

Satchel Paige

1

We still have radio contact with Cecil?" Ben asked his radio operator.

"Yes, sir. He's diggin' in for a fight. The last word I got was that Khamsin's people are really pourin' into Georgia."

"Setting up a line along Interstate Twenty?"

"Yes, sir."

Ben nodded and turned to Buddy. "Assemble your teams and get ready to move out. You'll be driving them hard, Buddy. Clear the way for us all the way to Sikeston, Missouri. We'll pick up Interstate Fifty-five there. We'll take that down to Jackson, Mississippi. From there, the column will cut straight east. I want us to come up under Khamsin's troops. We'll hit them from the south. Move out, boy, and good luck."

"Yes, sir." Buddy trotted off, shouting for his teams.

"Ike," Ben said. "Get in touch with Colonel West. Tell him to push hard. I want him to link up with Cecil in Georgia."

"Right now, Ben."

Ben stood and watched as Buddy and his teams pulled out, heavily armed, carrying as much ammo and food as they could. Buddy was in the lead Jeep, the ties of his dark red bandana tailing in the wind.

"Damn boy just won't wear regulation headgear," Ben said, smiling.

Ben saluted his son, and Buddy returned the gesture.

Then the teams were out of sight, pushing as hard as road conditions would allow.

"Godspeed, boy," Ben murmured.

"You sure this is going to work, Brother Emil?" Brother Matthew asked.

"I'm positive," Emil assured him. "You just make damn sure this gets in the men's water supply, and then leave the rest to Blomm."

Brother Matthew looked rather dubious about the whole thing, but finally he nodded his head. "Just the men's water supply?"

"Just the men's."

"Look, Emil. Don't hand me none of that Blomm shit. The Great God Blomm has about as much power as a pickle."

Emil looked frantically about him. "Shush! Don't say that too loud, you idiot. Somebody might hear you that isn't supposed to."

"This scam better work, Emil. 'Cause if it don't, I'm splittin'."

"It'll work. It's gonna take four or five days, maybe even a week, but it'll work."

"I hope you're right, Emil. For the sake of all of us, I hope you're right."

No more than I do, Emil thought.

After Brother Matthew had walked away, Emil looked heavenward; actually, he was looking more west than up. A bit north by west to be exact. Which was all right, as it would later turn out.

"Blomm, Zeus, Aphrodite . . . *somebody,* give me a little bitty miracle. 'Cause holy shit, I don't wanna have to go back to hoein' butter beans! I got it made here. Come on. Just a little teeny weeny miracle. Please?"

There is someone on the radio who is requesting to speak to you, general," Khamsin was informed.

"Who is it? Can't you see I'm busy?"

"My apologies, sir. But the person is very insistent."

"Name?"

"He says his name is Ashley, and he has news of Ben Raines."

Khamsin glanced at Hamid. "It could be a trick," Hamid said.

"And it could be worth hearing," Khamsin countered. "All right," he spoke to the messenger. "Tell this Ashley I'll be along presently."

"Yes, sir."

But impatience and curiosity got the better of Khamsin, and he was less than a minute behind the messenger in entering the radio room at his HQ.

"I'm having trouble holding the frequency, sir," Khamsin was told. "The distance is not that great, only a few hundred miles. But he's on very low band and keeps slipping away."

"Get him for me," Khamsin ordered.

"I'll keep this short, general," Ashley said. "I don't want the Rebels accidentally stumbling onto this transmission. You ten-four that?"

"I understand," Khamsin replied. "Can you switch to a scramble?"

"If they'll mesh, sure."

261

"We'll let the radio people on each end work on it. I'll talk to you momentarily."

The radio operators finally settled on a higher band, one that could be scrambled to both party's equipment.

"Now then," Khamsin said, taking the mike. "You may speak freely."

"Don't be too sure of that, general," Ashley told him. "Raines has the finest radio equipment in the world. They'll find us, and lock onto us and unscramble. Believe me, I know. So everything we have to say, we'd best say this go-around and save the rest for a face-to-face. Ten-four?"

"Perfectly."

"Raines is headin' your way with about thirty-five hundred combat-ready Rebels. Three of my battalions are with him; but only one is going to fight with Raines. You understand that?"

Khamsin looked at Hamid and both men smiled. "I understand," Khamsin said. "But why the generosity?"

"Simple. I hate Raines more than I distrust you."

"How do I know this is not a trick?"

"You don't. Yet. But hear me out. I just intercepted a radio message from Raines to Colonel West. Raines is going to take the southern route and come up behind your men, south of Interstate Twenty. The nigger, Jefferys, will link up with Colonel West and my people north of the interstate. To put your people in a box. Ten-four?"

"Yes," Khamsin said. "Ten-four. Your plan?"

"My men will wait until they've linked up with the nigger and then revolt. They have their orders. That agreeable with you?"

"Yes. But what do you want from me for all of this?"

262

"Not a goddamn thing, other than Raines being dead."

"Oh, come now! Surely you want something."

"All right. You stay east of the Mississippi River and I'll stay west. How about that?"

"How do you know you can trust me?" Khamsin asked.

"I don't, partner. But I've always heard that you were a man of honor. Is my information wrong?"

Khamsin drew himself up and bristled at the slur. "I am, of course, a man of honor."

"Then we have a gentleman's agreement, general."

"We have an agreement, Mr. Ashley."

"We'll both monitor this frequency at noon each day for messages. "Ten-four?"

"Agreed."

Both men signed off.

"I have discovered something, Hamid," Khamsin said. "With Ben Raines, there is no middle ground. People either love the man, or totally despise him."

"Or totally fear him," Hamid dared to say.

But Khamsin did not take umbrage. Instead he smiled. "Yes. You are correct, Hamid. Or totally fear him."

Ben pushed his people hard, driving first east, then due south on Interstate 55. Buddy and his teams were driving just as hard, clearing the way of obstacles, both human and accidental. A six-person engineer team was traveling with Buddy, in case the obstacles needed to be blown free, or a temporary bridge built.

The long stretch of interstate between Memphis, Tennessee and Jackson, Mississippi yawned before the Rebels, seemingly deserted, void of human life. But cook fires could be seen on either side of the concrete lanes as the Rebels drove south. But they rarely spotted any human life.

"I wonder about people like that," Buddy said to Judy as he pointed toward a slim finger of smoke, edging upward from a home in the distance. "I wonder what they're doing and how they are getting along."

"Warlords control much of this area," Judy said. "But the Rebels have crisscrossed this route several times before. They'll keep their heads down. They won't mess with us."

"How can people just allow themselves to be ruled like that? I mean, by outlaws and other human trash?"

"Roadblock up ahead," Buddy's radio crackled.

"This may answer your question," Judy said.

Buddy picked up the mike. "Location?"

"Five miles north of the Grenada Dam exit," the point team replied. "It's no small force, captain. We'll have a fight on our hands."

"Have they spotted you?"

"Yes, sir."

"Fall back and hold position. We're ten minutes away."

The column topped the hill and slowed, spotting the point team. Signaling his people to halt, Buddy walked to the Rebel squad leader. "Did you make verbal contact with them?"

"Yes, sir. They say this is a closed area. They'll allow us to pass if we give them ammo and women."

Buddy smiled. "In that order?"

The squad leader grinned. "Yes, sir."

Buddy was silent for a moment. "They may have just told us that they're short of ammunition. We'll lay back about five hundred meters and let the snipers have some fun."

Buddy waved several Rebels forward. They were all armed with heavy sniper rifles.

"Make things a little hot for the people down there," Buddy told them. "Let's see how heavy they return the fire."

The first volley from the long range shooters knocked three outlaws sprawling, all three with massive chest wounds from the rifles more than fifteen hundred feet away.

The returning fire was sparse.

"Low on ammo," Buddy said. "We can't just knock out this blockade and go on. They'll have it rebuilt in a day and then Dad will be held up. We've got to take the whole bunch out. Mortar teams up!"

Two mortars, each with a range of up to thirty-three hundred yards. "Blow it out of there," Buddy ordered.

The barricades were reduced to smoking ruins in less than two minutes.

"Clear it out and bring any still living up to me," Buddy ordered.

Three men and one woman were brought before Buddy. All were slightly wounded and dazed.

"The four of you are standing closer to death than you have ever stood before," Buddy told them. "And don't doubt that for an instant."

He could tell by their frightened eyes that they did not.

"What was the purpose of the blockade?"

The question seemed to confuse them all.

"You do not own the nation's highways." Buddy tried another tact.

"Neely Green claims this area for his own," the woman spoke. "We have formed our own nation here."

"Very admirable of Mr. Green," Buddy said, then

thought he'd give them all a mild jolt. "My father did the same."

"Your daddy?" a man asked. "Who's 'at?"

"Ben Raines," Buddy said softly.

The man peed in his dirty jeans. "Oh, Lard!" he said.

The other three began trembling.

"Where is this Neely Green?" Buddy asked.

"Grenada," the woman said quickly. "You want me to go git him for you?"

"How kind of you to volunteer. But would I ever see you again?"

The woman regained some composure. "Yes. Because you don't have enough people to whip Neely."

"I am in radio contact with half a dozen battalions," Buddy informed her. "General Raines commanding. Do you think that would be enough to contain your Mr. Neely?"

When she again found her voice, she thought that was probably enough troops to do the job.

"Why are you doing this to us?" one of the men with her asked. "We ain't done nothin' to you."

Indeed, Buddy thought. A fair question. He wondered how his father would reply to that. And Buddy was conscious of many Rebel eyes on him. "If you wish to set up small communities, to band together for safety and productivity, free of slavery and forced labor upon others, that, certainly, is your right. But you do not have the right to block highways and demand some sort of toll for others to pass."

"You're wrong," the woman told him. "The roads belong to them strong enough to take and hold them."

"And that is the feeling among all who follow this Neely person?"

"Yeah."

"You hold slaves?"

"Inferiors."

Buddy sighed. Would it never end? It seemed to be getting worse. He looked at the woman. "I don't expect you to tell me the truth, but I have to ask. How many men hold this area?"

"Fuck you!" she told him.

"Thank you, but no." He turned to Judy. "We'll need to know some estimate of how many we are facing. Send in a recon team?"

She nodded and left.

"Remove the prisoners, tie them up, and guard them."

He turned to the squad leader. "Set up perimeters. They may try to hit us. As much as I hate to say it, we're going to have to wait for reinforcements."

"There's no crime in that, captain," the squad leader said. "That's just good sense."

"But it's going to slow up my father's column."

"We're used to that, captain," the squad leader said. "We might not like it, but we're used to it."

Less than an hour passed before the first of the recon teams returned and reported to Buddy. "I'd say three to four hundred, captain. At the minimum. They're pretty well armed too. And not a ragtag-looking bunch, either."

Buddy went to his radio truck and called in. "Father, we are now approximately eight miles north of Grenada. We have cleared the southbound lanes of a roadblock, but are facing possibly four hundred armed men. However, I feel they are low on ammo. We are too small to launch any attack, but could hold until reinforcements arrive. Orders?"

"We don't have time to fuck around with some

two-bit warlord, Buddy. Hold your position and stand ready to repel any attack. Colonel Gray will be on his way within five minutes to beef you up until the main column arrives."

"Yes, sir. The colonel's approximate ETA?"

"Three to four hours."

"Ten-four, sir."

He turned to find Judy looking at him.

"My apologies, Buddy," she said.

"I don't understand. Why are you apologizing?"

"Because I said that no warlord would mess around with us."

"I think warlords come and go, Judy. This Neely person was probably pushed out of his last territory and came here; probably killed the outlaw leader who was here at the time. You had no way of knowing. Forget it. Get the people secured tight. We've got about a four-hour wait until Colonel Gray arrives."

Only an hour had passed before Buddy got the word handed down the line to him.

"We're completely surrounded, sir. Both sides of the highway and north and south on the interstate."

"Kind of like the old cowboys and Indians, hey?" Buddy said, his smile tight.

"Yes, sir," the young Rebel, no more than seventeen or eighteen, said.

But Buddy knew he was already a combat-hardened vet.

"Frightened?" Buddy asked.

The young man grinned. "No, sir. This is a piece of cake. I been doin' this since I was fourteen years old. I been in so many firefights I can't remember them all."

"What's your name?"

"Harris, sir."

"You've been a Rebel since you were fourteen?"

"Yes, sir. Me and four-five others come up out of East Texas to join the general."

"Where are the others who came with you?"

"All dead, sir. Fightin' the Russian, Striganov. Another got killed when the revolt went down. Another got his ticket punched out in California."

"A hard price to pay, Harris."

"Freedom don't never come easy, captain. I wasn't but two or three when the Great War came. I don't remember nothing 'cept hard times and fightin' to stay alive." He grinned, and his boyishness showed through. "But with all the fightin', General Raines made us all go to school for learning."

"You think a lot of General Raines, hey?"

"I think he's the greatest man that's walkin' the face of the earth today."

Before Buddy could agree with him, a voice sprang out of the woods on the west side of the interstate. An evil voice, filled with hate and ugliness.

"Mighty fine-lookin' bunch of cunts you got wearin' them fancy uniforms. We gonna do our bes' to take you gals alive. Then we'll all have fun."

No one from the thin and spread-out ranks of Rebels elected to reply vocally to that. Out of the corner of his eyes, Buddy saw Judy spit on the ground in disgust.

"Yes, sir," the voice spoke. "That old boy that come down here from Ohio and took over the area just east of here pays good for women. 'Course, me and other boys here will sample that pussy some 'fore we trade y'all off."

"Can you locate him, Harris?" Buddy whispered.

"I got him spotted close enough, captain."

"Judy?"

"Two more to his right. But I want them."

From the east side of the interstate, another voice was added. "How you reckon these fancy soldier boys will stand up to torture, Perry?"

"I reckon they'll do some hollerin'. Might be a right good show."

Buddy lifted his walkie-talkie. "East side. You have that voice located?"

"Ten-four."

"Ready, here?" he asked.

"Let's do it," Harris said.

"Now!" Buddy spoke into the cup.

The mid-morning quiet blew apart with the sounds of gunfire. One man on the west side of the interstate was lifted off his knees and onto his feet as his stomach and chest were stitched with M-14 rounds. He stood up on tiptoes and lifted both arms. Branches caught him under the armpits and stopped him. He hung there as the blood slowed its dripping as his heart stopped pumping.

Buddy heard the *thunk* of a rocket being dropped down a mortar tube, the slam and flutter as it took to the air. Screaming followed the explosion; more howling followed that. The mortar crew was dropping white phosphorus in on the enemy.

Buddy lifted his Thompson as a man darted into view across the median. The Thompson sang its .45 caliber song as the big slow-moving slugs took the man in the legs. Screaming, the outlaw pitched face forward in the weeds and lay howling until the pain dropped him into unconsciousness.

The *chug-a-chug* of the big .50 caliber machine guns joined in the smoky noise. The huge slugs knocked down small saplings and destroyed any living thing they came in contact with.

The returning fire was very light.

"Fall back! Fall back!" a man shouted. "We'll wait for Neely to get here. Fall back, goddammit!"

Then the Rebel snipers went to work. Any flash of color from either side of the interstate meant either pain or death as the outlaws raced to get away from the barrage of gunfire from the outnumbered Rebels. Firing beefed-up .308s and .30-06s, the snipers calmly and coldly did what they were trained to do.

Kill dispassionately.

"Cease fire!" Buddy yelled.

The firing stopped.

Moaning and yelling and weeping drifted to the Rebels from both sides of the highway.

Harris looked at Buddy and grinned. "I think those ol' boys are gonna be a tad more cautious next time around, captain."

Buddy returned the smile. "I couldn't have said it better, Harris."

2

There were no more attacks on Buddy's Rebels that hot afternoon. The day dragged on under the hot stickiness of late summer in Mississippi. There were no more taunting and threatening voices heard from the woods on either side of the interstate.

Buddy watched as Harris slipped from his position and knelt down on the shoulder, putting his ear on the concrete. He looked up, grinning. "I thought I heard something. Lots of vehicles comin', captain."

The Rebels opened the north side of their perimeter for Colonel Gray.

Smiling, Dan Gray stepped out of his Jeep and walked to Buddy. "A problem, captain?"

Briefly, Buddy explained.

Dan nodded his head. "Secure the area for a mile," he ordered his troops. "In all directions." He turned to Buddy. "General Raines can't take the time to knock out this warlord, Buddy. We'll just secure the area until the main columns pass. This Neely Green will just have to keep for a time."

"Yes, sir."

Dan waved to his batman. "Some tea would be nice," he said. To Buddy: "Your father is a few hours behind us. We've experienced some problems with the larger trucks. Let's go have a chat with the prisoners you took."

The three men and one woman looked up at the tall Englishman. "I say," Dan said to them. "You people are really in a frightful dilemma. And have placed me in quite an awkward position."

Buddy stood silent, not knowing what Dan had up his sleeve.

The men were badly frightened and showed their fear. The woman glared at Dan.

"What the hell are you?" she snarled at him.

Dan smiled. "Col. Dan Gray, madam. Formally of Her Majesty's Special Air Service, now a battalion commander with General Raines's Rebels."

"Well, kiss my ass!" the woman spat. "Ain't he just too sweet?"

Dan's eyes narrowed. Buddy had been told he did not like coarse women. "You are a rather crude person, madam. I might suggest, if you wish to continue breathing, you try to keep a civil tongue in your head."

She laughed at him and then proceded to hang together every cuss word she knew—which would have filled a dictionary—all directed at Dan and his ancestry.

When she paused for breath, Dan said, "Are you *quite* through, madam?"

"Yeah, motherfucker!" she hissed at him.

Dan's batman handed him a cup of tea and several crackers. He gave Buddy the same. Dan sipped his tea and munched on a cracker, all the while staring at the female with the foul mouth.

"They are your prisoners, captain," Dan said.

"What you do with them is your business. Personally, I'd shoot the woman."

He turned on his heel and walked away.

"You're stupid," Buddy told the woman. "Dan was probably going to cut you loose. Now I don't know what to do with you."

"Neely'll kill you, pretty boy," she said, grinning at him. "I'm one of his women."

"There is no accounting for some people's taste," Buddy told her, then turned and walked away.

The woman's screaming profanity followed him.

"Awesome," Joe Williams said to his driver. "Matt, we must be looking at three-four thousand troops down there."

"Yes, sir," the driver said, lowering his own binoculars. "Only good part about this is that we got the high ground."

"Yes," Joe said. "If only we can hold it until General Raines gets here."

Joe's troops were positioned just north of the interstate, running from Augusta west to Cadley.

A very thin line.

Cecil's Rebels were spread from Cadley over to Greensboro. The area between Greensboro and Conyers was patched together by Rebels who normally did not hold combat positions. The Misfits were lined up around Conyers.

An outnumbered line of Freedom Fighters.

Colonel West was driving his battalions as hard as he dared. He was now pushing across Central Tennessee, on his way toward Chattanooga; there, he would cut south on Interstate 75, then angle east and south midway between Chattanooga and Atlanta.

During one of their fuel stops, West called in company commanders and platoon leaders from his First Battalion.

"Second and Third battalions are up to something," he said, vocalizing a hunch. "I think Ashley hates General Raines so much he'd do anything to get him. Including sacrificing us to meet that goal."

"The commanders of Second and Third are sure buddy-buddy," a platoon leader said. "I'm with you, colonel. I think we're up to our ass in shit."

"So what do we do, colonel?" a mercenary asked.

"I'm going to split up Second and Third. Just as soon as we hit Chattanooga, I'm going to send the Third straight east, through the mountains, and order them to deploy north to south from Dillard to Tallulah Falls. I'll order the Second to stand back in reserve. If they bow up at those orders, we'll know they're up to something."

"And us?"

"That's what I'm going to find out right now."

West went to his communications van and told the operator to get General Jefferys on the horn.

"General Jefferys? Colonel West here. I think I've got a problem, sir." He laid out his suspicions to Cecil.

"What do you base this on, colonel?" Cecil asked.

"A soldier's hunch, sir. Ashley hates Ben Raines so deeply I think he'd do anything to see him dead. And there is this: I think we're better off without the Second and Third, even if my suspicions are wrong."

"They're that bad in the field?"

"The Third is the pits, sir. Useless. And the Second is not much better. And they are solidly Ashley's men. I don't trust them, general."

"If you split them, colonel, and your suspicions

275

prove out, you'll have them at your back."

West's sigh was audible over the miles. "Yes, sir, I am aware of that."

"I trust your hunches, colonel. You know these men in question; I don't."

"Thank you, sir. Where do you want me and my troops?"

"I'm very weak between Greensboro and Conyers. I need that area beefed up badly."

"I'll push them hard, general. With any kind of luck, I'll be there and in position by dawn."

"Thank you, colonel. It's good to have you with us."

"Yes, sir."

Emil hiked his robe up around his knees and began chanting, speaking in tongues as he did a combination of the jitterbug and the twist in the dust. Occasionally, he would stop and point in the direction of the camp of Francis Freneau and his Joyful Followers of Life.

Brother Carl began racing around the village. "Come quickly, come quickly. Brother Emil is in the spirit of Blomm, and the great god is speaking to him. Come quickly, come quickly."

Emil's followers gathered around, staring in awe and wonder as Emil began to get down and boogie right.

"Ughum, bugum, and doo waa ditty titty!" Emil shouted, working up a sweat under the summer sun.

He suddenly stopped his gyrations and flung his arms wide, his face to the sky. Fuckin' sun is tough, he thought.

"Blomm is angry," he shouted. "Blomm has told me there is an imposter in our area. A man who speaks with forked tongue." Come on, Emil, he berated himself. You can do better than that. "This man is subverting our worship of Blomm, and Blomm is raining down curses on this man's head."

Emil flung himself on the ground and began hunching and twisting and screaming.

Sucker is good when he wants to be, Brother Matthew thought. He just might actually pull this shit off.

The men and women, more than a hundred strong, oohed and aahed as Emil thrashed about on the ground, the dust flying, his mouth shouting words in a tongue known only to Emil and to Blomm. Suddenly, Emil stopped his frantic movements and stiffened.

Slowly he rose to his knees and pointed west with a trembling finger. "The great lie is *there!*" he thundered.

"Least he got the direction right," Brother Roger said. "Little sucker can get lost goin' to the crapper."

Emil heard him and shifted his eyes, whispering, "Shut your fuckin' face, ninny! I could win an academy award for this performance."

"Blomm is calling to me!" Emil shouted. "Yes, Great Blomm? Yes, yes, I hear and repeat your words."

Emil strung together some words from some 1970 rock songs, which made about as much sense now as they did then. Emil jumped to his feet, mouthed some 1980s rap, and ended with a chorus of Bo Jangles.

Minus the dog.

"Oh, Blomm!" Emil said, placing one hand over his heart. "Oh, no, not Francis Freneau!"

Emil lowered his head and slowly shook it from side to side. "Poor Francis," he said. "Thinking he

277

could fool the gods."

"What about dear Francis?" a woman called shrilly. "What is happening, Brother Emil?"

"He is being punished for placing himself in a godlike position. His behavior will become most erratic, and his followers will be unhappy."

"Oh no!" the ladies all shouted.

"And the men with him, too," Emil added.

"Oh no!"

"Fuckin' horny broads," Emil whispered. "He will be stricken with some terrible physical affliction. From his waist down!" Emil shouted.

"Oh no!"

Emil lowered his head. "And there will be nothing that anyone can do to save the poor misguided fool."

The ladies all began weeping and wailing.

"I am exhausted," Emil said. "I must rest." He looked at the crowd, a sly glint in his eyes. "It is very wearing on me to speak with the gods. But of course, you've never seen Francis Freneau do that, have you?"

"No," the crowd whispered.

"Come." Emil held out his arms. "Escort me to my quarters and bathe and rub my poor aching feet."

Soberly, as if they were handling the Mona Lisa, the crowd gently carried Emil to his quarters.

Ben stood with Buddy and Dan on the shoulder of the interstate, watching his columns roll past; a seemingly endless parade of the machines and people of war.

"What do you want to do with the prisoners, son?" Ben asked.

"Turn them loose. Let them wallow in their ignorance with their ignorant friends."

Ben looked toward Denise. "Cut them loose and have them guarded until the last vehicle is past."

"Yes, sir."

"You did a good job here, Buddy," Ben told him.

"Thank you, sir."

"Get your teams together and move out. Catch up and pass the columns. I want you at least fifty miles ahead of us."

"Yes, sir." He grinned. "I'll see you in Georgia, general."

As Buddy was yelling for his teams to gather and move out, Ike walked up.

"I'll be going on ahead, Ben. Joe Williams has got the easternmost section; I'll come up under him and be in position."

"All right, Ike. Good luck." He turned to Dan. "Dan, follow Ike. Spread your people from east to west. I'll take this section between these national forests here." He punched the map. "Just south of Greensboro. Tina? Your teams will be the last in position. Stay out of Atlanta. Spread out along this line from Conyers to, say, Covington. Let's roll!"

Khamsin's troops struck just at dusk, using mortars and light artillery. And had they not been so confident of victory, they might have punched through the thin lines in a spot not of Cecil's choosing. But the troops of the IPA had never full force tasted the fury of Ben Raines's Rebels. But on this bloody dusk, the last rays of the sun gone, the troops of the IPA were about to find out why Raines's Rebels had such an awesome reputation.

Khamsin's troops came across the interstate charging Joe Williams's position. The troops of The Hot Wind died in bloody heaps before even reaching the median.

Joe had armed every fourth Rebel with an M-60 machine gun. Every squad had a .50 caliber machine gun. And the Rebels had mined the median.

Joe, as had every commander, brought all the firepower his people could possibly use. And it was deadly awesome.

Then, for no apparent reason, Joe's troops pulled back and shifted positions, deserting the interstate, moving as silently and swiftly as ghosts.

"Where in the hell are they going?" Khamsin screamed the question as soon as he got the message.

"They are retreating, sir! We have broken through their lines."

But Khamsin recalled, bitterly, the last time his troops thought they had the Rebels on the run.

That little ruse had cost him a thousand men. He sat in his new command post in Augusta and worried thoughts around in his mind.

"Two companies," he ordered. "Send two companies after them. And do it cautiously."

The IPA who struck Joe Williams moved through the night, pursuing the retreating Rebels. They encountered no mines, no snipers, no nothing. But they did find tracks left by the Rebels as they ran away.

They reported this back to Khamsin.

"Fourth Brigade across the line and pursue the Rebels," he ordered. "Cautiously, cautiously, now."

Joe had pulled his people back, way back, all the way back to Highway 43, north of the interstate, leaving Rebel sappers in deep cover behind him, stretched out along a twenty-five-mile strip of interstate.

As the troops of the IPA moved across the interstate, into what had just been Rebel-held territory, the Rebel sappers came out of deep cover and moved across the interstate, carrying their deadly cargo of mines and explosives.

The sappers then formed up into small guerrilla groups and waited for the action to start.

Joe's troops were now in position, lying in wait, north to south, along Highways 43 and 78. That left the troops of the IPA with the river at their backs, the western fingers of Clarks Hill Lake to their north, and the deadly mined interstate to their south.

And a half a dozen guerrilla groups waiting in ambush in the darkness.

Cecil's thinly placed troops stood their positions and slugged it out with the IPA across the interstate. The odds were impossibly against the Rebels, but that was something they were, to a person, used to. They held their ground and fought savagely.

And Mark and Alvaro waited with their troops just south of Cecil's battle lines.

The hot late summer's night exploded in hate and rage along the interstate. Several companies of Khamsin's IPA, expecting little or no resistance, moved confidently across the interstate just east of Conyers. They died in bloody piles in the eastbound lanes. Lieutenant Mackey's Misfits were determined to prove themselves in the eyes of the other Rebels. The company of quick-trained Rebels fought with a ferocity that surprised even them.

The lines of Rebels, stretching thinly along the interstate, bent and buckled, but did not break as the night attack continued to ram its assault against the Freedom Fighters.

"Circle now." Joe Williams gave the orders, speaking into the cup of his walkie-talkie. "Quickly and quietly."

Rebels sealed off the few miles between the last south-pointing finger of Clarks Hill Lake and Interstate 20, just west of Highway 78. Other Rebels moved just east of Highway 47, putting the troops of the IPA into a box.

"Now!" Joe gave the orders. "Hit them hard. No prisoners."

The Fourth Brigade of Khamsin's invincible Islamic People's Army found themselves fighting shadowy ghosts in the night; they found themselves in a deadly no-man's-land, some of them facing men and women in vicious hand-to-hand combat, facing Rebels with knives honed to razor sharpness.

Some of Khamsin's IPA ran toward the north, toward the fingers of the lake, and became hopelessly lost in the maze of brush and timber and marsh, the country not tended by human hands in years. Others walked into ambushes. Entire squads were wiped out by two and three-person Rebels' teams lying in wait in the night.

Others of Khamsin's so-called superior forces ran south, toward the interstate. They ran into Claymores and Bouncing Bettys and trip-wired, electronically detonated C-4s. Brush fires sprang up into the night, set by Rebels to block escape routes. The fires grabbed greedily at the clothing of the IPA, creating running, screaming human torches in the darkness.

The night skies along the interstate became brightly lighted by the dry brush and wood.

"Get your people *out* of there!" Khamsin screamed the orders from his CP.

But it was too late for most of the ill-fated Fourth Brigade.

The summer night, normally filled with the scent of flowers, became filled with the odor of burning human flesh, excrement from death-relaxed bowels, and the sickly-sweet odor of death.

And once more, the taste in Khamsin's mouth was the copperlike taste of defeat.

"Scouts just radioed in, colonel," West was informed. "The Second and Third have linked up and are spreading out west to east. Looks like they're trying to box us in."

"Looks like I was right," West said. But he took no satisfaction in being correct.

Colonel West looked at his map. His troops had angled south and east in order to avoid the trashy and dangerous mess that was now Atlanta.

But they still had miles to go, over roads that were unfamiliar and, for the most part, badly in need of repair.

"I figure three-four more hours," West said. "We're ahead of schedule, but those assholes in Second and Third worry me some."

"That goddamn Ashley!" a company commander said. "He must really have the red-ass toward General Raines."

"If I ever get that son of a bitch in gunsights," West said, "I'll put an end to his quarrel. And you can tattoo that on your arm. Let's roll, boys."

Buddy's teams had barreled past Ike's slower-moving columns and were inside Georgia long before dawn.

At La Grange, Buddy brought his teams to a halt.

"Let's find out where everybody is," Buddy said. "String an antenna over there," he said, pointing, "and let's get set up."

"This is Captain Raines to any Rebel unit within

the sound of my voice. Come in, please."

At Conyers, Georgia, Lieutenant Mackey was darting from position to position during a lull in the fighting. She was approached by a runner.

"Lieutenant, there's a Captain Raines on the horn."

"A *Captain* Raines?" Mackey questioned.

"Yes, ma'am. Says he's Ben Raines's son; he's the lead recon commander. Has about seventy-five Rebels with him and wants to know where he and his people are most needed."

"This I gotta see," she muttered. "All right. Ask him if he can come up south of us and take some of the strain off us."

The request was made. The runner returned. "Says he can do, lieutenant. He'll be here before dawn."

Both sides facing each other across the interstate took the time to ease back and lick their wounds and review their situation.

And for the Rebels, it was grim.

"Order our people closest to Atlanta to break through." Khamsin radioed his orders. "And do it, without fail."

Cecil's CP heard the orders from Khamsin and informed Cec.

"Start falling back," Cec ordered. "Advise Mark and Alvaro we are doing so and to move out toward us. We've got to split up and send some people toward Conyers to beef up Mackey's Misfits."

"There is a Captain Raines heading that way now, sir. He's got a platoon with him. Who is Captain Raines, sir?"

"Ben Raines's son," Cecil told the startled Rebel. Cecil smiled. "That means that Ben and Ike and Dan aren't far behind. Any word on Colonel West's position?"

"Last report was Loganville. They should be getting into battle position any minute, now."

"How about Colonel Williams?"

"He creamed them, sir," the Rebel said with a grin. "From listening to radio reports, the IPA doesn't want any more of Joe Williams."

A panting runner slid to a stop. "Breakthrough, sir! The IPA just punched through at Barnett. They're trying to put Colonel Williams's Rebels in a box."

"Goddammit!" Cec cursed. "And I don't have a soul to send there. Any word on Ike's people?"

"Just crossing into Georgia, sir. They'll take Highway Sixteen and set up battle lines at Thomson."

"If there is anything left there to save," Cec said grimly. "Hang on, Joe," he said. "Just hang on, buddy."

3

Khamsin's IPA did, indeed, punch a hole into Rebel-held territory; but if they had thoughts of putting Joe Williams and his people in a box, they didn't know Col. Joe Williams.

But they were about to know him—far better than they wanted to, as it would turn out.

"Motherfuckers!" Joe swore, and he was not normally a profane man.

His driver and aide, Matt, glanced at him in the darkness. "They about to get you pissed-off, sir?"

"No, Matt," Joe said, his voice calm. "They have *got* me pissed-off."

Joe signaled for his radio operator to come over. Taking the mike from the backpack radio, he said, "This is Colonel Williams. All units form up north and south of my location. Take everything you can stagger with, and leave the rest. When you're all in position, bump me."

"What are we gonna do, colonel?" Matt asked.

"We're gonna charge, son!"

Matt grinned. "Yes, *sir!*"

Lieutenant Mackey almost jumped out of her

boots when someone touched her on the shoulder. She wheeled around, M-16 coming up.

Colonel West grinned at her. "Sorry, lieutenant. I walk rather softly."

"Softly's ass!" Mackey said. "You move like a friggin' ghost! Who the hell are you?"

"Colonel West, lieutenant. My battalion is in position just north of the interstate at Oxford. General Jefferys moved me to the east a bit. I'll explain his plan to you. Has Ben Raines's kid reported in position yet?"

"No, sir."

"He's a good troop. Not as savvy as his daddy, of course. But he's damn good." His eyes swept over what he could see of the Misfits. He grunted. "Strange-looking bunch."

Mackey grinned just as Billy Bob strolled up. "They're doing well for only five days' training, colonel." She introduced Billy Bob.

The men shook hands and West said, "*Five* days' training?"

"It's a long story, colonel," Billy said.

"I'm not even sure I want to hear it!" West said, softening that with a grin. "But if they're fighting and standing, that's all that matters."

He told them both of Cecil's plan.

"I ain't gonna second-guess no general," Billy said. "But if it don't work . . . we're all gonna be in one hell of a mess."

"That we are, sergeant," West replied cheerfully. "That we are. All right, lieutenant, I brought a platoon with me on this visit. Looks like you could use a few more people. Where do you want them?"

Before Mackey could reply, a shout rang out. "Here they come! Jesus Christ, there must be two-three thousand of them!"

"How about right where we are, colonel?" Mackey suggested.

"Considering the situation," West said, grinning a soldier's grin, "do I have a choice?"

Dan and his teams were just minutes behind Ike, and Ben and Tina only minutes behind Dan. All were pushing harder than road conditions would allow, and the trucks were showing it. But any vehicle that broke down was left, the gear and personnel transferred, and only a few minutes were lost.

Ike would travel on clear across Georgia, following 16 all the way. Ben would break off at Highway Forty-four, at Eatonton, coming up under Mark and Alvaro as they plugged the hole left as Cecil pulled back. Dan would roll about twenty-five miles past Ben's break-off point, and move north at Sparta, splitting his people, one group going up 22, the other heading up 15. Tina's teams had already broken off from the main columns and were racing toward Conyers. Those troops of the IPA who were pushing hard at the Misfits and at West's lone platoon. They were about to find themselves in a box with no way out.

Except death.

"Kill 'em all but six, people!" Williams roared into his mike. "And save them for pallbearers. Charge!"

Screaming their fury, the Rebels lunged out of the timber, the brush, the ditches; over the hills and across the old highway, cracked and worn from years of neglect.

The Rebels literally scared the living shit out of many of the IPA.

The Rebels had camouflaged themselves with touch-up paint, leaves, twigs, and mud. They looked and sounded like something straight out of hell.

And fought with the fury of ten times their number.

Teams of Rebels broke through the western lines of the IPA, then turned around and put Khamsin's people in the same box Khamsin had designed for them.

The Rebels took no prisoners.

The western edge of Khamsin's box had been broken, punched through at a dozen locations. Now there were no clearly defined battle lines; all along a twenty-mile stretch of highway, it was bloody confusion and death.

Selected teams of Rebels began stripping the uniforms off of the dead IPA troops and pulling them on over their tiger-stripe or lizard-battle dress, then slipping into the confused ranks of Khamsin's people.

To cut a throat or two.

Joe had given the orders for all his people, after doing as much damage as they could, to work east and form up between Highways 80 and 47. If they could just hold out until dawn, Ike and his people would be in position just south of Thomson. If they could just hold out.

If.

"Little Eagle, this is Big Sister," Tina radioed. "Are you in position?"

"Ten-four, Big Sister," Buddy answered. "I'm just south and west of Conyers. What is your position?"

"South and east of same. I've got Highway One thirty-eight to my back."

"Ready to go?"

"Sittin' on ready."

"Let's do it, Big Sister."

Buddy and Tina sealed off the south end of Conyers and began working their teams house to house, building to building; slow, dangerous work.

The first silver rays of sun were just beginning to slip through the darkness, giving the sky a tinted look.

Khamsin's people, now realizing they were caught in a box, dug in and began fighting from locked positions. And that action served only to spell out their doom.

"Lieutenant Mackey," Tina radioed.

"Mackey."

"You have mortar capability?"

"Negative."

"I do." West cut in on the transmission.

"Is this Colonel West?"

"Affirmative."

"We have a large force of IPA dug in hard. Downtown Conyers." She checked her grid map and gave him the coordinates. "Can you drop some surprises in there, colonel?"

"Ten-four. Are you in position to act as forward observer?"

"Ten-four."

"Keep your heads down. Mail incoming."

"Ten-four, colonel."

Downtown Conyers began exploding in showers of bricks and stone and dust as West's mortar men hit their targets. Bodies and bits and pieces of bodies soon littered the already littered streets of the Georgia town.

Tina lay behind the rusted ruins of a pickup truck and called the shots in.

As the troops of Khamsin tried to run from the deadly hail of rockets, Tina and Buddy's troops knocked them sprawling amid the litter with well-placed rifle shots.

To their credit, none of the IPA attempted to surrender.

They had been briefed beforehand that the Rebels did not take prisoners.

Tina called for a halt in the barrage.

The downtown area of Conyers was destroyed. Small fires were caused when WP was mixed with HE mortar.

"Northside friendlies," Tina radioed. "Please hold fire. We're commencing mopping up."

"Ten-four, southside friendlies."

Buddy and Tina soon linked up, standing and watching as their troops ended the dreams of world conquest for any IPA troop still left alive. Single shots sprang out of the smoky early morning mist. Rebel snipers lay in position, waiting to drop any IPA troop that might have escaped the deadly rain of mortars.

The morning dropped from a noisy, screaming battleground into a hush, broken only by the crunch of boots walking about the rubble.

South-side Rebels met north-side Rebels and Colonel West's mercenaries in the center of Conyers.

"Orders, colonel?" Tina asked West.

"General Jefferys has pulled back, opening a hole for the IPA to push through. The troops of someone named Mark and Alvaro are moving to plug that hole, trapping the IPA. I have my battalion waiting just east of here. But, there are two battalions of Ashley's troops moving in on us from the north. Let's do this: I'll take the north side of the interstate, you and Buddy and Lieutenant Mackey take the south side; we'll all work gradually east. Okay?"

"Sounds good," Tina said. "Let's roll."

Jake and his band of rednecks and white trash and miscreants had not gone far from Athens. Just about ten miles down the road to a little town called Watkinsville. There, Jake had licked his wounds and nurtured his hate, all the while gathering more human trash about him.

And Cecil had pulled his troops back and had set up his CP about four miles away, in what remained of a tiny town named Bishop.

As an undeclared cease-fire was occurring for a time, Ike and Dan and Ben were rolling into position.

The troops of Khamsin, who had pursued Cecil as he pulled back, were now positioned at the northernmost edge of the Oconee National Forest. The troops of Mark and Alvaro were only a few miles behind the IPA, filtering quietly through the forest.

A hush fell for a time on the one-hundred-and-twenty-five-mile stretch of battleground.

"We have lost contact with our troops near Conyers," Khamsin was informed.

"How long?" Khamsin asked, rubbing gritty eyes.

"More than a hour, sir."

"Our people in the northern Oconee?"

"Resting. They are only a few miles from the black general's position."

Khamsin lifted his eyes, meeting the gaze of Hamid. "I know," Khamsin said softly. "It is not necessary to speak the words; I can read them in your eyes."

We should have been content with what we had!

Hamid's eyes said. "I do not understand these people, Khamsin. We have conquered half the existing world, fighting forces that outnumbered us ten to one. Yet this little band of Rebels defeats us at every turn. I do not understand it."

"Could it be true, Hamid," Khamsin said, after dismissing his aides. "The rumor, the talk of Ben Raines being some sort of *god?*"

"Only Allah could answer that question, Khamsin. I certainly cannot."

"Issue the orders, Hamid. All troops fall back south. Retreat." But Khamsin was smiling. "But do not scramble this transmission. Not this one. After you have given those orders, instruct our radio people to go to the alternate frequency for one short message."

For the first time that day, Hamid smiled. "Yes, sir!"

4

"You no-good, lousy, son of a bitch!" Francis Frenau cursed Emil.

Emil grinned at him. "Why, Francis! What an unChristianlike thing to say. I'm ashamed of you, my boy."

"You asshole!"

Emil giggled. "Are you having some sort of difficulty, Francis?"

They were meeting alone, just outside a small town — or what was left of it — called Delhi.

"Difficulty!" Francis roared, towering above Emil. "You sorry bastard. Hite, I don't know exactly what you did to me. But I know that *you* did it. And I think I'm gonna kill you for that."

Francis was about two and a half times the size of Emil — in more ways than one; the porn makers didn't call him Long Dong as a come-on. In the porn-flick business one has to put up or shut up. Or perhaps rise up might be more apropos. But the big man stopped flat in his size thirteen sandals when Emil reached up his robe and hauled out a single action .45 about a foot and a half long and jacked back the hammer.

"Whoa, donkey-dick!" Emil told him. "Now you listen to me. You come swishing and yodeling your big ass into my territory, trying to screw up my scam. I'm the one oughta be killing mad, and I'm gettin' there, Bong Dong."

"That's Long Dong," Francis automatically corrected.

"Whatever, you freak. You know the rules of the game: no con artist moves in on another's territory. You blew it, dinosaur-dick!"

"What'd you do to me, Hite?" Francis demanded.

"Blomm put a curse on you."

"Blomm's ass! Save that crap for the stupids. Look, you shrimp. Whatever you done, undo it. My chickies are all upset."

"Good. Serves you right. Tell you what, Stanley, I might be persuaded to put in a good word for you, with Blomm . . ."

Francis/Stanley rolled his eyes.

". . . if you'll give me your word you'll get your ass, and your other attachments, outta my territory."

"Screw you, Hite!" Francis snarled. "I'll figure out what you did; gimme a little time. And when I do, I'll be back gunnin' for your skinny ass."

Out of the corner of his eye, Emil caught a glimpse of Sister Susie; the chick was even more beautiful in the daylight. He stowed the Buntline special and waved his arms. "Begone, you spawn of evil!" he shouted at Francis. "Begone from the sight of righteousness. Namely, me!"

"Friggin' nut!" Francis said. But he left, glaring at Emil occasionally. Emil would pat the butt of the .45 and grin at him.

"You big softie!" Emil hissed at him.

Sister Susie sauntered toward Emil. "You're so

forceful," she told him. "I just love a man that's sure of himself."

"Have you come to your senses, Sister Susie?" Emil said, frowning at the young woman.

"I'm sorry I was rude to you the other night. Will you forgive me?"

"Blomm would allow that, I suppose. Come, girl, let us sit by the creek and be comfortable."

Sitting on the bayou bank, Sister Susie's robe hiked up to mid-thigh. Emil reached up under what was left of her robe and squeezed.

"Oohhh," Sister Susie said. "Tell me more about yourself, Brother Emil. Are you firm?"

"Damn right. Plumb rigid at the moment."

"OOhhh," she said, as Emil gave her another squeeze. "That's good. All the men across the river have suddenly become so . . . so, flexible."

"Yeah. I bet they have."

She reached under his robe and grabbed his woody.

After that, neither one of them even noticed the old mossy-back 'gator on the other side of the bayou, watching them through unblinking eyes.

"I hate to say this, general," Colonel West told Ben. "But this has turned rather anticlimactic."

"It isn't over," Ben said softly. "Khamsin's got too much pride to let it end like this."

"What do you mean, Dad?" Tina asked.

Ben, Dan, West, Tina, and Buddy were sitting in Ben's temporary CP, just outside of Madison.

Ike had set up his CP at Thomson. Cecil had pulled back the northern Oconee Forest.

And Khamsin's troops had vanished.

"He's up to something, I believe. I think he's going

to show us that we're not the only ones who can play tricks and make them work."

"I am a bit curious as to what happened to those IPA troops who had followed Cecil," Dan said.

Ben walked to a map and pointed to an unpaved road leading east out of the Oconee. "I think they slipped out this way and then cut north. I think they're doing an end-around. Maybe a double end-around."

Colonel West walked to the map. He studied it for a moment, then nodded his head. "Sure. You're right, General Raines. They're going to link up with Ashley's two battalions north of our lines. And if they're pulling a double end-around, Ike is in for a bad time of it."

"If we could just be sure that's what he's got up his sleeve," Ben muttered.

"It's tough to have one's own game played against you, isn't it, general?" West said with that strange smile of his.

Ben faced him. "And you, colonel? Where do you stand in all this? You don't owe me a thing."

West shrugged his heavy shoulders. "I am a soldier, general. For hire. Since money, as we knew it, is useless, then I've hired out to you for the fight alone. I like your Rebels, Ben Raines. They're . . . unique. And to a person, by God, they'll stand. I think I'll stick around, general."

"Glad to have you, colonel."

"So you want me and my boys to link up with you guys, huh?" Jake told the CO of Ashley's Second Battalion. "Why the hell should I?"

"I, ah, understand that you had a small argument

297

with the nigger general, did you not?"

Jake flushed. "Maybe. So what if I did?"

"That's who we are going to fight."

"No shit! And just where might he be, fancy pants?"

"About twenty-five miles away from where we're standing. And if you'll join up with us, we'll have him outnumbered about eight to one. So how about it?"

"I want him alive," Jake said. "I got plans for that coon."

"If we take him alive, he's all yours, Jake. And that's a promise."

"Let's do it."

"Quiet," Cecil muttered. "We opened the door to the trap, but they didn't like the bait. I wonder why."

"Sir?" a Rebel said. "General Raines is on the horn."

"Cec! Good to know you're still alive."

"Something's up, Ben. I can feel it in my old bones."

"Yeah, I know." Briefly and quickly, Ben told Cecil of his hunch.

"Okay, I agree with you. But I'm sitting pretty good here. I've got Mark and Alvaro just south of me, and we're dug in deep; good cover. I don't think those renegade battalions want to try us in the woods."

"Yes, I agree. But Khamsin still has no telling how many thousands of troops. And they've got to be gearing up for something."

"Ike," Cecil said flatly.

"That's what Colonel West and I think. But goddammit, we don't know for sure."

"What's Ike say about it?"

"He's out of pocket for about an hour." Ben sighed. "How Colonel Williams?"

"Fat and sassy. That's why I'm not worried about my position. Joe's people are sitting just to my east."

"Cec, I've sent out a dozen recon teams, north and south of the interstate. What do you know about a two-bit warlord named Jake?"

"I whipped his ass about eight or ten days ago. Up in Athens."

"He's linked up with Ashley's renegade battalions. And they're not far from your position. That man carries a lot of hate for you, Cec."

"I should have killed him."

"Next time you meet, please do. Cec, recon teams are reporting that all signs, including civilian sight verification, indicate that Khamsin's people have moved east. I'm going to play out my hunch and bet that Ike's in for a bad time of it."

"All right, Ben. What are your orders?"

"I'm going to leave Ashley's battalions and this Jake person for you and your people to neutralize. I'll take Joe's bunch and what I've got with me and head east. Pray we're right, Cec."

"Will do, Ben. Luck to you."

Ben signed off and turned to Dan. "Dan, we know that Khamsin's people bugged out to the south. Indications are that they then cut northeast. They're after Ike. That's the only thing I can figure. I've got Buddy and Tina and their teams out working deep recon, gradually moving toward Ike's position. So here is what we'll do." Ben's eyes touched the eyes of Colonel West. "We'll all work east. All of us working south of the interstate. Work slowly and miss nothing, for we don't know what in the hell we're walking into this time around."

Dan and West nodded in agreement.

"I'll leave Lieutenant Mackey and her . . . Misfits," he said and smiled, "where they are. We've got to have somebody keeping watch on the backyard while we're gone. Order your people to get some rest, some food, and to check equipment. We'll be moving out at dawn tomorrow."

The mercenary and the Englishman exited the CP. Ben, Denise walking beside him, walked to his communications truck.

"Bump Ike again, please," he told the operator.

"Howdy, Ben." Ike's voice popped out of the speaker.

"Where in the hell have you been?" Ben asked.

"Oh, out lookin' around," Ike said, knowing Ben's sharpness was from concern, not anger. "Sure is quiet for all the rush it took to get here."

Ben told him of his hunches.

"Sounds right to me, Ben. But I'm sittin' pretty good where I am. Khamsin, so I'm told, has reached our status when it comes to heavy guns. He just ain't got 'em. He, like us, has got mortars running out the ying-yang, but no long range and heavy shooters."

"But he's gonna have you outgunned with those mortars, Ike. He can lay back and do a hell of a lot of damage."

"True."

"I've half a mind to order you out of there, Ike."

"Naw! Hell, we gotta face this dude sometime, Ben. Way I figure it, might as well do it now and get it over with."

"All right, Ike. Head's up, now."

"Five by five, Ben."

"I'll be pulling out before dawn."

"See you soon, partner."

West found Ben sitting alone, on the steps of a long-deserted house. He appeared to be deep in thought.

"Rather a pensive look on your face, general," West remarked.

Ben smiled. "Pensive? An interesting word for a mercenary to use."

West sat down and laughed. "What makes a mercenary, general? You were one yourself."

"I always preferred soldier of fortune."

West chuckled. "Semantics, Ben Raines. If you dip a rose in shit, you've still got a rose, haven't you?"

Denise was sitting a few yards away, listening.

"I guess I was pensive, colonel. I've just got this thought that Khamsin is pulling one on us. Some little . . . elusive feeling deep inside me. But I can't seem to pin it down."

"Some classic military move, general?"

"Could well be."

"Well, let's hope that in this case, history doesn't repeat itself and this turns out to be another Little Big Horn."

"That depends entirely on which side we elect to be on, doesn't it?"

Both men were silent for a few moments, listening to the sounds and smells of late summer. The thick smell of wildflowers and honeysuckle; the happy calling of the birds.

"Crazy Horse and Sitting Bull suckered Custer, didn't they?" West asked.

"Yes." Ben looked at him. "I think you've hit on it,

301

colonel."

"Maybe. It was just a thought."

"Colonel, if Khamsin's men run, don't follow them. Not even if it appears, *especially* if it appears, a victory is certain."

"I'll pass the word. Ike?"

Ben shook his head. "I don't know if Ike is in any danger, or not. I have this little feeling that Khamsin has decided to revert back to his roots."

"He was quite a terrorist."

"Yes. And that may be what he's heading back to being. I'm thinking that Khamsin's been shown he can't beat us by sheer numbers. He's taken some awfully heavy losses butting heads with us. I'd guess he's lost a full third of his forces."

"Yes. And that's got to be telling on the rest of his people."

"Maybe. But bear in mind that these people are fanatics. To die in battle means instant entry to heaven."

West glanced at Ben. "Oh, *shit!*" he whispered.

"Yeah."

West rose abruptly and walked off. Ben sat on the steps and watched him leave.

The mercenary was back in fifteen minutes, Dan with him.

And with Dan, a full platoon of Rebels.

"Now, wait just a goddamned minute!" Ben said, rising.

"Sorry, general," Dan said. "This is the way it's going to be. The colonel explained what you both feel is going down. Get used to the idea of being surrounded."

"And you probably spoke with Ike, too, didn't you?" Ben asked sourly.

"But of course!" Dan smiled.

"Wonderful," Ben muttered. He turned and walked off.

The platoon followed him. En masse.

Ben stopped and turned around. "I'm going to the *bathroom!* I don't need an audience."

"They'll turn their backs, general," Dan said cheerfully.

Ben walked off, muttering.

5

It took Emil a full half day to get over the sight of that alligator, just about ready to chew off his leg. Along with other parts of his anatomy.

What had saved them both was the hot breath of the gator on Emil's bare ass.

"I'm telling you!" Emil said. "That friggin' 'gator was forty feet long if it was an inch."

Emil's 'gator was closer to fifteen feet than forty; but still a good-sized 'gator.

"I wouldn't worry about that 'gator as much as I'd worry about Francis Freneau," Brother Matthew told him. "Francis has sworn to get even. And we're running out of that stuff to put in the water over there."

"I ain't goin' back to Monroe no more," Brother Carl said. "That place gives me the squirts just thinkin' 'bout them Night People."

"It's not just Monroe," Brother Roger said. "It's every city in the country."

"There isn't any more of it over there anyway," Emil said. "I thought sure he'd be gone by now. Hell, nearly all his followers are over here with us."

"Listen!" Brother Matthew said, holding up a finger. "Bagpipes!"

"Here comes Francis!" Sister Susie called.

"Wonderful," Emil muttered. "What the hell's he got up his sleeve now?"

"Them bagpipes is givin' me a headache," Brother Carl said.

Francis climbed up onto the hood of a rusting old car parked by the side of the road and opened his big arms. "Come gather around, my children," he called. "I have something of great importance to tell you."

"You reckon he's got a hard-on?" Brother Roger said.

Emil looked at Roger. "With him, believe me, you'd know it."

Emil and his immediate group hung back; the others gathered around.

"My heart is heavy, brothers and sisters," Francis said, placing one big hand on his chest. "An old, old friend betrayed me. Cut me with an invisible knife."

"Aaahhh!" the crowd said in sympathy.

"I trusted this man; loved him more like a brother than a friend. But," he said and gave a mighty sigh, "but as with Caesar, I must say to Brother Emil, Et tu Brute?"

"He et what?" Brother Carl asked.

Everyone ignored him. Emil felt many eyes on him. Hard, condemning eyes—coming from his own flock.

"You're a liar, Francis!" Emil shouted. "I ain't done nothin' to you."

Francis smiled lovingly at Emil. "There is no rancor in my heart for you, Emil. Your feet simply slipped from the path of righteousness."

"Say what's on your mind, Stanley," Emil said. "And then begone with you, or I'll call down the wrath of Blomm."

"Oh, you will, will you?" Francis said. He flung

305

his arms wide. "Call down the wrath of this Blomm, then. I challenge you to do that, Emil. For you see, brothers and sisters, there is no such god as *Blomm!*"

The crowd oohed and aahed and drew back, fearful of his blatant blasphemy.

"You lie!" Emil squalled. "Blomm is real. Don't push me, Ledbetter."

"Then tell this figment of your overactive imagination to strike me dead, Emil," Francis said. "I'm waiting."

"I wouldn't do that to you, Francis. You'd have to do a mighty hurt to me before I'd do anything like that. You see, Francis, unlike you, I am a gentle person."

Francis lost a little ground with that remark. He narrowed his eyes and stared at Emil.

"You poor fool," Francis said. "I didn't want to have to do this. But? . . ."

Francis lifted his arms and white doves flew out from his sleeves.

The crowd did some oohing and aahing.

The doves circled, dropping some shit on the heads of the faithful.

Francis did some of the colored handkerchief tricks: pulled a half dollar out of both ears and juggled a few balls.

The crowd loved it.

Francis said, "Let's all urge Brother Emil up here . . . I'll step down. Perhaps then he can explain why he sent some of his men slipping into my camp in the dead of night, like thieves, to poison me and my brothers?"

"I did no such thing!" Emil shouted.

"You are not truthful, Brother Emil," Francis said. Reaching into the pocket of his snow-white robe, Francis pulled out a small vial and held it up for the crowd to see.

Emil felt a little sick at his stomach.

He felt a little sicker when Francis held out his hand, and one of his men gave him the box the vials had come out of.

"Sister Susie," Francis said. "My dear sweet lovely child. Does this box look familiar to you?"

Susie said it did.

"When was the first time you saw it, dear?"

"In Brother Emil's car. At night. In Monroe. Near the hospital."

"That don't prove nothing!" Emil hollered. "There's boxes all over the damn place."

"True," Francis said. "But one of the men who has been poisoning me has a small cut on the sole of his right sandal."

"Well, shit!" Brother Matthew said.

Emil took a deep breath. Drawing himself up to his full height, which wasn't much, he pointed a finger at Francis. "Now you hear me, Ledbetter. And bear in mind this was your idea. I'm going into meditation now. Seclusion. And I'll be speaking with Blomm. At high noon, two days from now. We'll meet again. Right here on this spot. Then, *then* I shall show you the power of Blomm!"

"Bull-dooky!" Francis said.

"You'll pay for that, Ledbetter," Emil warned. "Blomm is angry; I can feel his mighty anger."

"Horse-poo!" Francis scoffed.

"Be here!" Emil told him. "All of you!" he roared.

"Emil," Brother Matthew said. "What are you gonna do two days from now, at high noon?"

Emil looked at him. "Hell, Matthew—I don't know."

Ben canceled all travel orders for his Rebels. His new orders: Hold your positions. Dig in. Keep your heads down. And be very wary of tricks.

The hours passed slowly and very quietly. The Rebels rested, ate, took much-needed baths, and cleaned equipment. Just like any army that was ever formed. That much never changes.

The Rebels constantly monitored any known frequency of Khamsin. The bands remained silent. If Khamsin was communicating with his troops, it was on a frequency not known to the Rebels.

"He'll strike," Ben said. "He's a very impatient man. That much I do know about him."

"What's the word from any recon team?" Colonel West asked.

"A lot of troops about forty-five miles south of us," Ben replied. "Stretching from Barnesville all the way over to Waynesboro. I got that word about two minutes ago. I was just about to call a meeting of COs and platoon leaders. I've ordered Buddy and Tina back in."

West sat for a time in silence. He wondered what emotions Ben Raines might be experiencing, knowing his two kids were out in the field with small units.

"I'll see that the word is passed, general," West said. "I'd like to see Kahmsin's new lines. I'm curious about them."

"Tina and Buddy both reported that Kahmsin has forced the people living south of us into forced labor camps. It looks like he's setting up a permanent barrier."

"Well, that's what I wanted to know," West said with a sigh. "General, you are aware that east of Atlanta, stretching south from Rome to Newnan, that area is controlled by outlaws and warlords?"

"I've heard." He glanced at West, accurately guessing what the man was getting at. "Well, now," Ben said softly, "that would put us in a box, wouldn't it?"

"Both of us were wrong, general," West admitted. "And those outlaws and thugs and warlords over east have only to take one look at Khamsin's superior forces and they'll join up with him."

Ben's laugh was short, holding no mirth. "That son of a bitch! He suckered us, colonel. He turned our own game against us."

"I fail to see the humor in it, general. We have gotten ourselves into a bind, my friend."

Ben waved at Denise. "Bring me my map case, would you please?"

Ben spread the map on the ground, just as Dan strolled up. Briefly, West told Dan about the new development, saying finally, "Whether it's fact or fiction, Dan, remains to be seen."

"Let's take it from the east, boys," Ben said, tracing a line on the map with a finger. "The bridges are blown from Hartwell to Augusta. Every one of them."

West glanced at him, and Ben explained the why of that.

"You had no choice in the matter, general," the mercenary said. "I would have done the same thing."

"North of us," Ben said, "we've got two of Ashley's battalions, the company that Ashley brought east with him out of Kansas, and the group that this Jake person has gathered around him."

Ben paused for a moment, silent so long, Dan said, "What's wrong, general?"

"I see Ashley's fine hand in all of this," Ben explained. "I'll be willing to bet you all that this stretch here, Interstate Seventy-five, running north

309

and south, is being closed down by Khamsin. And he's probably swung those outlaws and warlords north and south, leaving us one hole to run to."

"Atlanta," West whispered. "The city of the dead."

"And what is our fine and noble Gen. Ben Raines doing now?" Khamsin asked Hamid.

"Nothing, general," the XO replied. "Everything, along all fronts, is very quiet."

Now it was Khamsin's turn to worry. "What is that man up to, Hamid? It isn't like him to sit and do nothing."

"Perhaps he now realizes the box you have placed him in?"

"Perhaps. He certainly is not a stupid man. Just idealistic. Those thugs east of Atlanta?"

"Fell right into line, Khamsin. Our troops did not have to fire a shot."

"And they are being repositioned?"

"Yes, sir. Just as you ordered. They are surrounding the city from the north, south, and west."

Khamsin smiled. "I will have to reassess my first opinion of Ashley. His plan is a good one. But there is one weak part of it, Hamid. Our lines are not as strong as I would like them to be. Raines could possibly punch through."

"Begging your pardon, sir. But if that happens, it will not be through our people to the south."

"No, I don't think so, either. But I am not sure of the troops to the north."

"They are . . . not first quality, to be sure," Hamid agreed. "Perhaps I, myself, might take a battalion up to not only reinforce them, but to keep an eye on them."

Khamsin looked at the XO. The man was no

longer young. He sighed. "All right, Hamid. Perhaps that would be best. May the blessing of Allah go with you."

"Thank you, General Khamsin. I'll take the reorganized Second Battalion and leave at once."

Long after Hamid had gone, Khamsin called for an aide. "I'm going to take a nap. Wake me if any news comes through. Any news. No matter how unimportant it might seem."

"Yes, sir."

But sleep would not come to Khamsin. He tossed in his bed and finally, with an oath, threw back the thin cover and rose to sit on the side of the bed.

Ben Raines was up to something. Khamsin was sure of it. But what? He checked his watch. Time for prayers.

All good religious people need prayer. Even terrorists.

"I'm not going to order anyone to do this," Ben said. "And when I make my request for volunteers, I don't want a bunch of horseshit bravado jumping to the fore. Is that understood?"

It was.

Ben was addressing senior sergeants, platoon leaders, COs and XOs, along with Ike, Cecil, Dan, Tina, and Buddy. He had called them to his CP.

"What'd you have on your mind, Ben?" Ike asked.

"First I'll tell you how it's going to be done, and then I'll inform you of what is going to be done.

"First of all it's going to be done very quietly. There is going to be one team. Just one. Thirty people. Khamsin wants to push us into Atlanta. All right. But first let's check it out." He grinned. "If my idea works, all of a sudden Khamsin is going to be

311

facing an empty line, all filled with imaginary soldiers."

"Ever' time you start grinnin' like that, Ben," Ike said, "I get a funny feelin' in the pit of my stomach."

"I, of course, will lead the team, general," said Dan, who stepped forward.

"No, I will!" Ike said.

"That's nonsense," Cecil told them. "I shall lead the team."

Colonel West had joined the group late. "Whatever is going down, I feel that I should go in first."

Ben let them squabble and then made up his mind.

He winked at Buddy and said, "I've decided who will be team leader, people."

The hubbub ceased as they all looked at Ben. Finally, Tina asked, "Who, Dad?"

"Me!" Ben announced.

6

Ben pulled out at full dark, Buddy riding in the
Jeep with him. Behind them were several trucks and
Jeeps, filled with Rebels and supplies and ammo
enough for several days.

As they rolled past Conyers, Lieutenant Mackey
and Billy Bob waved at them from the shoulder of
the interstate. Both Ben and Buddy saluted the pair
and then drove on, entering the darkness.

Just about a mile from the loop that circled the
city, Ben halted the short column. "We'll camp here
until dawn. Four guards out and in close, two-hour
shifts."

Buddy climbed up on top of a rusted old truck and
stared at the outline of Atlanta. "I can see fire in
there, general."

"Colonel West called it the city of the dead."

"Have you ever seen one of these people?" Buddy
asked.

"No. Not that I know of. But from what I've
heard, they aren't pleasant to look upon."

"Is it their fault? The way they are, I mean."

"No. It isn't."

"That is what the Old Man told me. But he also told me to avoid them at all costs."

Buddy climbed down to stand by his father.

Ben said, "Your grandfather had seen some of these . . . people?"

"Many times. He said they are bitter about what they'd become, and they hate everybody not like them. I asked him once if there was not some good in them." Buddy paused.

"And?"

"He said he had not yet found any."

"I guess that about sums it all up then, doesn't it, boy?"

"And for that, we will destroy them?"

"Only if they open the fight, son. We're not here as a conquering army. Now go get some sleep. I want us standing on the edge of the city before first light." But Ben wondered about that first remark.

"Eerie," Ben heard one of his Rebels mutter.

And Ben could not disagree with the one word summation. The silent, windswept scene that lay before them was eerie. And it contained yet another one-word description: deadly.

"They are moving around us, father," Buddy said softly, walking to Ben's side.

"I can hear them, but I can't see them."

"I caught a glimpse of a few. They are robed, their robes dark. They blend in well with the night around them."

Gentle fingers of silver-gray began pushing up from the east, from the backs of the Rebels as they faced the stark outline of what had once been called the Hub of the South.

314

"Down," Ben called, his voice soft.

The Rebels crouched down, close to their vehicles, presenting no targets to whatever lurked in the darkness.

And no one among them knew for sure exactly what type of human being moved silently around them in the ink of night.

"The time is against us." All heard the voice spring out of the murk.

"Take them!" another voice called, a harshness in the command.

"The light! The light!" A third voice was added.

The dawning had intensified, the silver fingers becoming hands of silver, with just a touch of gold and white.

The Rebels couched beside their vehicles, listening as the scuff of sandals on concrete faded. The mutely lighted night grew silent.

Ben stood up, easing the slight pain in a bad knee. The road they were on became more clearly defined as the dawning continued to lighten the landscape.

"I'd guess at least a hundred had surrounded us," Ben said, looking around him. "But they're sure scared of the light. Fortunately for us," he added.

Ben glanced at his Rebels. They were calm, standing ready. Buddy was probably the youngest of the team. The rest were all in their late twenties or early thirties, hardened and seasoned combat vets. Men and women who had been with the Rebels for years. Ben knew them all on a first-name basis. And knew, too, that there was no backup in any of them. They would stand to the last person.

"Three groups," Ben said, walking to his Jeep and sitting down in the passenger seat. "We'll work a block apart, maintaining radio contact at all times." He laid his Thompson across his knees, the muzzle pointing away from the driver's seat. "Drive boy," he said to Buddy.

After only a half hour, Ben realized no one had anything to fear from the Night People—not during the day. For some reason, as yet unknown to Ben, those who lived for the night were very fearful of the sun. Why that was, he did not know. And wasn't particularly interested in finding out. He felt some degree of pity for the people; but it was not over-whelming within him.

Physically scarred and mentally traumatized by the bombings and aftermath of the Great War and the awful sickness that came a decade later, yes, surely they were. But instead of seeking out help from those able to give it, the Night People had banded together, electing instead to hate and despise those not like them. Instead of holding out the hand of friendship, asking for understanding and help, the Night People had decided to kidnap and God only knew what else, in order to salve their bodies and minds.

"Piss on them," Ben muttered, his eyes working from left to right. He was mapping out a route through the city.

"Beg pardon, sir?" Buddy asked.

"Look over there." Ben pointed.

The naked bodies of a man and woman were hanging from a power pole.

"Pull over there," Ben told him.

Ben got out and walked closer to the bloated and stinking bodies. They had been tortured, and tortured expertly, making the agony last a long, long time. And big meaty hunks of flesh were missing from their bodies.

"Why?" Buddy asked, not leaving the Jeep.

"I suspect because they are normal; not affected by the bombings or the sickness that followed. Now we

316

know what kind of pricks we're up against."

Ben got back into the Jeep. He lifted the mike to his lips. "Eagle One to West on tach."

"Go, Eagle One."

"I'm at Eastland Road and Twenty-three," Ben said. "Send two platoons with several days' rations and plenty of ammo to my sector, please."

"Ten-four."

The platoons rolled in at nine o'clock, led by Colonel West.

"Just couldn't resist it, huh, colonel?" Ben grinned at him.

"Got to go where the action is, general. What's up?"

"I've ordered everyone to start working their way west. Slow and easy, with no rush. They'll be working inverted—east to west first. In other words, Lieutenant Mackey and her Misfits will be the last to come out."

"I'm with you," West said.

"When I give the word, in about thirty-six hours, we're going to roll through Atlanta. At night."

West arched one eyebrow at that bit of news. He said nothing.

"When we start, colonel, nothing, *nothing* is going to stop us. Now we can't use Interstate Twenty to get through the city; we can't use the loops or the bypasses. The Night People have massive road blocks up damn near everywhere you want to look."

"If you've advanced no further than this point," West said, "how do you know the loops are blocked?"

"I don't know for sure about the northern loops; Two eighty-five, Eighty-five, and Seventy-five. But both Buddy and Tina tried the southern route getting in here. They had to circle around. I can only assume the same has been done to the north."

"And you want me and my men to do exactly what, general?"

"Help us find the best route through the city. Right down the heart of the city. And I don't have to tell you why it must be that way."

West nodded. "Khamsin will have spotters north and south, covering those areas for any signs of movement. But . . ." West paused, thinking. "How do we clear the route of the Night People without bringing attention to what we're doing? Gunfire is going to carry a long way."

"The Night People will be sleeping during the day, hiding from the light. We go house to house, building to building. We use knives and twenty-twos; use hollow-nosed shorts. If your people have sound suppressors available, use them."

"Going to be a distasteful and bloody son of a bitch, general."

"Yes. But if you have any doubts about what kind of people we're dealing with, take your men one block, that direction; take the first road west and have a look."

West and his men were back in half an hour. None of them looked too pleased.

"Find it?" Ben asked.

West nodded his head. "The couple . . . and more. We found some . . . normal-appearing children who had been tortured and disemboweled. Took them a long time to die. I have no more qualms, general."

"Then let's get to work."

It was bloody and awful and no one among them liked it. But after they found more tortured and mutilated bodies of "normal" people — men and

318

women and little children—the job became less distasteful.

The Rebels and the mercenaries found a breeding center in the ruins of a college. It was there that the Night People bred with normal people, mostly women, in the hopes of straining out the sickness with new generations. After the children were born, the women were usually killed, or kept as slaves. None of the women rescued by the Rebels knew where their babies had been taken. Or what lay in store for the children.

"Were the children free of the sickness?" Ben asked.

The looks in the eyes of the women gave him his silent answer.

"Hideous!" Colonel West said.

"Any idea how many of these . . . communities there might be scattered around the nation?" Ben asked.

"Hundreds," he was told. "In every city of any size."

"It appears that our next foe has been lined out for us, general," Colonel West said.

"*Our* next foe, colonel?"

West smiled. "It appears that action travels with you, general. I like that. I get bored with inactivity."

"Thought you couldn't live under my rules, colonel."

"A woman is not the only creature on God's earth with the right to change its mind."

Standing amid the fresh gore, Ben grinned and extended his hand. West shook it.

"Father," Buddy said. "I hate to break into such camaraderie." Both men looked at him. "But night is going to catch us right in the middle of this place."

West smiled. "The boy is right."

"There is something else, too, Father," Buddy said. "All these people are armed." He waved at the dead who walked the night. "So that tells me that occasional gunfire from within the city would not unduly alarm any of Khamsin's men on the outskirts."

"Smart, too," Ben said with a laugh.

They had cleared and secured more than half the route Ben had mapped out when one look at the sky told them dusk was about an hour away.

They pulled their vehicles into a covered parking area and made ready for the night — and the people from the night who were sure to come at them.

"Get as much rest as you can right now," Ben urged them. "I think we're going to be very busy later on."

They had seen areas where the Night People had, it looked to them, held open-air meetings. Many torches had been found; or pieces of torches. And that gave Ben an idea.

"Cocktails," Ben told his people. "Find as many small bottles as you can and fill them up with gasoline. They won't make as much noise as a grenade, and can do a hell of a lot of damage, physically and psychologically."

They soon had enough Molotov cocktails to withstand a siege. Which is exactly what Ben felt would be coming at them.

As dusk crawled into full night, robed and hooded figures began moving out of the murk. They darted from rusted old abandoned cars, slithered into and out of doorways, and appeared, disappeared, and reappeared in broken windows high above the closed parking area where the Rebels and the mercenaries were forted up.

"They have to eat," Ben said, more to himself than to Colonel West, who was standing beside him.

The colonel looked at him as if Ben had taken leave of his senses. "What?"

"They have to eat," Ben repeated. "And if they never leave the city . . . *what* the hell do they eat?"

"You pick the damnedest times to think about food, Ben."

"Where do they bury their dead?" Ben pondered aloud. "We've not found anyplace. And if they've killed as many people as those women over there told us," Ben said, jerking a thumb toward the small, frightened, huddled-together knot of rescued women, "it would number into the hundreds, right?"

"Yes, at least. What are you driving at?"

"The hanged and tortured bodies we've found. I think that might be some sort of ceremony; some sort of paganistic rite."

"I'll go along with that. But what does that have to do with food?"

Ben looked at him in the gathering gloom. "I think the Night People are cannibals. I think they eat any human they're ready to dispose of."

West looked at the half-eaten sandwich in his hand, grimaced, and wrapped it back up and stuck it in his pocket. "Shit, Ben!"

7

"They're all around us," one of Colonel West's men called softly. He was stationed on the second level of the parking garage. "I think they're tryin' to run a board across from the other building."

"Well, Jeff," West returned the call, "I hope you know what to do about that."

Jeff's laughter drifted down to Ben and West.

There were several sharp pops from above them as Jeff fired, using .22 caliber ammunition.

A short scream cut the night, the yowling cut short as a robed body hit the concrete, falling out of the second floor of the building on one side of the parking garage.

More small caliber pistols cracked spitefully. Choked-off screams ripped the warm night. Colonel West's walkie-talkie crackled.

"They decided to try another plan," a mercenary's voice informed him.

"They're massing behind the building!" another voice said from out of the walkie-talkie.

"Fire-bomb them!" West ordered.

The rear of the parking garage exploded in searing light as the gas-filled cocktails were hurled at the charging Night People. On the heels of the bouncing fire, the screaming of men in pain cut at the nerves of those inside.

Human shapes, encased in fire as the flames ate at clothing and flesh, ran helter-skelter into the darkness. Some made it only as far as the street, where they lay, kicking and howling in agony as the flames burned life away.

"Bastards!" Colonel West muttered.

A robed and hooded figure suddenly leaped in front of Ben; how he got inside was beside the point. He was.

Ben could smell the fetid, sour body odor of the man as his fingers snaked their way around Ben's neck. Ben butt-stroked the man with his Thompson, hearing the jaw shatter as the wood slammed against the man's face. The robed man fell to the dirty and oil-stained floor of the garage, unconscious.

"Tie him up," Ben ordered. "I want to talk to him later. And someone find the hole this bastard used to get in here and plug it up."

"The third level is full of the bastards!" a man shouted, his voice echoing around the curving concrete driveways.

"Guess that answers my question," Ben said. The reverberating sounds of weapons on full automatic hammered throughout the parking garage.

"Buddy!" Ben shouted. "Three or four of you get in Jeeps, put the lights on bright, and get up there, blind the bastards. Let's see how they react to harsh light."

"Yes, sir!"

Engines coughed into life, the Jeeps surging and

roaring up the levels. Howls of fright tore the garage as the Night People were blinded by the headlights.

Buddy's Thompson chugged in rapid fire, the big slugs knocking lines of stinking, robed men spinning and sprawling.

"Mop it up!" Buddy shouted, fast changing clips.

Ben lifted his walkie-talkie. "Bring me some prisoners, son."

"Yes, sir."

"They're falling back, Ben," West said calmly, as he lifted his M-16 and brought several more of the running Night People down. One pulled himself up to an elbow, his mouth screaming curses at the mercenary. Without changing expression, West shot him through the head.

The curses were abruptly and forever stilled.

"I never have liked for people to cuss me," West said, changing clips.

"Yes." Ben smiled. "I can see where it makes you a bit testy."

The two soldiers exchanged knowing glances.

The night settled back into a smoky, burning stillness, broken only by the moaning and crying of the wounded, the pop of fading flames from the cocktails, and the rattle of men and women changing clips of ammo.

"Report!" Ben shouted.

No one in his command, Rebel or mercenary, was dead; a few were suffering minor wounds. Nothing serious.

"Lucky," Ben said. "But you can bet those outside aren't through with us."

"Those at the windows and ramps stand back," West ordered. "Reserve up. Get some rest." He shifted his gaze. "Your son coming with several prisoners, Ben."

Ben ordered camp lanterns lit in what was once an office of some sort, and the Night People were brought in, a sullen bunch. Buddy and Colonel West sat with Ben in the room.

All three stared in shock as the hoods were jerked back, exposing the face of the prisoners.

Their faces were twisted and scarred; some were missing lips and nose.

One made the mistake of spitting at Ben.

Ben rose to his boots and knocked him to the floor. He reached down and jerked the man to his sandals, shoving him hard against a wall.

"Bring the others in," Ben ordered. He lined them up against a wall. "You all have my sympathies for what has happened to you. The Great War was not your fault. What happened to you, initially, was certainly not your fault. But that does not give you the right to attack people without provocation, to torture and rape, and to subsist on human flesh."

The Night People exchanged glances at that remark, and Ben knew he'd been right in his assumptions.

"Fuck you!" a scar-faced man hissed at Ben.

"So you don't deny that you live on human flesh?"

"We deny or admit nothing," another man told him. "Our way of life is none of your business, Raines."

"You know me?" Ben asked, surprise in his voice.

"We know of you," the man said. "Our leader has said you are our greatest enemy, and you will, someday, be destroyed."

"A lot of people have tried to do that," Ben said, sitting on the edge of a battered old desk. "I'm still here."

The stinking bunch glared at Ben. The one who seemed to be the spokesman said, "Kill us and have done with it, Raines. Our lives are scarcely worth living, so it doesn't really matter."

"In addition to all else that you may be, not much of it worthwhile, you're also a liar. No man wants to die. If you wanted to die so badly, you wouldn't be trying to improve your lot."

The sullen, smelly bunch glared at Ben.

"Eaters of human flesh," Ben muttered. "I don't know what to do with you."

"Keep them here until dawn, good light, and then throw them out in the street," West suggested. "It would be fitting."

"No!" one shouted. "We'll burn forever if you do that."

"Who says you will?" Ben asked.

The spokesman hesitated, then said, "The Judges."

"And who might they be?"

"They who judge."

"Are you being a smart-ass?" West asked.

"The Judges are the men and women who sit on the council," the Night Person told the mercenary. "They rule all who follow the night."

West shook his head and grimaced. "We had enough kooks and whackos and crackpots and nuts before the war. But what came after boggles the mind."

Ben asked a dozen more questions, but received no reply to any of them. It was obvious that the prisoners believed they were going to die and had made ready for it. "Buddy, take them to a secure room and lock them in. We'll decide what to do with them later on."

When they were gone, West said, "What are you

going to do with them, Ben?"

"I don't know. Suggestions?"

West shrugged. "Kill them now or kill them later, I suppose. But I have never enjoyed shooting unarmed men. What we did today and will be doing tomorrow with the sleeping Night People was necessary, I guess. It's all come down to a matter of survival for us all. Was war ever fun for you, Ben?"

"What an odd question at this time, colonel. Fun? I don't know whether that noun fits, or not. But maybe it does. For the sake of argument, I'll say yes."

West smiled. "War is what it's all come to, Ben. This is it." He slapped the palm of his hand down on the desk. "All computers and their banks of knowledge; all the statesmen and intellectuals, and writers and thinkers and doers. Well," he sighed, "the machines are rusting and the trillions of words are gathering dust. The statesmen and the thinkers and the teachers . . . all gone. It's all come down to you and me and Ike and Cecil and Buddy and Tina and Dan. Modern day cavemen. With automatic weapons instead of clubs."

"West, you're a frustrated intellectual. You know that?"

The mercenary laughed, the sound echoing in the small concrete room. "You're correct to a degree, you know, but don't let it get out. That would ruin my reputation."

The Night People kept the Rebels and the mercenaries awake that seemingly endless darkness before dawn, but no more hard attacks were launched by them. They had learned that while they might outnumber those in the parking garage, their fighting

327

skills were not nearly so honed to perfection.

At dawn, Ben and his people once more began their grisly hunt and kill mission, mapping out a clear route of escape.

Teams rescued a few more handfuls of women and kids, and one of the groups gave truth to Ben's awful theory. The Night People were cannibals.

It made the hunt and kill mission a bit easier to take.

At noon, the Rebels moving west began calling in.

Ike and his bunch were on the outskirts of Atlanta. They had traveled all through the night, gathering people behind them as they came. They had seen no sign of any of Khamsin's troops.

"How far is the next column behind you?" Ben radioed.

"Sittin' right on my ass."

"Get inside the city proper," Ben ordered. "Get them all in. We're going to be busting out of here at dark. Did you and the others set up the dummy installations?"

"Ten-four, Ben. From a distance, they look just like the real thing."

"Come on, Ike."

"Rolling."

The Rebels had left behind as many trucks and other vehicles as they could spare. They had dragged in others and placed them around their positions. They had made straw dummies with real weapons before them. They had left behind many tents and clothes hanging on the line. From a distance, the camps appeared the same.

It would appear to any spotters that some Rebels were staying, others were moving out to beef up the long battle line that was the interstate. Ben hoped, at least.

"So we're going down the big fat middle of Atlanta, following this road, until we intersect with Twenty at Carroll Road?" Ike asked.

"That's it," Ben told him.

"It's worked so far, Ben. From all indications, Khamsin thinks we're just spreadin' out a little."

Buddy strolled up. "The bridge over the Chattahoochee is intact," he told his father. "I left a team there to see that it remains so."

"Good," Ben said. To Ike: "Where the hell is Cecil?"

"Relax, Ben. He's about a half hour behind me. And he's going to stay that way," Ike added.

Ben's look was sharp. "What the hell do you mean?"

"Cecil's pulling rear guard duty, Ben. Told me early this morning. Said you wasn't gonna like it, but that's the way it was going to be."

Ben opened his mouth to protest, then closed it. There was no point in arguing. Once Cecil made up his mind, that was that.

Ike waved a Rebel to him. He outlined the plan and said, "Take it back to General Jefferys. And son . . . tell him that I said to watch his ass. He may be a night-fighter, but he still bleeds red."

The scout grinned. "Yes, sir."

West had listened without comment. He said, "Cecil Jefferys is a very brave man, Ben."

Smiling, Ben said, "For a black person, you mean," he said, needling the mercenary.

"Like I said, Ben: There are exceptions to every rule."

Ben checked his Thompson. "West, if you ever decide exactly where you stand, you are going to be a

329

person to be reckoned with."

"I am a soldier, Ben. Nothing more, nothing less."

But Ben wasn't so sure of that. He wondered what the mercenary really was—and wondered if he'd ever find out.

And finally, he wondered if he really wanted to know.

8

The western-most team, a squad of West's mercenaries, radioed back that the route was clear. The route had been cleared of all blockades, living and stationary.

It was late afternoon in the dead city of Atlanta.

"All units in?" Ben asked.

"Everybody here, Ben," Ike told him. "Joe Williams's gang pulled in right behind Mark and Alvaro's team. Cecil and his battalion have bivouacked out at the old federal prison farm, just south of Interstate Twenty."

Big Louie's timer, back in Kansas, had about twenty hours to go before the bird would fly.

"It worked," Ben said. "I had my doubts, but it really worked. But the next few hours are critical for us."

"I've ordered guards out and the rest to relax," Ike told him. "It's gonna be a wild ride to the Chattahoochee tonight."

"We bug out at full dark. Tell Cecil I want his people to pull in closer. And that isn't a request, that's an order."

Ike nodded his head.

Ben continued. "I'll be waiting at the bridge for him. We'll blow it just as soon as his people are past."

"It would be an honor if you would allow me to do that, Ben," West spoke up.

Both Ben and Ike glanced at the mercenary.

"Do I have to ask if you know what you're letting yourself in for?" Ben questioned.

"I am fully cognizant of the consequences, general."

"Very well. Get your men in position."

Ben held out his hand and the mercenary shook it.

"See you all on the fair side of freedom, general," West said, then turned on his heel and walked away, shouting for his men to join him.

"That's a strange fellow, Ben," Ike observed. "Likable ol' boy; but strange."

"I had my doubts for awhile, but he's on the level. He's with us all the way."

"But why?" Ike questioned.

"That, old friend, is something we shall probably never know."

"Something is wrong," Ashley radioed to Khamsin's CP.

"Why do you say that?"

"It's too damn quiet! Ben Raines is up to something. And no, I don't know what it is. But I've known the man for twenty years, and I'm telling you, he's up to something."

"The front?"

"That's just it, Khamsin. My spotters report that nothing is moving. *Nothing!*"

332

"No signs of life? Nothing!" Khamsin felt his blood pressure soaring.

"Nothing."

"Move your spotters in closer. I'll do the same from the south."

Khamsin leaned back in his chair and let the forbidden obscenities fly, startling those in the room with him.

Tomorrow is the big day, Emil," Brother Matthew said. "What have you got up your sleeve?"

Emil glared at him. "I'll come up with something. Bet on it."

"I've already packed my gear. Just in case."

"Oh, ye of little faith!" Emil wailed. "I am being deserted in my time of need."

"Eighteen hours and counting, Emil," Brother Matthew reminded him.

"I wonder what that fuckin' Ledbetter is doing?" Emil asked.

"Havin' a party on the riverbank. All the cute chickies have returned to his camp."

"I hope he gets eaten by a goddamn alligator!" Emil spat out the words.

"Brother Emil's gonna come up with something," one of the faithful announced firmly. "The Great God Blomm will not desert us."

Emil sighed with great patience, wondering how in the hell he ever got mixed up with all these yo-yos!

Jake had already figured it out. He put it together when one of his rednecks told him, "Sumthang queer goin' on down there, Jake, and I ain't talkin' 'bout no

333

wienie-chewin', neither."

"Whut you talkin' 'bout, boy?"

"There ain't no movement. Some washin' on a line done been blown down more'un a hour, and ain't nobody snatched it up. That ain't rat."

"No movement? None a-tal?"

"Nuttin'."

Jake stood up. "Git the boys together. And don't say nuttin' to nobody 'bout it. We gonna cut them fuckers off at the pass. I know whure they's a-goin'."

Two hours and counting," Ben muttered. "If we pull this off it'll be a miracle."

"I'm surprised they haven't discovered us missing hours ago," Tina said.

Ben put one arm around his daughter's shoulders. "Just between us, kid, so am I."

Already, long purple shadows were creeping about the city, casting pockets of gloom amid the sunlight. Ben could feel Tina shudder under his hand.

"Damn place spooks me, Dad."

"Steady, girl. We'll be home free in a few hours."

Ben made no mention of Tina's husband. And she had not brought up his name in a long time. He suspected they had split the sheets. But he had never interfered in her life, and wasn't about to start now.

Tina abruptly giggled, quite unlike her. "I think Buddy's getting serious about Judy."

Good cue, Ben thought. "And, you, girl? How's your love life?"

She was silent for a moment. "Static. I am totally committed to the Rebel cause. He wanted a stay-at-home person."

"Sorry to hear it."

"You don't see me weeping, do you, Dad?"

"I seem to recall that you're not the hysterical type."

"I learned that from Salina. Did you love her, Dad?"

"I was . . . content," Ben replied.

"There is an old proverb that reads, 'A woman should always marry a man she likes, and a man should always marry a women he loves.'"

"How interesting." Ben's words were dry. "But where is this leading?"

"Just making chit-chat in the middle of ghosties and ghouldies and things that go bump in the night, Pop."

Ben laughed and shoved her away, slapping her on the butt. "Get outta here!"

"Oh, by the way," she called over her shoulder. "Colonel West said he'd like to prepare dinner for me some evening . . . when we're free."

"You could do worse," Ben told her. "And I sure can't say a damned word about him robbing the cradle, now, can I?"

Tina walked away laughing.

The shadows deepened across the land.

"Come on!" Jake screamed into his radio. "Push it, goddammit. We've still got sixty miles to go."

Khamsin intercepted the message. He was just west of Thomson, in a rage after discovering the Rebel camp was deserted, with straw soldiers and junk vehicles.

He lifted his mike. "Khamsin to base. Order all units to converge on Atlanta. All units push hard. Raines is in *Atlanta!* Cut them off. Order all units around the city to seal it off. Now!"

"They know we're here, general!" came the shout that reached Ben.

Ben ran to his Jeep and turned up the volume on his radio.

"Coming under heavy attack, Ben." West's voice was calm.

"Can you hold, colonel?"

"Ten-four, general. But it's going to take all of us to punch a hole clear through."

"Ten-four, colonel. On the way." Ben stood up in the seat and shouted, "Bug out! Bug out! Roll!"

Dropping back in his seat, he got Cecil on the horn. "Pull back, Cec. Block the streets as you go. Use the junked vehicles; they're all over the place. And fall back to my position. That is not a request, Cec. That is an order. Do you acknowledge?"

"Ten-four, Ben. Bugging out." Cecil's voice was calm and professional.

"Buddy! Tina! Link your teams up with Dan. Fall back to the river and beef up Colonel West. Roll, kids!"

He looked at Ike, standing by his side. "Join the others, Ike."

"Is that an order, Ben?"

"That's an order, Ike."

"See you at the river, Ben."

Ben motioned for Lieutenant Mackey to come to him.

"Sir?"

"You have any doubts at all about your Misfits, lieutenant?"

"Not a one, sir."

336

"That's good. Join up with my people and get ready to bug out."

"Yes, sir."

She saluted and ran over to where Billy Bob was waiting with the Misfits. "General Raines just made us a part of his outfit," she announced. "But before you all start cheering, bear this in mind. General Raines's troops usually lead the way."

"I'd damn shore rather lead than follow," a man spoke from the ranks.

"Everybody's in," Ben said, walking up to Cecil and shaking his hand. "You're the last ones."

"They're right behind me, Ben," Cecil told him. "In the thousands." He smiled. "With the warlord, Jake, leading the parade."

"You want him, Cec?"

"That would be nice, I think."

"This time, kill the son of a bitch."

Cecil nodded his head and walked back to his Jeep, taking out and holding up a Weatherby 300 mag, with scope. "That answer your statement?"

" 'Deed it does." Ben smiled and stuck the needle to his friend. "But you're getting so damned old you probably won't be able to hit him."

Cecil snorted. "I refuse to dignify that remark with a reply. "Hang around, sport."

"Oh, I shall. And judging from the sounds of all that traffic heading our way, we won't have a long wait."

Jake's column, if it could be called that, came roaring into view, Jake's vehicle leading the way. The big 'neck was standing up, hollering and waving to his people.

Cecil waved at Jake.

"There the black son of a bitch is!" Jake hollered. "Git 'em, boys!"

Cecil lifted the 300 mag and sighted Jake in. He gently squeezed the trigger, allowing the rifle to fire itself. The slug struck Jake in the center of his chest, toppling the man over into the back seat.

Cecil dropped to one knee and sighted in again. This time he took out the driver, the slug punching through the windshield and striking the man in the center of the face. Half the driver's face was blown away. The vehicle slewed sideways, toppled over, and began howling down the concrete, sparks flying.

The vehicle immediately behind the downed Jeep swerved to avoid it and rolled over, smashing into the sideways-moving Jeep. Both vehicles burst into flames as gasoline ignited. The other cars and trucks behind the flames managed to come to a halt — with about a half a dozen of them crashing into the one in front of them. The entire street was blocked.

"Let's go!" Ben yelled.

Dark was only minutes away.

Already, hooded shapes were moving, staying close to the darkness that was forming in the city.

Jake's outfit was now totally disorganized, milling about, not knowing what to do. Jake wasn't there to tell them.

Shore wasn't.

Rocks and stones and bottles and pieces of concrete block and bits of iron were being tossed down on the Rebels as they roared through the city. But only a few of the more daring of the Night People were risking the half light of that time between light and dark, and only a few of the thrown objects managed to inflict any damage, most of that dents in

338

vehicles and not cuts on flesh.

Those Jeeps and APCs with mounted .50 caliber machine guns soon cleared the rooftops of the Night People.

With Denise driving, Ben sat in the passenger seat, burning powder and tossing lead from his Thompson.

They were only halfway through the city when full dark fell on them.

"I thought darkness creeped." Denise shouted, fighting the wheel.

"Crept," Ben automatically corrected, the writer in him surfacing. "Not this time of the year. We're going to be in for a hell of a time of it, baby!" he yelled.

"Okay, baby!" Denise returned the shout.

Ben laughed aloud and exchanged Thompsons. This one was fitted with a drum instead of a clip. A hooded, robed figure appeared, with a AK in his hands. Ben stitched him, working from ankles to waist, the slugs tossing the man, or woman — Ben wasn't sure and didn't particularly give a damn — off the sidewalk and into a store window.

A half a dozen Night People began pushing an old car into the street, attempting to block the Rebels' way. Ben got a firm grip on the Thompson, pulled the trigger back, and held it back.

The powerful old SMG chugged in rapid fire, the .45 caliber slugs howling and splattering and sparking and richocheting off the street as the SMG worked up, from left to right. The lead cleared the street of Night People.

The Rebels rolled under and over and through loops and expressways and interstates, finally hitting Gordon Road. They were about five miles from the Chattahoochee River bridge.

And Khamsin's troops of the IPA were just entering downtown Atlanta as full night fell.

Ben began laughing.

Denise looked at him. "What in the hell do you find so funny?"

"Khamsin. The Night People won't know or care that he's chasing us. To them, he'll be just another person to hate. The terrorist is about to get terrorized!"

9

"Pull back! Pull back!" Khamsin screamed into his mike. "It's a trap. We don't know the city and don't have any idea what's facing us. Pull back!"

But for several companies of the IPA, it was too late. The Night People, during that time between Ben's passing and the IPA's approach, had blocked the streets, trapping those first few pursuing Ben.

The guns of the IPA knocked down the first wave of Night People, then the mass of the robed and hooded swarmed the vehicles.

The soldiers were dragged screaming from their trucks and Jeeps. They were stripped naked in the streets as the blades of sharp knives flashed silver in the glow of headlights, and then dripped with blood as the choice cuts of human flesh were carved away from the living, screaming, terrified, agonized men.

No orders from anyone less than Allah could have forced the remaining IPA into the dark streets of the city, and Khamsin didn't even try. He ordered his men back, back into the county, away from the city.

"Do we swing around to help the outlaws and our

341

people west of the city?" Hamid asked Khamsin.

"No," the terrorist replied. "By that time, it will be all over."

Knowing that Khamsin would be forced to break off his pursuit, Ben ordered mortars set up and began pounding the positions of the remaining IPA and the outlaws to the north, south, and west of the river.

The ending was rather dull, as Dan put it. The Rebels knocked a hole through the thin lines of outlaws and warlords, and the IPA and rolled west. They were in Alabama several hours later.

Ben halted the column. "Put out guards," he ordered. "Everybody else get some rest. They won't be coming after us."

Two Rebels from Mark and Alvaro's team walked up to Ben, a prisoner between them.

"General, we got this man yesterday; he got too close to our position. He has something to tell you."

Ben looked at the prisoner. "What outfit are you from?"

"Ashley. You don't know who he really is, do you?"

"And you do?"

"Yes, sir. You turn me loose and I'll tell you."

Ben was feeling generous that night. "All right. Speak."

"Would you untie me first?"

Ben signaled for the guard to cut the man free.

Rubbing his wrists, the man said, "You don't 'member me, do you, Raines?"

"No. Should I?"

"I lived not too fur from you, outside of Morriston."

Ben stared at the man, then shook his head. "I don't remember you. Sorry."

"Don't make no difference. You always was thinkin' yourself better than others. That damn fence around your house and all that."

Ben sighed. "The term is reserve; not believing I'm better than you. Say what you have to say."

"Ashley's his middle name. His first name is Lance and his last name is Lantier."

Ben chuckled, for a moment lost in memory recall. "Well, I'll be damned! Fran Lantier Piper's big brother, Lance. My God. I whipped his ass more than twenty years ago."

"Yes, sir," the prisoner said. "And he's hated you ever since."

Ben nodded. "All right. You'll stay here tonight with us. We'll turn you loose when we pull out in the morning."

Ben walked away, into the night, wondering how a man could nurture such hate for such a long, long time.

He also had a hunch he'd be seeing more of Lance Ashley Lantier in the very near future.

He was still smiling as he lay down on the blankets and went to sleep.

There hadn't been much to Lance twenty years ago, and not much to him now.

Except his hatred.

10

The sounds of bagpipes and tambourines and singing filled the hot air. Cute little white-robed chickies danced ahead of Francis Freneau, sprinkling petals from flowers before him.

Emil stood alone and glared at the big con artist.

Back in Kansas, the hands of the clock and the date on the calendar meshed. The concrete shields rolled back, and the missile fired.

It soared up, turned, and nosed southeast.

Francis moved close to Emil and whispered, "Your scam is all through, little buddy. In five minutes, you won't have a single follower left."

"Give it your best shot, Stanley."

Francis stepped back and sang "Danny Boy," bringing tears to the eyes of most present. Gave Emil a case of heartburn.

Francis preached a short sermon, proclaiming himself as the new spiritual leader of North Louisiana.

"Blomm is going to give us all a sign, Francis!" Emil shouted. "He'll . . . he'll make the heavens thunder, showing his disapproval. Fire will spring

344

from the sky!" I hope, Emil thought. Hell, just a little-bitty thunderstorm might do it.

But there was not a cloud in the blue skies.

Francis laughed at him. "Blomm! There is no Blomm. If the heavens thunder and fire springs forth, I will acknowledge that you, Emil Hite, are the spiritual leader of all the earth."

"And you'll leave?" Emil asked, stalling for a little more time.

"I shall exit and nevermore return."

Emil hiked his robes up around his bony knees, took a deep breath, and began speaking in tongues and dancing, his feet kicking up dust. He did the bebop, the rebop, the jitterbug, the twist, and even invented a few steps. *Dance Party* would have hired him on the spot.

Almost ready to drop from exhaustion, Emil flung his arms wide and shouted, "Blomm! Give me a sign!"

Big Louie's rocket ran out its string and blew, directly over North Louisiana. The sky erupted in flames and violence. A great ball of fire glowed in the skies.

Francis Freneau yelped once and then gathered his robes up off the ground and, quite ungodlike, hauled his ass out of there. The last anyone saw of Francis was of him loping westward, on Highway 80.

"Holy friggin' shit!" Emil breathed, awestruck. "There really *is* a Blomm!"

Emil rose to his feet (he had hit the ground in fear when the rocket blew) and glared at the people around him.

"Are there any doubters among you?" he screamed.

The men and women shook their heads and bowed to the Great Emil.

"Pulled it off again," Brother Matthew whispered. "Okay, Emil. You're the main man."

"Bet your ass, I am!" Emil turned, tripped over the hem of his robe, and fell flat on his face in the dust.

11

"Hell of a bang," Ike said in his radio message to Ben. "What the hell you reckon that was?"

"I think that was Big Louie's last surprise, Ike," Ben radioed. "I'm just glad the damn thing blew a couple of miles up and not on the ground."

"Where are we headin', Ben?" Ike asked.

"Back to Louisiana, Ike. Once there, we'll start gearing up for the building of outposts across the nation."

"Not far, now, Father," Buddy radioed. "I have the Mississippi River bridge at Vicksburg in sight."

"Ten-four, son." Ben replaced the mike in its hook.

Denise looked at him, noting the expression on his face. "Odd look on your face, Ben."

"This is where it all began, Denise. I woke up one morning, and the whole world had gone crazy."

"Are you going to live in your old house? If it's still standing, that is."

"No. Too many memories there."

"The mental faces of old girlfriends?" she teased.

He smiled. "Well, yes. That, too."

"There will probably be Night People all around us."

"Yes. We'll have to deal with them. And Khamsin

347

isn't going to forget or forgive. He'll be along, bet on that."

"And Ashley."

"Him, too. And more Jakes and warlords and outlaws. We'll just take it as it comes."

The long column rolled westward, through Vicksburg. Buddy was waiting in the center of the big bridge.

"Post guards on the bridge, boy," Ben told him. "But we'll deny no person the right to enter our territory to live free."

"Yes, sir."

Ben looked at the handsome young man for a long moment. Then he smiled. "When you get the guards mounted, you and Judy come on in. I'll be set up by then. We'll have supper . . . my son."

William W. Johnstone
The *Mountain Man* Series